THE INTERCESSOR

THE INTERCESSOR

Cover by: Arlene Goldbard

ISBN: 9798292799894 (print)
ISBN: 978-0-9891669-5-9 (ebook)

www.theintercessor.info

Email: arlenegoldbard@gmail.com

ADVANCE PRAISE

The Intercessor is the novel we need for these times of despair and divisiveness. Through interconnected tales, you'll experience the humor, mysticism, compassion, inclusivity, and hope of a little-known aspect of Jewish life: the Jewish Renewal movement, combining 18th century Hasidism with 20th century feminism. Goldbard's characters prize justice and equality side-by-side with spiritual introspection. Theirs are stories of continuous growth in the embrace of community, exactly what we need now. Just like the old ads for Levy's rye bread, you don't have to be Jewish to love Arlene Goldbard's latest book! You'll learn a lot, even if you are!

—Rabbi Phyllis Ocean Berman

In *The Intercessor* seasoned author Arlene Goldbard spins a tale of mystery, magic and healing in the visible and beyond-visible worlds. We meet Sharon, a diminutive, salty private investigator who finds herself serving as spiritual advisor to an unlikely assortment of folks in her small Jewish community. Allowing her characters to speak in their own voices, Goldbard reveals their redemptive journeys with wry humor and psychological savvy, weaving a rich tapestry of Jewish mystical lore and ultimately challenging readers to open our minds to the possibility of unseen powers guiding us all. A delightful and engrossing read!

— Rabbi Diane Elliot, author of *This Is the Day* and *Traces*

A wise meditation on identity and values in today's polarising world, The Intercessor is rich in powerful narrative and vivid characters. Rarely have the spiritual and the everyday been brought into dialogue so convincingly. Though it is rooted in a distinctive culture, The Intercessor is universal in its spirit. I highly recommend this thoughtful novel to every reader with an open and curious heart.

—François Matarasso, community artist and author of *A Restless Art*

If Jewish renewal, and indeed our human species, survives and flourishes over the next thousand years, Arlene Goldbard's book will likely be part of the canon.

—Barry Barkan, Ashoka Fellow, Founding Co-Director, Elders' Guild

To Rick always, and with gratitude to the deep teachers of the
Jewish Renewal movement

THE INTERCESSOR

ARLENE GOLDBARD

TABLE OF CONTENTS

THE MAIN CHARACTERS

Sharon Marks is a private investigator who has a sideline as a *melitz yosher*, someone who intercedes with higher powers to help a person who is ill or facing another challenge. She's a small person in late middle age who's sometimes told she bears a slight resemblance to Yoda.

Jonathan Fox is a Jewish Renewal rabbi who succumbed to COVID in 2020 at 62 years of age. His wife Judy died half a dozen years earlier, leaving him to raise his daughter Sarah. He was educated in Orthodox yeshivas, but was drawn to engage with countercultural spiritual movements, bringing both streams to his work as founding rabbi of the Or Chadash congregation.

Nomi Riordan comes from coastal South Carolina, where she was raised a blonde, blue-eyed Baptist. Since childhood, she was pulled toward Judaism without really knowing it. She completed her conversion at 34 in 2000 and left behind her former profession of librarian to start and run the Khegev Center, promoting inclusion in Jewish community.

Rivvy Rosenblatt is a Jewish Renewal rabbi, married to Sam Maimon, who teaches philosophy at Berkeley. She has an earth mother presence, a full figure, wears flowy clothes and jewelry. She is founder and head of a Jewish retreat and learning organization, the Rachamim Center.

Ken Simon—gray crewcut, freckles, wiry and typically dressed in black—is an early 70s writer of modest success, estranged from his mother and sister, who rejected him. His best friend is fellow writer Lucy Perelman.

Isamu Goodman, Iz to all, is a half-Okinawan, half-Ashkenazi graduate student with a double major in Asian and Jewish studies.

Anya Applebaum is the Shomer—essentially president—of Or Chadash, the Jewish Renewal congregation founded by Reb Jonathan Fox. At 77, she does her best to bridge the community's generation gaps, and isn't quite ready to retire.

SHARON

Imagine a doctor who must swallow some of her own medicine or else the patient won't get well. When I took on this work, I knew I'd be playing with a whole handful of wild cards. But this side effect has to be the wildest.

You see, people come to me for help. The sign on my office door says "Sharon Marks: Investigations," and mostly I make my living from the ordinary types of human troubles: insurance scams, missing persons, hidden assets. Those are the clients who come through referrals from attorneys or other satisfied customers.

But people also find me through a very different kind of network. You might call them spiritual seekers. They aren't exactly sure what they want. "A vague anxiety" and "a nagging feeling" are the two commonest presenting symptoms. They come to me because they've heard I have a way of looking beyond the complaint to discover what a person really needs and how to get it. My method doesn't always succeed, but a lot of the time it works in ways I never could have expected. For about half the cases, whatever remedy I prescribe, I have to do the same thing myself, swallowing some of the medicine I'm dishing out.

So that's how I found the answer to my family's secret.

But wait—I'm getting ahead of myself. *Start at the beginning, Sharon*, like my friend Nomi always says. "Take a breath, sugar, and start at the beginning."

Okay. Probably the beginning is before I can even remember. Maybe I overheard something in my mother's womb. But I'm going to start quite a while ago, a few years after I met Reb Rivvy.

I'm a spiritual seeker too. But instead of running off to India to find serenity in the lotus position, for the past couple of decades, I've been investigating my own tradition as a Jew. Rivvy is a local rabbi who has taught me a lot and become a friend along the way. She likes to categorize people. When we first met, she put me in the pigeonhole for "culinary Judaism": kids who were brought up eating chopped liver and chicken soup, whose families celebrated all the Jewish holidays with the same humongous meal, and who got sent to some kind of Sunday school for their weekly hour of Jewish education.

She's right, I admit, but just by one generation. Bubbe Fay, my Dad's mother, was observant if not entirely Orthodox. They kept kosher, Daddy said, which also included eating *treyf*—like the cheeseburgers he loved—off paper plates once in a while, blessing the Shabbos candles every Friday night, and making challah French toast on Sunday mornings, a custom my parents carried on. All the Judaica in my parents' house came from her: a brass Seder plate from Israel with a special green patina, silver candlesticks that my parents lit maybe once a year; a *hanukkiah*, the menorah used annually for the faux Christmas my parents made out of that holiday. Now it all sits on my shelves along with things I've acquired—my *havdalah* set, a special candle and cup used to mark the division between Shabbat or holidays and ordinary time, my *tzedakah* box where I save coins for charity—and gets more use every season than my parents gave it in a lifetime.

Bubbe Fay died when I was two, so I don't remember her except to recognize her photograph. But I cherish my personal legacy from her: a tiny *kiddush* cup—a silver goblet for wine to be blessed on Shabbos and holidays. There is engraving around the cup's foot: "*yaldah tova*," "good girl" in Hebrew, and "*Shira*," my Hebrew name.

Still, I don't think Rivvy's pigeonhole tells the whole story. I also belong in the pigeonhole for kids whose families thought FDR was God, who were brought up believing that being Jewish was a guarantee of progressive politics. I don't think I knew there could be Jewish Republicans until the Reagan administration: Norman Podhoretz, Irving Kristol and all that gang—what a rude awakening that was!

Anyway, for me, actually learning the Jewish texts and stories and "spiritual technologies" (that's what Rivvy likes to call them, so I do too out of loyalty to her, even though it sounds a little more new age-y than I like), this has been as exotic and eye-opening as a trek to India was for my friend Steve. Two years of traveling by rail from ashram to ashram ended with Steve sitting in a cave while a teacher whacked him on the knee every time he began to show signs of drifting off. "You're sitting on a rock in a cave!" the teacher shouted each time, bringing Steve back to earth. Thinking he might as well be sitting on a chair in a house, he bought passage home.

Me too, at least home to my roots. So I investigate divorce cases and insurance claims by day, and by night I study, dipping my toes into the waters of *Zohar* and other mystical texts and practices. I want to tell you right now that I am not one of those Hollywood *kabbalah* fans: no magic strings, no magic potions—really no magic at all, in the sense of believing that buying something insures future happiness. But here is what I have discovered: there are things to be learned, real things, once you let go of the rationalist tic. What, you may ask, is the rationalist tic? Faced with anything mysterious, the mind

          Arlene Goldbard

emits a prerecorded message that blocks all incoming information: *Whoa!* it says, *I don't believe in that kind of thing. I'm sure there's a rational explanation.*

Maybe so. I don't check my brain at the *shul* door. It seems obvious to me that we have these big brains to explore creation, to learn, and to repair the world. It doesn't take anything away from God or Spirit or Infinite Source or Mystery, whatever you want to call Him-Her-It-Them, to accept evolution or nuclear fission or the Big Bang as part of our reality-map. But mystery is mystery. How can spiritual certainty—including died-in-the-wool convinced atheism—be anything other than an act of faith? So, if you want to tie yourself in a knot coming up with alternative explanations for my experiences, knock yourself out. But as for me, I know what I saw, I know what I felt. I know what happened.

Ken Simon first arrived at my office by way of his friend Lucy Perelman, who was a member of the same Berkeley-style, Hasidism-meets-feminism (meets shamanism) community I belong to, Or Chadash. My office is pretty much what you'd imagine if someone said "one-person office." Filing cabinets, desk, chairs, a ficus plant that has just about outgrown its pot, overstuffed bookshelves, a tweedy carpet, tan walls. I don't like to be distracted. Ken had a no-nonsense look too: Gray crewcut, black T-shirt, black jeans, black sneakers. I bet myself he was an artist. We shook hands and he folded himself into the chair opposite my desk.

Rubbing one long hand across his freckled brow, he told me he was a writer. "I don't know what's happening," he said. "All I can say is I feel blocked. I sit and stare at the keyboard and my mind goes blank. It's as if a door has slammed shut and I can't find the way to open it." His watery blue eyes darted down at me, a wary sidewise glance.

I am not tall. Five-two on a good day, although in truth, I haven't peeked at my height reading for a long time, afraid that at 61 the doctor's scale will tell me I've shrunk even more than I imagine. I like to think of myself as heightless, the way some people seem ageless. But I suddenly saw myself through Ken's eyes. I looked like Yoda, if Yoda had gray-streaked brown hair pulled back into a ponytail. I could see how that might be unnerving. I sat up straighter, trying to look taller.

"I was telling Lucy—you know her, Lucy Perelman, the writer—that I'd felt blocked since my mother died two years ago," Ken continued. "She said maybe my mother's death had something to do with the block. Normally, I wouldn't go there…" he paused, looking even more uncomfortable.

"You don't really believe in this sort of thing," I said.

"Yeah," he said, breathing freely for the first time. "Not really. But I'm desperate." A flash of panic crossed his face. "Do I have to believe for it to work?"

"No," I assured him. "You may not have to do anything at all. But if you do, you'll have a choice, and there won't be any penalty if you don't want to do it. So relax, okay? We'll just schmooze awhile."

How did I get here? Half a dozen years ago, in 2013, Reb Rivvy offered a course called "*Melitz Yosher*: On Being an Intercessor." I knew the root word—to intercede, to act on behalf of someone—but I had no clue what this meant as a Jewish practice. I had taken other courses from Reb Rivvy, but this sounded different. The tag line kept nagging at me: "take this course if you want to deepen your spiritual practice." So I did. It turns out there is a sizeable body of Jewish knowledge on interceding in higher realms for people who need help. (Time to do me a favor and put your rationalist tic in your pocket, please. You can always pull it out later.) Some people take this very literally. If you want to read a straightforward eighteenth-century account of how "the spiritual realm…contains courts of justice and deliberating bodies, with appropriate rules and procedures," pick up Luzzato's *The Way of God*.

It was raining as my friend Nomi and I drove to Reb Rivvy's, so the roads were clogged. Californians can only drive if there's absolutely no weather. Good thing we left early. Chapter six of Luzzato was our advance reading for the class. Nomi was newer than I to all this stuff and I knew just a little, but we both found it unnerving to read about heavenly courts, judges, and advocates, a feeling we attempted to discharge by making gentle fun of it. "What kind of outfits did the judges have in your vision?" Nomi asked. "I saw the whole place as kind of a Westminster Abbey set-up: high ceilings, stained glass," she sketched with her hands as she continued. "Lots of little pointy carvings, ranks of pews on either side of a rectangular space. People in funny hats and long black robes."

"That's your heritage coming through, my friend," I said. I knew I wasn't supposed to refer to the fact that Nomi is a convert. That is considered very bad form. But what can I say? We'd become best friends. We teased each other all the time, me about how she still preferred tuna salad with lots of mayo and sweet pickles and thought of Rice Krispies treats as comfort food; Nomi about my tendency to eat pickled herring for breakfast, and the way I loved those little neon-colored half-moon jellies you can buy for Passover. "The whole cathedral thing," I told her, "that's the other team."

"And what authentically Jewish imagery did you conjure, sugar? Educate me." Even though she'd lived in Berkeley for ages, Nomi's South Carolina accent tended to thicken when she was the least bit peeved.

"It was sort of vague," I admitted. "Kind of like a class picture, three tiers of smiling people in ethnic finery. Not much décor."

"Thirty-six Rivvies," said Nomi. "Much better."

Sitting in a circle in Reb Rivvy's living room, peering at the ancient masks and musical instruments on her wall, trying to make out the Hebrew titles of battered leather-bound books on high shelves, I wondered what the hell I was doing there. Some kind of incense was wafting through the room. People were talking about their personal "councils" of the dear departed, how they used pendulums to get advice on life problems and presumably, on which shampoo to buy. *Whoo-whoo*, my rationalist tic said, *I don't really believe in this kind of thing.*

A few minutes after the appointed hour, Rivvy's sturdy hands adjusted the multicolored scarves wrapping her springy black curls. She straightened the gold and silver chains around her neck, making sure the charms hung properly, then smoothed the folds of her embroidered caftan over her knees as she sat. By that time, the room was silent. Closing her eyes and taking a deep, sighing breath, she said, "Shalom."

"Shalom," we chorused, seven women of a certain age and one plump, cheerful young man with a rainbow *kippah* perched atop his light brown hair, baby-fine wisps encircling his ears. Some of us sat on couches, others on big floor pillows. There were plants everywhere, some with long trailing vines that had been tacked to the ceiling molding with pushpins.

"If you are here," said Reb Rivvy, focusing her black eyes on each of us in turn, "you have been drawn to this work enough to find out about it. What you find may seem like the answer to your prayers, or it may not be for you at all. After the course, you will know if you are moved to carry on. For now, just be here, Okay?

We all nodded obediently.

"Did you do the reading?"

I guess enough of us nodded yes, because Rivvy plunged right in. "An intercessor," she said, "in Hebrew a *melitz yosher*, is like a defense attorney. You go upstairs," (this cozy expression mimics the Hebrew vernacular for higher realms, *l'malah*), you advocate for the person, you find out the price, you bargain."

This produced some uncomfortable laughter. Evidently, some people had trouble parsing spirituality with the language of commerce. But that's when I began to get interested. Midway through the second lesson, Rivvy asked us what qualities an intercessor needed. Taking notes, I filled a whole page with my fellow students' offerings of sweetness and light: "courage, humility, strength, compassion, sensitivity, honesty, balance, desire to be of service…"

Something seemed to be missing. *What the hell*, I thought, raising my hand: "A talent for negotiation?"

"Bingo!" said Rivvy and for the first time, I thought, *Maybe this is for me.*

I was right. I'm not a lawyer, but people have told me I sound like one, which makes sense when I plead as a *melitz yosher*.

Ken settled in as he answered my questions about his situation. He seemed to subside a little and I seemed to grow, so we felt more face-to-face. "My mother worked very hard to support us after my father died suddenly," he told me. "She'd been one of those Hadassah women, card parties with the girls, that kind of thing, and then one day my father dropped dead at his desk, and everything fell on her. She got a lot wrong: she coddled my little sister—I guess she knew what it was like to be a little girl—and even though I was only ten, she decided I had to be the man of the family. I had after-school jobs, weekend jobs, hours of chores around the house.

When I wanted to go off to a state university rather than staying home and taking a few courses at a local school, she felt betrayed. She told me I was abandoning the family. I think she took all that anger she'd suppressed with my father—how mad she was at him for dying—and dumped it on me."

"I heard a voice in my head," he said, scrubbing both hands over his gray crew-cut as if he had a headache that wouldn't quit, "and it said *Run! Save yourself!* So I did. I worked two jobs the entire time I was in college, sending

     Arlene Goldbard

every penny home that I could, but my mother never forgave me. She and my sister just hunkered down in that apartment...."

I could almost see the place as he talked, clean newspapers spread over worn, much-washed linoleum, that atmosphere of long habitation, curtains that had absorbed the smell of a thousand reheated meals, faded doilies on the arms of overstuffed chairs.

"Thank God it was rent-controlled," Ken said. "They always had enough to eat, they always had warm clothes. When I lived in the east, I came home for every holiday and birthday. They treated me like an unwelcome guest. I started bringing dinner with me, takeout from a deli they liked; otherwise, I'd arrive at dinnertime on my mother's birthday and they'd be sitting in front of the TV, nothing cooking on the stove, always pretending to be surprised to see me. Every year they looked more like twins, even though my sister Doris was nearly thirty years younger than Fanny.

"I tried to talk to them about it. But they acted like nothing was wrong. You know what my mother said?"

Looking into his reddened eyes, I shook my head no.

"Why are you making out like there's something wrong with us, Kenny? I see families like us on the TV all the time. Why are you always picking on your sister? Doris is a good girl. Leave us be." Ken's laugh was bitter.

"In the end, my sister hung up on me every time I called. One time I got through to my mother—Doris must have been out getting groceries or something. We hadn't talked in maybe two years, and Fanny said 'Oh, hi, how are you?' in the kind of distantly polite voice you would use with a friend who'd called the week before. I could hear the TV blaring in the background. I asked if she'd like me to come visit and she said 'No thank you.' Nothing more. Just 'No thank you.' Doris didn't even phone me when my mother died. A cousin called a week later, wondering why I hadn't been at the funeral. I phoned Doris, but she just hung up on me again. I was in New York a few months later and went to the cemetery. I'm not much for praying, but I said *Kaddish* all by myself. Then I went home."

For me, all the stuff about the courts and judges upstairs is deep metaphor. I can't quite wrap my mind around the idea that angels and sages sit in judgment, rendering verdicts with all the trappings of bureaucracy. But the basic analogy to a court of law is sound. You use prayers and blessings to contact the higher authorities—whatever forms those energies may take—on behalf of the person you wish to help. If you get permission to go forward, you describe the situation, receive a message, and based on what it says, you negotiate for the help you seek.

Messages come in different forms. For me, it isn't like being struck by lightning. No voice booms out. The nearest thing I can say is that when I ask what the person needs, something arises in my mind—usually right after I have the thought *Nothing is happening*—and that it is almost always clear and specific. When I ask what it will cost, what the person has to do in return, usually another highly specific something arises in response. Sometimes I have to ask clarifying questions. For instance, an assignment may include reciting certain prayers or psalms and I need to ask how often or how long. But when the energy flows, there is no ambiguity. The task is clear.

Ken's assignment had a few parts, but the main one involved writing. It happened that he visited me a couple of weeks before Rosh Hashanah, the new year. It arose in my mind that to break the shell that had hardened around his writing, he had to write his own personal Torah between then and Simchat Torah, the final installment of the High Holy Days, when we celebrate by reading the end of one year's Torah, the final passages of Deuteronomy, and the beginning of the next, the beautiful opening section of Genesis.

Ken's assignment was to write the story of his personal awakening and exodus, faithfully representing his own feelings and experiences. It was to be addressed to his mother, he was to write at least a few lines each day, and he had no obligation to share it with anyone else. I advised him to write before sundown on Friday and after sundown on Saturday, because these repairs tend not to work if you do them on Shabbat. He was not to think of it as a literary production, I told him, but a repair of the fabric of his life.

I felt satisfied with the assignment as soon as I had given it. It seemed fitting. I pulled out a calendar to count the days before Simchat Torah. There were thirty-six. Hebrew letters have numeric values used in mystical interpretation to add a layer of meaning to words. The value of *chai*, the word for life, is eighteen. Ken's assignment was twice *chai*, a very auspicious number.

The intercessor has to be careful that her own weak spots don't distort or impede her work. Reb Rivvy taught me that as part of my preparation, I should always ask to be shown anything in my own life that relates to the situation in which I am attempting to intercede. You ask that it be revealed to you, so you can proceed in awareness. You ask to be shown how to heal it, so it doesn't get in the way. So that's how I'd started. Then, before Ken and I were finished, I did what I always do to end the session: I asked if there was anything else, especially anything I personally needed to do to support Ken's work. That's when I understood I had to perform the same writing assignment he'd received, all 36 days of it.

I made sure again that Ken understood there would be no consequences if he decided to refuse his assignment, but if he accepted it, he would have to execute it faithfully or it would have no effect. He thought for a minute, looking much happier than when he came in, and said yes, extending his hand to shake on it. Thanking me, he took his leave, promising to call if anything came up that he needed to talk about.

That evening I sat down at home to write, choosing my big armchair— and the matching footstool so my feet wouldn't dangle. I felt very ready, the floor lamp casting a warm light, a glass of wine on the end table, a little dish of salted almonds if I got hungry, an extra pen if ink ran short. Softly, in the background, I played a favorite recording, "Echoes of Reb Shlomo Carlebach." Reb Shlomo had become a controversial figure, but there were tracks on this compilation that tuned my spirit to something higher than ordinary time, so I focused on the good. Rabbi Akiva Mann was singing Psalm 23. His deep, resonant voice always went straight to my heart.

But when I tuned in to my assignment, I discovered that I was a little uncomfortable with my part of it. In contrast to Ken's psychodrama of manipulation, my family story had been sort of normal: no huge betrayals, two parents who stayed married, both dying in their late seventies, one from a stroke, one from a heart attack. My big complaint about my parents had been that they'd always been a little distant, a little opaque. In contrast to the stereotype of the Jewish mother, Estelle didn't try to find out all my secrets, nor did she treat everything I did as a comment on her. If I was tempted to confide, she'd always be understanding. She generally had something useful to say. But she never opened up. Harry's life was shaped by routine: off to work after a bagel and coffee, home every day with the afternoon paper folded under his arm. Daddy liked to watch boxing on TV, also the six o'clock news. I never heard them fight, in the sense of knock-down drag-out, but sometimes a trickle of raised voices leaked from the bedroom door.

Born in 'fifty-eight, I was a little young for the sixties. But like Nomi says, since the sixties lasted till the late seventies, I managed to catch that counter-cultural urge.

I used to take Estelle and Harry out for her birthday every year, dinner and a movie. She adored anything with a Jewish subject or a Jewish movie star, like rooting for the home team. When I sat down to write the first entry in my personal Torah, one particular birthday came to mind, so that's what I wrote about.

> Mom, remember when I took you to see *Running on Empty* for your birthday in 1988? I thought I'd found the perfect movie for us: you got Judd Hirsch, a bona fide Jew and your favorite from *Taxi*, and I got one of those stories of the sixties revolution that makes me nostalgic for what I never experienced. Sidney Lumet, cool movie stars running from the police, what more could we want? When we came out, I said "That family felt like us, didn't it? The same energy, almost as if we'd been living underground or in witness protection or something all these years."

> You just shrugged and made a joke: "Oh, yeah, big revolutionaries we are." But I saw something flash in Daddy's eyes, a brief guilty look, like a petty thief caught in the act. I think he saw me watching, because he turned away and got real interested in something in a shop window. That made me remember a nagging feeling I'd had almost as long as I could recall: that you and Daddy had a big secret, something you always hid from me. "That wind is making me chilly," you said, hustling us into the car and turning on the radio.

> When I was in therapy, I told my shrink about it. I couldn't come up with anything more concrete than a feeling, though. She said it might be akin to the sense some kids have that they're adopted. Maybe they find a shred of evidence. Or its lack. I had a friend who decided he was adopted because, leafing through family pictures, he saw his brother and sister in diapers, but he couldn't find his own photo as an infant. My therapist told me that people invent the adoption story because it resonates so strongly with something they feel deep inside: *I don't belong here.* She said that maybe the feeling that there are hidden secrets is what made me decide to become an investigator.

Starting with this sense of all that had been suppressed or unspoken, I found it challenging to write frankly to my parents, even if part of me doubted

   Arlene Goldbard

they would ever know what I had written. (*Whoa! I don't believe in that sort of thing.*) But I have to live up to my reputation for bravery, so I made myself do it.

I wrote all the things I'd never said out loud: how I wished my mother had pried into my life a little more; how I wish she had taken me in her arms and told me secrets about how she'd felt when she was my age and experienced exactly the same sort of childish disappointments; how I would rather have heard the facts of life from her lips than be given a little printed booklet that described human reproduction in terms that were positively horticultural. Despite my reservations, once I started to say what hadn't been expressed, the writing flowed.

But after a while, reading over it, I began to feel annoyed with myself, like I'd been kvetching a lot, and kvetching into the silence to boot. I wondered what I was supposed to learn from the exercise. But an assignment is an assignment. If I stopped, Ken's task might have been affected. I had accepted the assignment, so I had no choice but to do it every day.

About three weeks after our meeting, Ken left a message on my voicemail. "Sharon," he said, sounding shaken, "something very weird happened. Could you call me back?"

He told me this story: he'd been writing daily, a little stiffly at first, but soon it began to hum, as if the story were writing him. "I realized that still, after all these years, I wanted my mother to understand. So each time I wrote, I found myself ending with a plea, 'Dear Fanny, please understand, please see it now from my side.'

"Nine days in, I heard a voice. Honestly, I can't say I remember my mother's voice, but I felt it was her. 'And if I see your side,' she asked, 'what will happen? You'll forget all about me again.'

"At first, I felt wronged. Why would I do that? My one Jewish observance is lighting a candle and saying Kaddish every year on her *yahrtzeit*, just like on the anniversary of my father's death. So I started to argue with her. Then I thought, *No, she's right, I don't think about her from one year to the next.* If I think at all, I think about my grievance, how righteous I was, how she hurt me. When I wrote my next entry, I apologized. I said I'd never thanked her for all her hard work after my father died, nor stopped much to think about how lonely and scared she must have been to need Doris so badly. I said that despite the real hurt I still felt, I saw that I could have considered things from her side too, instead of sitting on my resentment all these years.

"The next day," Ken told me, "as I sat down to write, I heard Fanny's voice again. This time it was loud, insistent, and it had a simple message: 'Go to the cemetery.' The funny thing is, I had a conference in New York at the end of that week—I was flying the red-eye the next day. I thought, *Okay, I'll go after the conference.* The entire six hours across the country, I swear, the airplane engines kept repeating it: 'Go to the cemetery, go to the cemetery, go!' I got off the plane and into a taxi. Instead of telling the driver to take me to Manhattan to check into my hotel, I asked him to drive me to the cemetery in Brooklyn. It took a while to find the section where my parents are buried. When I looked at the spot next to my father's grave where Fanny's temporary marker had been the one and only time I visited, there was nothing but grass. Empty grass."

I could hear Ken's quick intake of breath, a ragged scrap of choked-back sob. "I felt sick," he said. "I told myself all sorts of stories: I'd gotten the spot wrong, she'd been moved, I didn't know what. When I checked with the cemetery office, they told me that no one had ever ordered a marker. I called my old home number, hoping to speak to Doris. But someone with a West Indian accent answered; they'd had that phone number for a year and a half and they'd never heard of my sister. I called the cousin who phoned me after Ruth's funeral. She said that Doris had sold off all she could from the old apartment and given the rest to Goodwill. Doris told my cousin she had enough in the bank from Fanny's insurance and savings—this was the money I'd been sending all these years—that she could live on it the rest of her life. She said this was good-bye."

He paused for breath. "My cousin is an old woman. She'd gone to the cemetery around the time she expected the unveiling, eleven months after my mother died. But like me, all she found was a patch of grass. She called Doris to ask when the marker would be ready. Doris said she didn't owe Fanny a stone. She had given her mother her life; now *she* would be Fanny's marker. The cousin said she'd put up part of the money to buy a stone that matched my father's grave, that she'd call me to get the rest. Doris said that if she knew what was good for her, she'd do no such thing. If she went behind Doris's back and put up a stone, Doris would find her grave after she died and spit on it.

"My cousin cried when she told me this. She was scared. I told her not to worry. I called the cemetery and ordered the marker. I was half afraid they'd tell me I needed Doris's signature, but of course they were happy to take my

 Arlene Goldbard

money so long as what was written on the marker matched their records. So now I'm waiting. It will take nearly three months to be ready."

"Oh my God," I said. *Oh my God.* I repeated it several times. "So how do you feel now?"

"That's the strangest thing," Ken said. "I feel good. Even though I sent Fanny money all those years and Doris absconded with it, even though I had to lay out more money I don't have for the marker, I feel like something has been completed. I feel like the past has settled into the past. I don't resent anyone anymore. It just feels over."

"I think you're right," I said, "but be sure and complete the assignment to wrap it up. Don't let it go."

Ken laughed out loud. "Are you kidding? I haven't written like this in years, it's just flowing out of me. I'm so glad I came to see you."

That night, when it was time to write an installment of my personal Torah, I went out to my tiny back yard to rest for a minute. It held a small patch of lawn, a few neglected garden beds, a concrete patio supporting a little table and two lawn chairs. Nothing much, but I loved it. It was one of those rare Bay Area nights when neither clouds nor city lights disrupted the blackness or blocked the brilliance of the moon and stars. I sat on cold metal and somehow didn't mind. I looked up until my neck threatened to lock, drinking it in. I could hear all kinds of night sounds, a barking dog here, music from someone walking past my place. Everything rose and fell, like breathing.

The garden was flooded with my favorite scent. They call it petrichor, that delicious smell when rain hits dry earth. It makes me feel like getting on all fours and sniffing the ground like a dog, just to take as much of it as possible into my lungs. I told myself I need to come out here more often instead of being busy, busy. I was forgetting to notice what lay around me, and I didn't want that.

When I went back inside, I did a meditation to focus myself, hoping to clear Ken's story out of my head. I sat in my armchair and closed my eyes, imagining that I could breathe light into my heart through the top of my head. I saw the top of my head opening like a flower. Light poured across the petals like spring rain, saturating the length of my spine. As I breathed in the light, my parents' images arose in my mind. I saw their heads from below, as if they were peering over the petals. Their hands clasped the petals' edge, giving the whole scene the aspect of an excursion, mountaintop tourists holding onto a handrail to admire the valley view.

They were much, much younger than I remembered them—they looked like kids. My father wore his Navy uniform, but he'd gotten out of the service before I was born. My mother's hair was swept into a French twist with high, springy bangs. They both had sweet, tender expressions on their faces, two mouths echoing the shape of a coo. I imagined they must be gazing into my cradle, looking down at my baby face and baby tummy. I was flooded with the sweetness of being held like a baby, tears prickling my eyes.

Then my father said this: "What a brave little boy! Facing the *mohel* without crying a drop!"

My mother brought one hand to her eyes, dabbing with a sodden handkerchief. "Can't say the same about me," she whispered.

I felt a sizzle in my stomach. He? The *mohel*! They were talking about a *bris*, a ritual circumcision. One hand went to my breasts, the other to my crotch. Everything felt real, everything felt like mine. What could this mean? I took out my notebook and wrote:

Mom and Daddy, if that was real, then you already know what I saw. What 'brave little boy' were you looking at? My Torah doesn't have any brothers in it, does it? Is this the big secret? Tell me, please!

That's when I really got that finishing Ken's assignment also amounted to interceding for myself. I had been surprised to learn in Reb Rivvy's class that you can intercede on your own behalf so long as you follow proper procedure and you get permission to forge ahead. I had already discovered that you can ask too much. The penalty for that is not getting an answer to your inquiries. (I had a spate of tough cases for a few months last year. Then, after Nomi and I giggled about it, I asked if I should do online dating. It seems I asked once too often, temporarily wearing out my welcome upstairs. Still, I took that as a no.) So now I do my *melitz yosher* thing only when truly necessary. This seemed like one of those times. I called in the big guns: my parents, to be sure, but also a wonderful, holy man I knew who'd died some years before, and the ranks of colorfully costumed beings I'd described to Nomi that rainy night in the car on the way to Rivvy's first class.

I pled my case, and here's what arose in my mind: the image of a silver goblet, wrapped in cloth and stuffed into a large burlap bag.

     Arlene Goldbard

My Jewish studies come in handy here, because the forces upstairs tend to communicate with me using a highly specific, symbolic lexicon. I immediately recognized this image as part of the story of Joseph and his brothers.

Joseph's brothers were resentful of him on account of his being his father Jacob's favorite and having some dreams they found tremendously unflattering. So they sold him to traders who took him into Egypt and sold him in turn to Pharaoh's steward, Potiphar. Potiphar's wife lusted after Joseph, but he refused to cooperate. Spurned, she set him up for a prison sentence. The fabulously resilient Joseph made himself indispensable to the warden, also interpreting the dreams of some of Pharaoh's staff temporarily indisposed behind bars, thus ingratiating himself. When Pharaoh needed help with his own troubling dreams, Joseph was fetched. He did such a great job that Pharaoh made him overseer of all the land, shepherding Egypt through seven years of famine.

Meanwhile, thinking their brother long dead, Joseph's starving siblings traveled to Egypt from Canaan to see the grand overseer and plead for food. Servants ushered them into Joseph's opulent quarters where they were wined and dined. And intimidated. Joseph chose to conceal his identity, toying with his brothers, using deception to compel them to return for a second trip, this time with his youngest brother Benjamin in tow. One of Joseph's tricks was to hide a silver goblet in Benjamin's bag before the return trip to Canaan, then send a servant after his brothers to accuse them of stealing the goblet. Having forced his brothers back into his power, after toying with them a little more, Joseph revealed his identity and forgave them all. I'd like to say everyone lived happily ever after, but Joseph's brothers never stopped fearing him despite his late-breaking generosity. And as for the Israelites in Egypt, since Joseph's coziness with Pharaoh led to the population's eventual indenture and a few centuries of slavery, that's another story. As my friend Anya—she's Shomer of Or Chadash, Reb Jonathan Fox's congregation—says, the law of unintended consequences is never broken.

So I understood the image, but not what it had to do with the brother I was becoming increasingly sure had been the big secret at the heart of my family.

Intercession works in strange and indirect ways. When I took up my assignment to write to my parents the following night, I asked again for help.

> Mom and Daddy, I am really confused. I have been thinking about this all day. I think I have (or had) a brother. I think Joseph's goblet has something to do with it. But more than that I don't know. Can you give me another clue?

Total air silence. I phoned Nomi, thinking that talking out loud about it might help. I told her the whole story.

"*Gevalt!*" she said (only it sounded like "Gev-a-a-a-lt" with that South Carolina drawl).

"*Gevalt* indeed. So I guess there was a big secret after all. It wasn't just my imagination."

"Yeah, but what is it?" Nomi's words were muffled by the soggy sound she made chewing on the end of her long blonde braid, something she liked to do while thinking. "I mean, the poor baby could have died, right?" she asked. "That's probably it, because if he hadn't, you would have known him, wouldn't you?"

"You would think," I said. "But who knows? Maybe they gave him up for adoption for some reason, like when my father was in the war, maybe my mother couldn't handle a baby alone."

"Yeah," drawled Nomi, thinking it over. "I guess there are quite a few possibilities. You're an investigator. Isn't there some way to find out?"

"Duh!" I slapped my hand on the desk. "I think I have brain lock." I might like to see myself as fearless, but it takes everyone's cooperation to keep a family secret, I've found. I had to admit the part of myself that was scared to learn this one had slowed me down. Would I find something I didn't want to know? *Those are the breaks*, I thought. "Why don't we start by googling 'Joseph Marks,' just for ducks?"

I found 833 entries, the typical *tzimmes* of genealogical records and links to doctors and insurance agents. If this putative brother had been born before me—if Daddy was still in the Navy at the time—he'd be in his mid-sixties, give or take. I clicked on the links that seemed promising, but no one whose picture I found appeared to be the right age or have the Marks family features: dark brown eyes, short noses, round jawlines.

"There is nothing as stimulating as sitting on the phone while someone else surfs the web," said Nomi, her voice slightly thickened by a mouthful of blonde braid. "You just keep doing that all night, honey, and don't worry a bit about me."

"I'm sorry, Nomi. Unless he's one of these CPAs in Dallas or he owns a florist shop in Encino, I don't think any of these guys are likely to be him."

     Arlene Goldbard

"Don't you have any old papers or scrapbooks or anything like that from your folks? I thought you told me you wanted to go through a few cartons of photos and stuff, but you never got around to it."

This was really challenging my self-image as intrepid investigator. "Okay, I'm going to go through it all tonight."

"Want me to come over and keep you company? I could bring a pizza?"

"Only if you promise not to scoff at the disorder of my garage."

"Let me think that over," she said. "Scoffing is most of the fun."

"Okay, okay. But no hurtful scoffing, alright?"

"Agreed. Mushrooms and four cheeses, okay?"

Nomi slouched back in the old gray armchair, one foot resting on the opposite knee, dangling the point of a pizza slice just above her open mouth. She made such an orderly public self-presentation, hair combed back into her neat braid, crisp solid-colored shirts, ironed jeans, just a dab of lipstick on a cupid's-bow mouth. "If they could only see you now," I said. "Miss Manners in the flesh."

"Who? Well, whoever *they* are, if they could only see you trying to investigate your own jam-packed garage. You know, I hear you can actually park in these things if you take the crap out."

I knew that in theory, but since it was almost impossible for me to throw anything away, in practice the garage was a dumping ground for my past. To me, there was an order. If I knew what I was looking for, I could usually go straight to the correct corner, even the right layer of boxes if not the precise box. But to the outside observer, it was a chaos of cardboard and paper with patches of oil-stained cement floor peeking through.

I'd already dug through two battered cartons of family photos, failing to find a single bouncing baby boy, although I did stare at quite a few unnamed (and now forever unknown) sepia-toned cousins posed stiffly against drapery and moonbeam backdrops. Carton number three was piled with miscellaneous artifacts. Most of what Estelle had thought worth saving before she and Daddy moved to the assisted living complex had become my good dishes and silver, my knickknacks. The leftovers in this box included a trophy I'd won for an essay contest in tenth grade, a brown velvet jewel box containing a cameo brooch, and a folder with my father's mustering-out papers from the Navy.

Fortifying myself with bites of pizza, I examined each object, laying them in turn on a towel I'd spread over the cracked gray floor. I was admitting to myself (but not yet to Nomi) that when I was done, I would put it all back in the box and stack the box exactly where it had been since I brought it home from my parents' place. I couldn't use any of it, but I wasn't about to throw it away either. I pulled out what appeared to be the last of the artifacts: a clouded plastic bag containing an old embroidered tablecloth; rather ugly, I thought, cross-stitches in shades of brown and gold, but hours of painstaking needlework for someone. But lurking in a corner of the box was one more object: one of those bags jewelers use to pack silver—soft gray flannel or moleskin with a little drawstring at the top.

When I picked it up, I felt a jolt, as if the bag had been wired with electricity. Whatever was inside was light, weighing less than an egg. Laying the bag on the palm of my hand, I extended it for Nomi's inspection.

"Well, well, well," she said. "What have we here?"

"I don't know, but I'm getting some kind of buzz off it."

"Open it up," she demanded, laying down her pizza crust and licking her fingers in preparation for wiping her hands on a wad of paper napkins.

Inside was a miniature *kiddush* cup, the twin of my own. It was so tarnished, I had to hold it up to the light and squint hard to make out the engraving. "*Yeled tov*," it read on one side, "good boy" in Hebrew, and on the other, "*Binyamin*," the Hebrew equivalent of Benjamin.

"Joseph's youngest brother," I said. "I guess I forgot to consider the obvious."

I put everything else back in the box while Nomi gathered up the scraps of dinner. We trooped upstairs to the computer. That first google search got me 442 links (which was interesting, because Joseph orders the goblet to be concealed in Benjamin's pack in Genesis 44:2, but I know, *you don't really believe in that sort of thing*). I'd like to say that Benny turned up in the first link, but it took me two whole days and all my investigative chops to eliminate a bunch of real estate agents, dentists, and stockbrokers. Nomi made the point that it was unlikely my brother would be alive and thriving in some profession: what then would have explained my parents' choice to keep him a secret? I gritted my teeth and started searching records of a different kind. It took me another two days to find a Benjamin Marks, 65, in a care facility for mentally disabled adults.

     Arlene Goldbard

Nomi offered to go with me, but I decided to go alone. My plan was to face him if I could, or if I couldn't, at least to find out as much as possible about my mystery brother. I filled my briefcase with Daddy's mustering-out papers post-Korean War, a clump of family photos, my own birth certificate and anything else I could find that would substantiate to the powers-that-be that this stranger and I were related. Even if I didn't know whether I wanted us to be.

I needn't have bothered. The care home was cheery, pastel walls and silk flowers everywhere. A young woman with the characteristic features of Down's Syndrome was coloring with crayons at a small table. She welcomed me with a big smile, which I returned. I explained my errand at the front desk and a nice lady with glasses on a chain and a flowered blouse came out to greet me. I showed her the contents of my briefcase and filled out a few forms, wondering why these bureaucrats were being so cooperative. "Benny's room is right down this hall," she said. It was pleasant and comfortable-looking, painted a soft blue. There were the expected furnishings—a chest of drawers, a small table, a couple of upholstered chairs. But also a large open toy chest filled with dolls and cars and puzzle boxes.

As soon as I saw Benny, I realized it had been the photos that turned the key, making me welcome. Seeing him was like seeing my father, only the picture was slightly out of focus, the eyes didn't quite line up.

Benny took one look at me and his pupils dilated. He turned his head to the side and said "Mommy?" in a tentative, quizzical voice. I suppose he was wondering how Estelle could reappear as her younger self. I said I wasn't his mommy, but that we were family, and he could call me Sharon.

The doctor in charge told me that Benny had lived his entire life in the home, that my parents had set up a fund to support his expenses, and that they'd come to visit him at least once a month as long as they lived.

I don't expect I will ever know the real story, but I think I may have guessed one of the elements. Working out the dates, I think that my father was still in the Navy when Benny was born, and that when his profound mental deficits began to be apparent, my mother couldn't cope. Whether what she couldn't cope with was shame or disappointment or the obvious difficulties of being left alone with a fast-growing child whose mental age would never come close to his physical age, I can't say. Whether Benny was concealed from me with the idea of protecting me, giving me a "normal" childhood, or for some other reason—some nineteen-fifties mental hygiene theory of what would be fitting and proper—I can't know. I think of my friend Ron, who grew up with a sister not so different in her abilities from Benny. He was left with a lifelong ambivalence: admiring his parents for their dedication and sacrifice, resenting them because everything went to his sister, there was no room for him to be anything other than responsible and self-denying. I don't think what my parents did was "right," but I can't see that makes any difference. What's done is done. Am I satisfied with understanding the big secret? Wouldn't you be?

So now I come once a month to visit Benny, bearing gifts of fruit and candy, small toys—he especially loves things that wind up and jump around, frogs and bunnies and like that. We sit for an hour. We play with blocks and dolls. We do a puzzle meant for toddlers. We look at pictures of Estelle and Harry. Sometimes I tell him a story, sometimes he tells me one. He hugs me when I leave.

The home has Benny's birth certificate, so I was able to learn his birthday. On the first birthday after we met, I brought him the little *kiddush* cup. I guess I was hoping for a spark of recognition as I took it out of the bag, as I showed him the Hebrew letters that spell out his name. In his plump hand, the cup looked like something you might buy for a doll's tea party. He held it up to his mouth and pretended to drink. Then he gave it back to me, saying, "Would you keep it for me, Sharon? I might lose it." I said I would. I put it on the mantle, right next to my own cup from Bubbe Fay.

Imagine a doctor who has to swallow some of her own medicine.

     Arlene Goldbard

JONATHAN

People like my friend Sharon Marks, who acts as a *melitz yosher*—offering prayers of intercession for those who have a problem or an illness—have a funny way of talking about pleading a case before a heavenly court. They say they "go upstairs." So let me begin by saying I am writing this from upstairs.

I am one of the one million-plus Americans who succumbed to the COVID-19 virus. All were unfortunate, but I hope I can be forgiven for sometimes thinking I was especially so, because I was neither exactly elderly at 62 nor apparently ill when I contracted the disease. I say "apparently" because I did have a little cough at the time. Spring allergies, I thought, getting out the neti pot and homeopathic remedies that kept me breathing each year. But it turned out to be chronic obstructive pulmonary disease, most likely the start of emphysema that would have evolved for years had COVID not accelerated things. When I died in the fall of 2020, three earth years ago, there were ventilators around, but a shortage of people who had the knowledge and availability to deploy them properly. I died, exhausted, holding the hand of a kind and traumatized "essential worker" who had done her best to handle the volume of patients in the ICU. People just couldn't keep up.

Upstairs, however, I breathe like a bellows and never seem to get tired.

I'm not going to answer the obvious question: "What is it like in the world to come?" It's not that I don't want you to know. It's that there is no fixed reality here. The closest I can say is that it's a little like beaming up on *Star Trek* and a little like tripping on LSD. We souls envisage where we want to be, a place of memory or imagination, and in the next moment, there we are. You'd think that not having a body would be somewhat abstract, but you can also imagine yourself into the body you used to inhabit and all the sensations—sights, sounds, smells—that went with it. So while I'm not *actually* chewing on my bubbe's challah, or sipping bitter coffee while schmoozing with fellow souls Martin Buber, Hannah Arendt, and Edward Said (when we died didn't matter as our souls are here forever, offering a huge range of opportunities to connect), hiking the Grand Canyon in spring, or strolling slowly around the enormous sunlit brick bowl of the Piazza del Campo in Siena, my experience comes very close to what I remember as reality.

When I was in *Assiyah*, the most material of the four concentric worlds described by the Kabbalists—in other words, when I was grounded on Planet Earth—most of my life focused on spirituality, Jewish primarily, but also depth psychology and Ram Dass and The Mother and pretty much any window into the non-material worlds I felt all around me, even if I could not touch or taste them. For me, spirituality, cosmology, psychology, feminism, all these could be mapped onto our experience in a way that teaches us something deep and valuable.

When I was alive, it was sometimes hard for me to distinguish what I *wanted* to be true from what I *knew* to be real. If you perceive every ordinary thing as a sign or reminder of holiness, then messages from a force beyond the material world arrive constantly. An apple reminds me of Adam and Eve (or Chava, as we call her). At the seashore, I imagine the waters parting to allow our people to cross the Sea of Reeds on dry land. A bird in flight calls to mind my favorite psalm, 91:

> With pinions you will be covered;
> you will find refuge under God's wings—
> whose fidelity is an encircling shield.

If back then you had forced me to say whether what I saw was real, I would always have replied that I didn't know. Why reject what cannot be resolved? My friend Sharon told me that almost everyone who comes to see her for an intercession is desperate for help and clutching at her as a last resort. She usually has to tell them a few times that she knows they don't believe in what she's doing just to get them to relax enough to actually experience it. Life is uncertainty. Why pretend otherwise?

Death, on the other hand, is certain. It turns out the best part of being dead is absolute certainty about the true nature of existence. But knowing that wouldn't have helped me much when I was alive, because the true nature of existence is infinitely, perpetually mutable. In the time it takes to say *Now*, that now has passed, only to be replaced by another and another and another.

Which doesn't mean you can't plan things or fix them or figure them out, just that in all likelihood, you will have to plan them or fix them or figure them out all over again.

Up here, however, we have certain powers I lacked when I inhabited a body. So far, I'm really enjoying using them for the greater good. I'm a channel or helper for people like Sharon who are stuck in the material world hoping that all the things they do as a *melitz yosher*—the prayers and chants and pleas and bargains—will help whomever they're interceding for. I don't plead before a court like a defense attorney, but I try to give a little boost to the people like Sharon who do that work.

     Arlene Goldbard

When earthbound intercessors open a session, they start with prayers or chants that are intended to provide spiritual protection. Sharon seems to like "*Emet v'Yatziv*," meaning true and enduring. It has a nice rhythm and traditionally follows the recitation of the morning *Shema*—the foundational Jewish prayer. It is basically a series of adjectives: "genuine, established, enduring, upright, faithful, loved, cherished, desirable, pleasant, awesome, mighty, correct, acceptable, good, and beautiful is this affirmation for us forever and ever." Sharon does it three times, patting her hand on a table or the arm of her chair as she chants.

"Protection from what?" you may ask. From the *Sitra Achra*, the "other side," the realm of evil. If you are trying to go upstairs and bargain with the forces there, how do you know if you have contacted good angels or imposters, evil spirits? Intercession is a process of negotiation. What if you inadvertently find yourself negotiating with a pretender, a spirit who does not wish the person well, but would be quite happy to increase the suffering of whomever you are interceding for? The consequences could be terrible.

If Sharon were here (and let me say there is absolutely no rush to come upstairs, may she live 120 healthy years!), this is where she would say "I don't really believe in that sort of thing." This is because to her, it sounds like a Manichean universe in which forces of good and evil contend for each life, and that does not fit her idea of truth. Yes, she's heard a million times that the *yetzer hara* (the evil inclination) and the *yetzer hatov* (the good inclination) are active in each person. She even likes the saying that "where the *yetzer hatov* dwells, the *yetzer hara* seeks," which seems a handy explanation for why so many clergy of all faiths are tempted to descend into sin and exploitation. But it isn't truly a Manichean understanding, because it's not like two powerful outside forces—a God of light and a devil of darkness—are pulling us in opposite directions. Both inclinations are built into the human subject. The battle rages within each of us, but some people mistakenly feel they are immune.

That's not Sharon, though. I'd say she just underestimates the evil inclination. She recites *Emet v'Yatziv* and maybe a few other psalms or prayers before she starts an intercession. She asks the Source of Blessing to protect her, to let her know if she herself needs to do *t'shuvah*—to cleanse herself—before she is worthy to intercede. But from knowing her when I was alive, I don't think she feels intensely at risk of being deceived by the *Sitra Achra*. This is a thing about humans. Not all of us, but as a rule we see evil but don't see ourselves as potential evil-doers. Yet everyone is equally susceptible to both the *yetzer hara* and the *yetzer hatov*. So that is where I now come in.

You don't need special talents to be a *melitz yosher*. In fact, a common thing to say when someone passes away is "May he (or she) be a *melitz yosher* for us." The idea is that such persons are now closer to the heavenly court and so more able to plead a case. Jews don't have a formal practice of ancestor worship like some other peoples. But we like the idea that someone who cared for us while alive would want to be an intermediary if we need the mercy or blessing of higher powers. Mostly I engage with people like Sharon whom I know to be good-hearted and knowledgeable, whose accounts of what they are doing (which I overhear if I tune in) are believable to me.

When I eavesdropped on Sharon's second session with Ken Simon earlier this year, I had no trouble comprehending. His complaint was writer's block. It had been going on for a while. The issue was self-doubt induced by the madness of social media and other public discourse. Did he have something worth saying to offer? Could he be heard?

Before listening to Ken's story, Sharon started with *Emet v'Yatziv* as usual. She asked if she was authorized to continue, and didn't hear a *No*. But I could tell that something gnawed at her, a subtle feeling that perhaps she was doing this wrong, or for the wrong reasons. One way a message like that comes through is thinking of yourself as wanting to help, and then getting a chagrined feeling that maybe what you really want is to be admired or appreciated for helping. If that builds for a while, you either run away with your ego or start putting yourself down for being ego-driven. Either way, you're no help at all.

That's where I dropped in. I didn't think Sharon could sense the internal battle that was just beginning to form, but I could hear it as clearly as if a person were whispering in my ear. You see, the essential thing about interceding for someone is to not get caught in thinking you have magical or healing powers, because the person who needs help will often lay that on you. *You're a miracle worker! I can't thank you enough!* That kind of stuff goes to your head, sometimes in such a sneaky way that you aren't even aware of it. But if you listen closely, you will be able to discern it because something starts blocking what had been a clear channel of listening, a true receptivity.

The antidote to the *Sitra Achra*, to the negative voice that may answer you in the guise of helping, is to think of yourself as *nothing*. It isn't your thoughts or feelings, your words or actions that will help the person you are interceding for. You are not your thoughts. You are not your feelings. Those move through you like weather through a busy sky. If you are doing the work, you let them pass, concentrating every iota of your being on listening. If you listen with caring and patience, the remedy—the assignment—will be revealed.

   Arlene Goldbard

So I slipped onto the same plane as Sharon and felt the *yetzer hara* trying to wrap itself around her heart. "This one is easy," it was telling her. "Just give him the same assignment you gave that artist. Painter, writer, what's the difference?" I slipped my hand (I know, I know, I don't have one anymore, but stick with me, the metaphor works just as well as the fleshly organ) between the *yetzer hara*, which had taken the form of a serpent, and Sharon's heart. Then I squeezed the serpent tightly, cutting off its breath.

In the next world, we have a way of communicating without words. I sent Sharon this thought: *Keep listening, that is not the message. Listen more deeply.* And she did. I knew she could because I remembered that the first time she helped Ken, a year before I died, she listened so hard that underneath the message she received for Ken was one for herself, just as profound.

Here I take advice from Rabbi Simcha Bunim of blessed memory, who taught that every person should keep guidance in two pockets. In one pocket should be a piece of paper saying: "I am but dust and ashes," words spoken by Abraham in *Bereshit*. In the other pocket should be a piece of paper saying: "For my sake was the world created," which comes from the Babylonian Talmud. You titrate the dosage, reading one text when your ego swells, the other when life has you down. Neither truth cancels the other.

It took me a while to come up with a title for my job. To be clear, nothing is actually a job up here: no bosses, salaries, working conditions. I guess you could say everything we do is a hobby, but that doesn't really fit either, as there are things souls may do for play—believe it or not, there's a sizeable group of people who want to play golf for all eternity—and things we do because our desires to learn or to help or to expand our consciousness somehow persists even when we no longer have bodies to express them. When I thought of myself as being a kind of guardian for the *melitzim yosher* of my acquaintance, one step removed from the role of intercessor, I gave my role a title, *Tsofah*— watcher, observer, scout.

In Assiyah, back on Planet Earth, my title was Rabbi, of course. Observing was a big part of it, but thinking, feeling, acting, and caring were bigger. People used to ask me why I decided to be a rabbi, but in truth, it wasn't a decision. I came from a not very religious family—High Holy Days and Pesach Jews— but from an early age, I was drawn to study and practice. I was sent to a sort of Conservative Sunday School (the name tells you everything). My parents thought I should have some type of grounding in Judaism, at least know something of the holy days and histories, maybe learn enough Hebrew so it wouldn't be a struggle when I had to prepare for my bar mitzvah. But I was lucky to be given a teacher who wasn't just going through the motions. As soon as I walked into Daniel's class and saw him sitting on the edge of his desk singing a *niggun*—a wordless melody great teachers such as Rebbe Nachman believed had the power to heal or uplift or transport—I felt as if a soft cord had been looped around my body and I was being reeled in, hand over hand. I didn't even know what *it* was yet, but from that moment I wanted more. Always more. I sometimes seek out the Besht—the Baal Shem Tov, a towering figure in the development of Hasidism—to hear "The Niggun of the Besht" from the source. I close my eyes and remember my teacher Daniel, and sometimes that brings him to me too.

That great desire to learn never left me. My young brain's neuroplasticity helped me learn languages and memorize sacred texts quickly. For this, I was praised. My parents didn't quite know what to make of me. Looking back, I see they were half-afraid I would be taken away from them, not in the sense of abducted, more seduced. But I pleaded with them to let me study much more than that one afternoon each week, and before long, I was enrolled in Cheder Chabad, a school for boys run by an Orthodox Hasidic movement that by now has an empire spanning the globe.

Their flavor of Judaism is closely observant. You will see Chabadniks on the streets of most cities wearing white shirts with fringes—*tzitzit*—peeking out at the waist, black suits, black hats, full beards and *payess*, side curls. They are the men dressed that way who corner Jews around the time of major holidays or at prayer times, asking if they want to take part. It's an old lineage, dating back to the 18th century. Unlike some other expressions of Judaism, Chabad prizes ecstatic practices—mystical teachings, dancing, giving oneself over to God—as much as learning Torah and practicing the *mitzvot*, the rules that guide religious life.

In other words, it was a total immersion experience, and I dove in without hesitation. I received accolades for my learning and diligence. By the time I was ready to graduate from yeshiva, it had been made clear that people had high hopes for my future. I got to meet with the Rebbe, which was a great honor. And yes, you may have guessed it, all this went to my head. I began to wonder why I, admired as a prodigy, should abide by the same rules and prohibitions given to every ordinary student. I began wanting to see more of the world than the four walls of the *shul*—the synagogue—and the *beit midrash*, the study

    Arlene Goldbard

house, could show me. I wouldn't have said so, but I decided to test God.

I invented a doctor's appointment and snuck out to Philadelphia. I bought a wig to cover my Chabad haircut, short on top with long *payess*. I don't think it did the job very well, because people stared at me wherever I went, even though I'd tucked in my *tzitzit* and changed my white shirt for a T-shirt. I went to a movie that featured half-dressed women. I ate *treyf* (non-kosher food). I waited to be struck down or at least punished, but the only punishment that came was my own guilt at having such secrets. I would venture out, repent for a while, and after a time transgress again. I felt sure the *Sitra Achra* was pushing me, and increasingly I was scared of being pushed too far.

But instead of having to make a decision, time moved on and chose for me. Yeshiva ended, and I thought I might take a break before what was likely to be my next assignment, maybe teaching in Cheder, maybe taking my place as one of the envied ones who spent their days learning, praying, and writing. To my surprise and delight, I was invited to study at Chabad in Israel for a year. So that's what I did, only I ended up staying for three years, at the end of which I was ordained as a rabbi.

At this time, there was a great spiritual ambition throughout Chabad to connect with Jews who had fallen off the path—or completely secular Jews, who had never been on it in the first place—and bring them in. Starting in the late sixties, emissaries were appointed to go into cities with significant Jewish populations and act as shepherds, rebuilding the flock. A decade or so later, this became my mission, going to college campuses and neighborhoods where hippies gathered, and connecting young people who had strayed into Yoga or Zen to the elements of their heritage that addressed the same spiritual needs.

As so often happens, the one who is appointed rescuer rescues himself. Enough deeply intimate spiritual conversations with newly fired-up adepts of Eastern philosophies and I began to see that it might be time for the world of Judaism to let in a little air and learn from them. It turned out I wasn't the only Chabad emissary who was thinking along these lines. There's a story I won't tell about a bunch of us dropping acid together and seeing the shining features of Abraham, Isaac, Jacob, and Moses superimposed on our friends' faces. I was the youngest, the junior of the group, but that gave me access both to people I honored as teachers and people my age who weren't so easy for the others to reach.

That led to a lot of travel, to study in ashrams and zendos, and ultimately to a post as rabbi in one of the hippest of the hip centers of new Judaism, where Torah study was always an experiment and Jew was always a verb. We were

Jewishing. Men and women shared the *bimah*—the table on which the Torah was read. Women were ordained, men and women receiving personal *s'micha*—ordination—from those considered senior teachers. Not me. I didn't have the gravitas or chutzpah at that age. But some of the other emissaries who'd become rabbis at Chabad before venturing out gathered quite a few acolytes. And all of that was good. We called it Jewish Renewal because it was renewing the tradition, refreshing what had grown stale for us.

That time led to the most important spiritual insight of my life, and one of the things that makes me sorriest my life was cut short. I realized you can make an idol out of anything.

The Jewish prohibition against idolatry is well-known. The Torah is full of injunctions against carving figures out of wood or casting them in bronze and worshipping them as deities. There is a most famous *midrash*—a story that adds incident and dimension to the core sacred texts—that makes the point perfectly.

Our patriarch Abraham, when he was still the young boy Avram, was the son of an idol-maker. One day his father Terah left him in charge of his shop. Avram took a stick and shattered some of the idols. Then he positioned the stick in the arms of the largest idol. When his father returned, saw the mess, and asked what had happened, Avram explained that someone had come to make an offering and the idols began to fight over who would consume it. The largest idol won out and smashed the others. Terah said this was impossible: these figures can neither eat nor fight. Avram's reply? "Why then do you worship them?"

The prophet Isaiah outright ridicules the practice in 44:15:

> He takes some to warm himself,
> And he builds a fire and bakes bread.
> He also makes a god of it and worships it,
> Fashions an idol and bows down to it!

The idolators depicted in Torah invested their creations with power, not just symbolism. I realize that many of those whose worship involves images of saints, prophets, and deities don't necessarily endow objects with divine powers (though don't get me started on miraculous healing relics). They see the objects as symbols of something much greater, as pointers to holiness. But we Jews are forbidden to worship such objects.

     Arlene Goldbard

When I say you can make an idol out of anything, this is what I mean: part of the hubris intrinsic to human beings is our capacity and desire to worship our own creations.

Social media! Computer projections! QAnon! Artificial intelligence! When I left *Assiyah,* I feared for the future of humanity not only because of the epidemic, but also because of the enraptured credulity with which people were believing things that had obviously been made up to profit from their gullibility. When my daughter Sarah was small, she sometimes asked me if she could do some outlandish thing. Her defense would be that a friend was doing it. I would give the usual parental reply: "If Debby told you to jump off a bridge, would you do that too?" I died afraid that half the country was ready to jump off a bridge, or at least drink bleach. And the root of it all was worshipping their own creations. The *yetzer hara* loves viral technology.

But when I first learned the full implications of this lesson decades earlier, it was before anyone I knew even had a personal computer. When I took that first rabbi job with the hip *shul,* Ahavat Olam (roughly translated, "eternal love"), most of the members were bona fide hippies. They'd resisted the draft, smoked dope, lived in communes, questioned anything their parents believed, and so on. The community was loose, but it had grown to the point where quite a few members felt it would be good to have an actual rabbi rather than rely entirely on lay leaders. The lay leaders were knowledgeable, but there were a lot of them, some more determined or entitled than others, so what would start out as a civil discussion about who would give the *d'var Torah*—the teaching on that week's Torah portion—could easily end up as a shouting match or worse between contenders for the limelight, however dim it was.

When I was hired, one of the conditions was that I shouldn't capitalize the word "rabbi" in my title. You could take it as an e.e. cummings gesture, but it carried a lot of symbolic rather than literary weight. I was told that a capital letter would make me seem like I was trying to be better or more important than everyone else. So I decapitalized.

I wish that had solved the problem, but the truth was, the personal history this group of Jews shared included resistance to all forms of earthly authority. The most popular bumper sticker I saw in those days read "Ignore alien orders." I tended to think of myself as mild-mannered and cooperative, but in a meeting to plan the next week's services, if I suggested that something should be done a certain way, I was instantly chastised for dictating to the group. Almost every meeting ended with people walking away feeling bad. There were many group sessions and mediations intended to cool things down, but none of them worked for long.

How is this idolatry? I'll tell you. The Ahavat Olam crew worshipped their freedom from authority and convention, the way of being they had created for themselves. They had constructed a culture in which everyone constantly judged whether others were overstepping their bounds, and if they deemed it so, chastisement would surely follow. When I left to start Or Chadash, the Jewish Renewal *shul* I served until I died, someone who had been a friend and ally said this to me: "Some people are slaves to their own freedom." I thought that was apt.

Why did the lesson about idolatry make me especially sad that my life was cut short? Because it was one of many things I wanted to teach my daughter. She and I were a team, more so than ever since her mother passed when Sarah was just ten years old, six years before me. Judy had stomach pain the doctors told her would go away if she avoided certain foods and stresses. But when we insisted they listen to us, that it was only getting worse, that she was losing weight and couldn't feel rested no matter how long she slept, the tests they hadn't wanted to order revealed advanced pancreatic cancer.

Sarah and I missed her every day. When COVID started, it felt like just the two of us, marooned. Everyone else was a ghost or a shadow on Zoom. When I got sick, the most beautiful kindness emerged. Sarah was my heir, of course, but too young at 16 to care for herself. I made Sharon the executor of my estate, put the big house and everything we owned in trust, and Sharon and her good friend Nomi moved in with Sarah, determined to support her through the rest of high school and beyond. I knew they would be perfect guardians, just as I knew that Anya Applebaum, Or Chadash's *Shomer*, would shepherd the community through what was to come.

Another reason I became a *Tsofah*, watching from upstairs over Sharon's *melitz yosher* experiences, was that it gave me a way to glimpse Sarah from time to time, to discover that laughter had snuck back into her life in the spaces between grief and fear, to see that she could accept comfort from the women she now called her "aunties."

I see Judy upstairs all the time, of course. We put on our old bodies, the healthy ones, and sit across from each other, holding hands. It's hard to explain about sex upstairs, because there is no space for desire, since everything can

     Arlene Goldbard

be manifested just by imagining. But love is everywhere, and learning that—immersing myself in that, swaddling myself in it like a blanketed baby—is the very next best thing about being dead, right after understanding the nature of existence. Judy isn't interested in being part of this *melitz yosher* thing, but she likes me to keep her posted. She's been a member of a chorus up here, souls who loved to garden. Each member adopts a tree or flower or even a blade of grass, and at regular intervals, each sends a whisper in that plant's direction: "Grow," they croon, "grow, grow."

Yesterday, checking in on Sharon, I found Sarah telling her about a problem. Sharon offered to intercede for her. They were sitting on the dark blue velvet couch in the living room I remembered so well. I could almost feel its slippery softness.

Sarah was holding a pillow to her stomach and crying. "Yasmin won't even talk to me. My heart hurts. I can't focus on anything." She blew her nose on a tissue, then crumpled it and tucked it into a sweater sleeve. Judy used to do that. In fact, I thought I recognized what Sarah was wearing as one of Judy's sweaters, a bluish green color like seawater. Sarah had so much of her mother in her, her smile, a way of tilting her head when she was listening, old Kleenex drifting out of sleeves onto the floor of her closet.

Yasmin Shaheen is Sarah's girlfriend. They've been together for years.

"Start at the beginning," said Sharon. I could see how much she loved Sarah. I was so grateful for her friendship and Nomi's too. Sharon was grayer now, but still as full of energy as a spring. She was giving Sarah her full attention.

"Well, you know I'm a big peacenik when it comes to Israel-Palestine, right?" Sarah looked a little shy as she asked this.

Sharon nodded.

"Yasmin too. We were like our own little coalition, Jew and Muslim. Our love proved you could connect and care across lines that some other people wouldn't cross."

"*Proved?*" asked Sharon, stressing the d, "not present-tense *proves?*"

I was pretty sure what was coming. We don't play politics upstairs, except schmoozing in the coffeehouse and even there we know it will take eternity to sort things out in *Assiyah*. But some of us still pay attention to what is going on. In the earthly year of 2023/5783, the horror of Israel-Palestine had not escaped us. Buber and Said and Hannah Arendt took no comfort in the fact that they had warned of this. Many wise people had counseled Jewish-Arab cooperation in a binational state, but Ben Gurion's vision of a Jewish-run homeland had won out. Neither did they pretend that the forces that cared more about winning the contest of blame than making peace would be able to lead the way out of this hell. From what we all could see, what had been bad had gotten worse, and the wrong people were in charge of everything. I guess you could say the main thing we shared with those still living was a sense of powerlessness. And now Sarah was feeling it too.

"Yasmin's brother Ahmed is this big revolutionary," Sarah said to Sharon. "He's never liked me. Yasmin pretends we're just friends when he's around—he doesn't like lesbians either. On October 8, he was posting paraglider memes and celebrating Hamas' righteous act of resistance."

Sarah put her head in her hands and sobbed for a few moments, then continued. "I thought Yasmin and I were on the same side, the side of justice and peace. I thought if two people showed it could happen, then two more and two more would do the same until the tide turned. But the death toll in Gaza! Blocking the aid trucks! Iran! Lebanon! It's going on and on! Yasmin knows I'm sick about it. She knows I hate Netanyahu. I know she hates the way Hamas uses and abuses its own people. Human shields! But she says she can't see me anymore. It's not only her brother but her father, her uncles, a bunch of her friends. She feels like she's being torn apart. I want to comfort her, but she won't even answer my texts."

I could see that Sharon understood. All Jews who called themselves "progressive" knew how it felt to be pushed out of movements filled with people who couldn't hold two realities at the same time. I heard the wails echoing from Jews who mourned Israeli deaths in October, before Israel's retaliation started, and were told that by doing so, they had betrayed justice. You had to pick one side, and it was based on identity. There were only two choices, oppressor who deserved no human rights and oppressed who were justified in whatever they did.

An upstairs friend of mine listened in on his son wrangling with all this. The kid was part of the first college protest encampment at Brown in December. Skipping classes, he had lots of time to sit around and talk with other protesters. He came into the encampment a supporter of Jewish-Palestinian peace coalitions like Standing Together and Combatants for Peace. Pro-Palestinian kids told him that those groups were tools of the Israeli state to normalize a kind of both sides false equivalency. *Normalize* was a very bad word. You were supposed to denounce any kind of cooperation between Jews and Palestinians. My friend wished he could explain to his son that if you couldn't negotiate or cooperate with the other side, war would never end—unless one people were obliterated. He wanted to ask his kids' friends what America would do if members of a mistreated group had parachuted into a big rock concert in California, Outside Lands maybe, to kill or rape or abduct a thousand or so people. But we're not supposed to interfere that way, so he didn't.

Sharon stroked Sarah's hair. My girl has that beautiful soft golden brown hair, just like her mother's. With a sad half-smile, she said, "I'm so sorry, honey. You know I'm a big peacenik too." Sarah nodded through her tears. "Like most people," Sharon said, "I have a lot of political opinions about places I don't live, places I have no power or influence. But I don't think our political opinions matter so much right now. Your problem is about love that got knocked off-course by ideology—and by family, you can never underestimate that."

Pulling tissues from a box on the couch to wipe her eyes, Sarah looked up. I thought I saw a glimmer of hope.

"Give me a little time, honey," Sharon asked Sarah. "Just sit right there and let me consult with the folks upstairs." She closed her eyes and took a few slow breaths.

I slid into her consciousness for a little eavesdropping, not intending to interfere. I didn't detect any alien energy.

"Okay," Sharon said. "I'm getting two things. One is about love, like I said. I'm getting that you should read *Shir HaShirim*, *The Song of Songs*. Have you ever read that?"

"Some," Sarah said.

"Do you remember the parts where the lovers praise each other?" Sharon picked up a book from the end table and began reading aloud.

"My beloved to me is a bag of myrrh
Lodged between my breasts.

"My beloved to me is a spray of henna blooms
From the vineyards of En-gedi.

"Ah, you are fair, my darling,
Ah, you are fair,
With your dove-like eyes!"

"I'm blushing!" said Sarah.

She was. She looked about eight. I remembered sitting with her on that blue couch, reading out loud from Harry Potter, which she loved. Her teddy—his name was Dov, Hebrew for bear—was always propped up next to her, listening too. It was good to see her smile again.

"Okay," said Sharon, slightly businesslike. "The first part of your assignment is to read *The Song of Songs*, then write your own poem to Yasmin. A song of praise, pure praise." She hesitated. "Hold on a minute. I have to get the rest of the assignment." Sharon closed her eyes again, sank back against the couch cushions. When she opened them, she said "Eighteen stanzas, one each day for 18 days. You can think how you want to give them to Yasmin, but I wouldn't advise texting. Maybe write them on cards and mail them, or take photos and send them, or even email. That's up to you. But your aim is to make her feel your love as an outpouring, a flow, and not a pressure. Okay?"

Sarah sighed and nodded. She picked up her coffee mug from the end table. It was bright red with her name and a geometric design on it. She made it in junior high art class.

"I was told there is a second assignment," Sharon said. "Now I have to receive it." After a few minutes she opened her eyes again and said "Okay."

During those few minutes, I whispered in Sharon's ear, not the physical one, but the ear of her *neshama*, her spirit. Her forehead had wrinkled in a way that made me want to check in again, and when I did, I sensed she needed a little push. What I whispered was a text from I Kings 19:12:

> After the earthquake—fire; but GOD was not in the fire. And after the fire—a still, small voice.

Then I helped an image arise in Sharon's mind: the golden calf forged in the wilderness by the formerly enslaved when they lost heart after Moses' long sojourn on Mount Sinai.

Sharon's eyes popped open, startling Sarah, who'd been staring vaguely in her auntie's direction. "No one can win this battle with Yasmin's family," Sharon said. "Arguing won't do any good. Everyone is wounded. Everyone needs calm and quiet, but they're too busy dancing around a golden calf, hoping it will save them. You need to identify the golden calf. What idol is being worshipped here? How can you and Yasmin turn away from it and toward each other?"

"I don't know," Sarah said, crumpling her wad of tissues. "What could it be?"

"I can't answer that for you," Sharon told her, "but I can give some examples.

     Arlene Goldbard

One could be ideology, that you or Yasmin can't see your love through the screen of assumptions and fixed ideas being thrown up around the war. Like if Yasmin's brother adopts an ideology that says identity equals virtue, then for him it follows automatically that you are the wrong identities to be together. Another could be authority, that Yasmin's family cannot say her older brother is wrong to be so harsh with his sister because of his position in the family. Another could be the ideas about relationships you may have inherited from Hollywood: if you're meant to be together, nothing else matters. Love conquers all. That could have you believing that Yasmin's only right choice is to abandon her family. And that could leave her with an impossible dilemma. Whenever we think there's only one way to look at something important, a golden calf, a false idol, is probably blocking the view.

"If you want to accept both assignments, Saraleh, then on each of the 18 days, in addition to your stanza, you'll need to write something exploring a possible golden calf that's taken up residence in your mind or Yasmin's. Think for a minute now, then tell me if you accept the assignments, both of them."

Watching Sarah's face as she considered this gave me joy. She was always such a thoughtful girl. Her expression was like an old-time engraving illustrating the word "pondering": brow wrinkled, mouth pursed, eyes staring into the distance without focusing on anything. She still clutched her little cushion, the one she'd embroidered with multicolored yarn flowers and given to her mother on her last birthday. I wished I could take her in my arms.

Right then, Sharon stretched out her arms to welcome Sarah into a warm hug. She brushed back my girl's hair and looked her in the eyes. "What do you say we get some ice cream while you think about it, sweetie?" Sharon asked. Arm in arm, they walked to the kitchen, my favorite room of the house, a large open space painted a creamy ivory, with pots and pans hanging from a rack on the ceiling and a big planter full of herbs in the window overlooking the garden. The sun shone in, making everything sparkle. Sarah picked chocolate chip, always her favorite. Sharon had a small dish of vanilla. I sent them both a silent blessing of well-being in all ways: health, happiness, love, community, meaning. Then I thought about telling Judy what I'd seen and suddenly, we were together.

Sarah did accept, and she followed through diligently. That poetry must have been something, because on day 18, Yasmin phoned her, crying. Laughing, too, as she said "I surrender. Who could resist?" They couldn't pick right up where they'd left off. Ahmed would make Yasmin's life miserable if he saw that. But Yasmin snuck out for a meal with Sarah at the house. They sat in a pool of light cast by the hanging lamp above the dining table. It reminded me of an old-fashioned spotlight, which seemed fitting. With Sharon and Nomi as witnesses, Sarah shared the list of possible golden calves she'd compiled. The ones Sharon had suggested were on the list, but also the obsession with who is right and who is wrong, arguing about who is to blame, and the feeling that each of them had to keep their worst fears to themselves, which pulled them apart.

The two of them pledged not to be distracted by idols, but to always try to see each other with open eyes. It was beautiful. I took Judy to a bench in the terraced Rose Garden high above the Bay with the sight and scents of full blooms everywhere and told her all about it as we held hands. She appeared just as she had right after Sarah was born, radiant, soulful, like a freshly lit Shabbos candle, letting me know how happy that made her.

I can't tell you that everything worked out happily ever after, because souls upstairs don't have the power to see the future. We aren't bound by time in the same way as life in *Assiyah*, because we can jump from one remembered moment or imagined scene to the next. There's no arrow of time. But there are many branches. It turns out the future isn't preordained, or if it is, we aren't privy to it.

There is a way we can be part of it, though. We souls upstairs have been told that we can apply to return to Planet Earth, not as our former selves, but as an old soul in a new body. I have no illusion that I can rejoin my daughter and my friends that way. Even the use of the pronoun "I" is all wrong. After all, Buber and Said are still here. For that matter, the prophet Isaiah is still here, as is Moses' sister Miryam. Even, God help him, Amalek, whom we are told to both remember and blot out. No one really wants to hang out with him, which amounts to the same thing, no? But their presence here doesn't mean they never joined *HaGilgulim*, the reincarnated, just that the I that asked permission to return to a body remains here. It's the new I and the new body that exist in *Assiyah*, animated by a Divine spark transmitted from another soul. I have no idea whether, if I took this path, I would remember my loved ones. Nor do I know if when the new I dies, the upstairs world will be familiar or entirely new.

So what should I do? Judy doesn't love the idea, even though she understands that the I she knows will remain here with her. "What if you're born in a war zone," she asks, "or in a village with contaminated water?" She doesn't want any

     Arlene Goldbard

part of me to suffer. I admit those are very good questions. I really need a *melitz yosher* to advise me, or maybe I'll just intercede for myself. No rush, though. After all, I have all the time in the next world.

NOMI

My name is Nomi, but in another life, I used to be Nancy, little Nancy Riordan. I grew up Baptist and took this Hebrew name when I decided to convert. That was 10 years ago, and it's the story I want to tell now, in 2022.

I think it's taken me all this time to tell it because I was intimidated.

You see, there's still a little voice in my head saying not to share this story. There's this caution in Jewish law against calling attention to anyone's status as a convert in case it makes them feel bad, feel puny and less than. There are tons of stories about converts in *haredi* communities—very, very Orthodox—having their conversions challenged, being forced to go through a second and more stringent conversion process before they are accepted, being asked for their conversion papers to prove their Judaism. This is extremely fucked up because we are commanded not to oppress the *ger*, the stranger: "You shall not wrong or oppress a stranger, for you were strangers in the land of Egypt." That's Exodus 22:20, and it is cited in the Talmud as the justification for this prohibition: "If one is the child of converts, another may not say to him: Remember the deeds of your ancestors."

I'm not in the *haredi* world, so that's not my experience. I'm 55 years old and still single, but I definitely won't be going to a matchmaker to find a husband or enrolling a kid in yeshiva. No one has asked me for my papers. Sometimes I fantasize that if anyone did, I'd respond *Treasure of Sierra Madre* style: *I don't need no stinking papers*. But I wouldn't do that. I'd probably shrink to the size of a pea.

My flavor of Judaism is Jewish Renewal, which we tend to shorthand as Hasidism meets feminism. Think of blending mysticism and feminism under the banner *y'all welcome.*

So I would like to be able to say that we are therefore much more likely not to make converts feel like strangers in places that should welcome them. And maybe we are if the convert doesn't advertise that fact and looks plausibly Jewish in that stereotypical way. But at one *shul* I sometimes used to go to, the last time I attended Rosh Hashanah services there, I saw a woman who'd been a member forever spot a Latino-looking couple taking their seats. She rushed up with a stiff smile to ask if they were Jewish. At last, I think it's finally beginning to dawn on the world that not all Jews are white. Rabbis and cantors with African or Asian or Latin roots are more and more often in positions of responsibility

  Arlene Goldbard

and influence in our communities. But to most American Jews and non-Jews alike, Jews are white and those who aren't have to prove themselves.

Or Chadash is the community that's least like that, the one I feel most connected to. Reb Jonathan Fox, who founded it, was the amazing teacher who helped me learn and guided my conversion process. Things aren't quite the same there since Reb Jonathan passed away early in COVID, but the longtime folks mostly feel like some kind of family. Anya Applebaum, the Shomer (which would be the Moderator or maybe the head of the Deacons in the Baptist world I grew up in) is excellent at mothering one and all. And Or Chadash is all about belonging.

Not every Jewish community is like that, so I have a little mission here in the East Bay Jewish world, and that is to make sure everyone is welcomed wholeheartedly. I'll tell you more about that soon. For now, though, know that my motivation for walking this path was partly because even though I don't raise the racism flag since I appear whitely white ("Too white?" my friend Sharon once wondered), with blonde hair, light blue eyes, and pale skin, I wasn't welcomed by one and all with open arms.

Sticklers will press me on this point, so just to be clear: there is a tradition that a person who wishes to convert should be turned away three times. If that person tries again after those rejections, then they are accepted into the conversion process. The language describing this is grounded in two different aspects of Jewish experience: a stringent idea of observance and the history of persecution. Is the person willing to accept the "yoke" of the *mitzvot*, the commandments that govern the life of an observant Jew? That's one question. But "yoke" is also understood as describing the burden of being othered, hated, oppressed. Every time I hear it, I have a mental image of people tricked out as oxen, heavy wooden yokes around their necks. So it could be argued that not feeling welcome is par for the course. But the people who made me feel unwelcome didn't have the power to block my conversion. They were just ordinary Jews expressing ordinary prejudices. Judge for yourself.

I was born in 1967 in a part of South Carolina you've probably never heard of: Beaufort County. (That is pronounced *Byew-fert*, by the way.) It's on the south coast—if people know the area, it's probably from visiting Hilton Head. But my part of the low country isn't all cocktails on the verandah, darlin'. There are more facilities housing Marines than tourists near the tiny, majority-white, solid Republican town I came up in. It's hot and steamy and Palmetto bugs hugely outnumber Palmetto trees. My parents still live in the butter-yellow clapboard house I grew up in, but I haven't visited for a very long time.

You could say I was a problem child. I never felt at home in my hometown. For that matter, I never truly felt at home in my house, our church, or the local "white school," as everyone called it back then. Segregation had been outlawed, but when the integration order came down, white parents started "Christian academies" to keep their kids from having to attend the public school, or as they called it, the "black school."

I had friends. We played with dolls and jacks and watched cartoons in my pink room with the lacy pink curtains and matching bedspread. My mother always looked so happy to see us when she came upstairs in her apron to offer milk and cookies. When the memory visits me now, her expression telegraphs relief that I was doing something "normal" instead of curling up alone on the window seat with a book that had no pictures. It seems a little cuckoo to say so, but when I did the normal things, hoping they'd make her happy was a big part of why. But if I was doing something Momma liked, inside myself I was mostly counting the minutes to get back to my book.

I liked to read the Bible, but just the part that folks called the "Old Testament." I never got around to making the profession of faith that got you baptized. Most kids were 12 or so when they did it. I just kept postponing until I was gone. I was shy and bookish. The library shelf I visited most often held twentieth century history. I checked out all the books on that rickety shelf one at a time and read them on the porch swing one high school summer vacation, cooling myself by rolling a glass of iced lemonade along my forehead. I'd gotten a Walkman for Christmas that year, and I kept it tuned low to a radio station that specialized in Southern blues and rock. When I see one of those books again, the Allman Brothers start playing in my head. I can hear "Dreams" right now. I still love them both, the books and the band.

I had dreams, or rather the same few nightmares over and over. I saw myself packed into a crowded train car, trying to hang onto my mother's hand even though I was so hungry and thirsty I could barely stand. I clutched a doll with blonde hair like mine and a white dress with lace trim. The train lurched and I felt her slip out of my hands. I woke up crying. In another dream, I saw myself entering a large room with low ceilings and blotchy concrete walls, filled with people standing naked. A soldier pointed his bayonet at me. I heard myself screaming over and over until I woke up. It was hard to go back to sleep.

     Arlene Goldbard

I got out of Beaufort County as soon as I could after high school, making a beeline for U.C. Berkeley in 1985. My waking life took a turn for the better. I made a few friends. I learned a little about other cultures and parts of the world. I saw every foreign movie the art houses showed, learned how to smoke cigarettes and drink wine and roll joints. I took walks along the bay, a very different ocean, windy and cool, pelicans and herons galore. I scared and thrilled myself with how new everything was. I had to pep-talk myself in front of the mirror just to gin up the courage to leave the house: "Toughen up, honey. You may look like a Girl Scout, but you pack a punch." I made myself do it every day and I can't recall regretting it once.

Gradually I came to feel like I belonged in the East Bay. Undergrad in English, then graduate school in what was then called the School of Library and Information Studies. I got a job on campus. I liked being a librarian: the smells of paper, ink, and leather, the cool surfaces of the tables and chairs, people asking me questions and me actually finding them the answers, the changing cast of characters, street people and professors emeriti. I also loved learning, so my main hobby was extension classes. From this distance, I think it would be fair for someone to say I'd found a way to continue doing what I'd wanted to do as a kid. But without the watchful eyes of my parents keeping track, it was all much lighter and more fun.

One day I was having coffee in my favorite old, funky, dark coffee place. I was a sucker for wood-paneled booths. Bach was playing in the background. Every other table was filled with people staring at laptop screens, half-full cups beside them. Sharon Marks, a new friend I'd met in a world literature extension class, sat across from me. This was 2012, quite a few years ago now. Lifelong learning, you know?

Sharon was fast-talking, sophisticated, comfortable asking any question she wanted. She was a little bit of a thing, but her energy was huge. Sometimes for a minute or two I wanted to be her. I complained that I was tired because I hadn't slept well the night before. She wanted to know why, so I told her about the dreams. They'd never stopped, but you could say I'd become more used to them.

"*Oy, gevalt*," Sharon said. She looked pale, even a little shaken. I told her I didn't know what that meant. "It's what we Jews say if something is shocking or forceful," she said. "Kind of like "holy shit" but not rude."

I didn't know she was Jewish. I hadn't developed much Jew-dar at that time. "Why did you say it then?" I asked.

"Because you're having dreams of the Holocaust, the transport trains, the gas chambers. Have you watched many World War II movies?"

"Not really. I used to read a lot of history of that period, but no, not much film."

"Did you ever think the dreams were about that?"

I felt a little stupid as I asked myself why not. "No, not really. When they started, I had no frame of reference. If I yelled, one of my parents came and sat with me till I fell asleep again. They'd say, *Don't fret, honey. It's just a bad dream.* After that, they were just repeats of something from childhood. I never gave them a context."

Straightening her arms as if to push the table away, Sharon took a deep breath. "Do you have any idea why you've been having these dreams?"

"You're making me nervous," I told her. I started shredding my paper napkin into tiny pieces. "I've been having them since I was six or seven. A lot of people have recurring dreams. I looked it up."

"There's a mystical concept that Jews murdered in the Holocaust were reincarnated in non-Jewish bodies, because there weren't enough of us left to go around. *HaGilgulim*, the reincarnated. They have memories of things they haven't experienced in this lifetime."

"You're saying I'm one of them?"

Sharon shrugged. "What do I know? But let's see if we can ask someone who might."

Sharon took me to see Jonathan Fox, a local rabbi—a Renewal rabbi, she told me, though that meant nothing to me at the time. We found him sitting behind a desk heaped with papers. Photos and posters covered his walls.

Some looked like mystical symbols, the figure of a human being formed from graceful strokes Sharon said were Hebrew letters, a geometric shape surrounding the image of a tree. There was a framed photograph of a dark-eyed woman who I later learned was The Mother, Sri Aurobindo's collaborator and founder of the Indian ashram city of Auroville. She had been born a North African Jew in Paris. Reb Jonathan wore an elaborately embroidered beanie that fit his head closely—a *kippah*, but I hadn't heard that word yet—and a mismatched outfit, striped T-shirt under a green plaid shirt. He had a kind smile, a short, curly, brown beard with a few gray threads, and twinkly blue eyes behind thick glasses.

After Sharon introduced us, I told him the story of the dreams. He asked me several questions, mostly details, nodding each time I replied. Then the same question Sharon had asked: "Why do you think you have these dreams? With dreams, usually there's some detail that connects with experience, some feeling or image that rhymes with waking life. Where do you think these dreams come from?"

I had a fast sinking feeling as I again admitted to myself that I'd never really considered the question. Like I said to Sharon, I'd told myself recurring dreams were pretty common. Every time one old friend of mine was stressed, she dreamt she was back in high school, late for a test, can't find the right classroom. I had a boyfriend who sometimes dreamed he missed his flight. But I couldn't really connect my dreams to stress. They just came.

"Do you ever make a note of the date when you have one of these dreams?" Reb Jonathan asked.

His question startled me. "How did you know?"

"Just a hunch," he said. "Some people keep dream journals."

"It's just a regular journal," I told him, "but I write a page or two every morning, so if I've dreamt, it's on my mind when I wake up."

"I have some thoughts," said Reb Jonathan, "but I don't want to push them on you. Let's do a little experiment, okay?"

I nodded, a tad nervous.

"How would you feel about going through your journal for this year and noting down the dates when you had one of the dreams?"

"Okay, I guess."

"Why not?" Sharon asked. She'd been standing off to the side, quietly pulling volumes off a bookshelf. I'd almost forgotten she was there.

"Yeah," I sighed. "Why not?"

When I had the list of dates, I showed it to Sharon. Up till then, I'd thought of her as a friend who shared my interest in literature classes. Now I was starting to think of her as an expert on all things Jewish.

Sharon pulled out her phone and checked each of the dates on my list, making a few notes as she went. When she looked up, that pallor I'd seen in the coffeeshop was back.

"Okay," she said. "I want to show you something and it's a little woo-woo. Does that sound doable?"

"I was the most woo-woo white girl in Beaufort, South Carolina, sugar. But coming to California has made me look pretty square. Show me."

Next to every one of the dates on my list, Sharon had written a number and some foreign-looking words. It started in January with "15 Shvat/Tu b'Shvat," and continued through the year. Notes were clustered in the fall and then there was a break till sometime in December. I looked up from the list, puzzled.

Sharon looked me straight in the eye and said "You didn't even skip *Ta'anit Esther*."

"What's that?"

"The Fast of Esther. It comes right before the holiday of Purim. Have you heard of that?"

"It's the Book of Esther, right?"

Sharon looked surprised. "How do you know that?"

"It's right there in the King James version," I told her, "after Nehimiah and before Job, right?"

She looked even more surprised. "You tell me," she said. "I tend to skip over some of those little ones."

"I know my Old Testament," I said. "Practically by heart."

"We don't call it that," said Sharon. "We say *Tanakh* or Hebrew Bible or Torah. Ever since this one Christian Bible-believing girl turned her laser-like logic on me—'You people accept the Old Testament as the word of God, so why don't you accept the New Testament?'—I got the point that to some gentiles, calling it 'old' meant 'outdated.' Did you know the Christians have their own word for that—supercessionism—though why don't they just call it replacement theory like the white nationalists? It basically says Christians have a covenant with God that replaces the Jews."

"I never heard that. Me and the church aren't such good friends," I told Sharon. "I never did get baptized. But I also never heard the answer to that girl's question. What is it?"

     Arlene Goldbard

Sharon sighed. "Well, one rabbi I know used to say that we Jews have an allergy to Christianity because we got overexposed too early, meaning they tried to force it down our throats. But I tend to look at it this way: the Torah says the messiah will come to reign in King David's place. We think Jesus was more than a little premature and definitely overconfident. These days, few of us are hoping for a king on a white horse. To Reb Jonathan and me and a lot of people I know, our hope is a collective shift in consciousness, a new era of redemption, love, and justice. Jonathan calls it '*moshiach* consciousness,' messiah consciousness."

"That makes sense," I said. And I meant it. It pretty much matched my hopes, though I tend to keep them to myself. So that was a first, hearing that my secret wish for the dawning of peace and love was shared. The more I learned about the kind of Judaism Sharon and Jonathan embraced, the more I felt its pull. But not right then, not just yet. Right then all these coincidences or whatever they were just made me feel like I was in a slightly spooky novel.

"I want to say more about your list," said Sharon. "Remember I said it was woo-woo?"

I nodded, trying to ignore the little knot in my stomach.

"Well, my friend who looks like butter wouldn't melt in her mouth, hold on tight. Your dreams coincide with every Jewish holy day on the calendar, including fast days and holidays so minor I don't know anyone who observes them." Sharon kept her eyes fixed on mine. I didn't know if she expected me to faint or leap up, but she looked watchful.

"What am I supposed to make of that?" I asked. My neck prickled.

"Let's ask Jonathan."

We walked over to Reb Jonathan's. It was a beautiful day, a different kind of beauty than I remembered from the low country where it was hot and wet and there was so much green you almost choked on it. This part of California was a dry place whose residents were devout irrigators. I could see the drip irrigation systems spouting like mad all along our route. Berkeley was a gardener's paradise. When we came to a pale green stucco one-story house Sharon pointed out as Reb Jonathan's, we saw rows and mounds of greens and tied-up onion plants filling the places where a lawn or flower beds might be. A woman with long soft brown hair tied back was on her knees in the dirt, wearing gardening gloves and a smock, weeding.

"Hi!" called Sharon. "Looking good."

"Thanks," the woman replied. "I just heard water restrictions may be coming on account of drought. I've been thinking of what we can do to conserve. Maybe a gray water system or rain barrels."

"That sounds smart," I said. "I'm Nancy, by the way."

She stood, pulling off one glove and reaching to shake hands. She had a lovely face, even features a little smudged with dirt. "Judy. I'm Jonathan's wife."

"I'm taking Nancy to see Jonathan," Sharon told Judy. "We have a Jewish mystery to solve."

Judy laughed. "You and your mysteries!" She pointed over one shoulder. "He's in his office." In less than two years, she would be dead. By then, I would be Nomi.

Sitting at his desk reading my list of dates, Reb Jonathan looked as if he were sucking on an especially delicious piece of hard candy. His lips formed a little smile, but his cheeks moved as if they were having trouble containing their contents. He pushed some piled-up papers aside, making room on his desk for my list. Then he twirled a tiny corner of his beard.

"I need to tell you a story," he said. "It's a little far-fetched, but I'm sure it's also true. Are you with me?"

When I nodded, he explained that there's a line of Jewish thinking that goes back to medieval kabbalists describing the *gilgul neshamot*—more or less the recycling of souls. Some stories talk of great teachers having been reincarnated through many generations, ascending to heights of wisdom and holiness. More common, he said, is the idea that the divine sparks released from a soul whose body is passing can be received into multiple bodies. I was to learn that Reb Jonathan was a bit of a science nerd. He often surprised me by dropping tidbits about physics or whatever. He said it was a little bit like the scientific law of conservation of matter, which says it cannot be destroyed, just transmuted.

One particular wrinkle on that idea—and here, he said we were coming to the heart of the matter—is that when six million Jews were murdered during the Holocaust, there weren't enough Jewish bodies left to receive them. "As a matter of fact," he said, turning his head so he was looking at me sideways, "80 or so years on, there are still fewer Jews on the planet than there were in the

1930s. Post-Holocaust, some believe, many of those souls wound up in non-Jewish bodies, and some of those soul-bearers felt it. They say the signs are visions, fears, déjà vu experiences." He paused for a beat. "And dreams."

Something sizzled in my stomach like a hot rock dropped into a pond.

Reb Jonathan said he thought I could be one of them. He reached for a book on a high shelf and handed it to me: *Lovesong: Becoming a Jew*, by Julius Lester. "This man was a well-known writer and civil rights activist in the sixties. He grew up in the south, son of a Christian minister. He had dreams and experiences like you, and he also had a powerful calling to discover their source. He became a Jew. If you'd like to read this, I think you'll find it useful."

"He's black," I said, looking at the dust jacket.

"Jews come in all colors," Sharon and Jonathan said in not-quite-unison.

Reading that book was the true start of my journey. It frightened and attracted me. It made me want to go home, if I understood home as a place I'd never actually lived.

Reb Jonathan had classes each week in his crowded office. Usually just a few people came: me; Sharon; a man who seemed to know the whole Torah and many commentaries by heart, but whose Asperger's had him asking inappropriate questions a few times each evening; a changing cast of Reb Jonathan's congregation members. He was rabbi of a Renewal congregation called Or Chadash, New Light. I started going there sometimes too, sitting next to Sharon, or if she wasn't there, sitting in the back and trying to figure it all out.

For class, we read things that related to upcoming holidays or Torah portions—a reading that's assigned for each Shabbat—and then we talked about them. We said a blessing for studying Torah first, and in between topics, we sang songs in Hebrew, or wordless *niggunim*, spiritual melodies. It was interesting and informal, a no-stupid-questions type of situation. I wasn't sure why I was there except that I liked it. I was learning, and it had become something Sharon and I did together, deepening our friendship. We'd go out for a glass of wine after and chew everything again. I couldn't explain to anyone who knew me back in the day why I loved it so much, but I left every class wishing I didn't have to wait for the next class to begin.

A few months in, though, I was asked to explain my presence. Or maybe justify it. An older woman started showing up. She was chunky and serious, with short, straight gray hair and black-rimmed glasses. She vaguely reminded me of a teacher whose presence always tied my tongue, that aura of knowing much, including how little I knew. There was a right and wrong for Batya Stein, and she was fine with telling you when you were wrong, which in my case was obviously a lot of the time. I stumbled over names and concepts. I'd learned the Hebrew letters enough to sound out words, but not yet well enough to comprehend their meanings. I'd gotten used to asking a lot of questions, and up till then no one seemed to mind.

One night we were all sitting around a tableful of books and papers. It was dark outside, but the room was filled with golden light from the assortment of old lamps Jonathan had perched on every available surface. Batya sat next to me. It was a little chilly, and she was wearing a warm-looking gray wool jacket, buttoned all the way up. There was a lull in the conversation. She turned to me, staring right into my eyes, and asked this: "Why are you here?"

My first impulse was to escape by joking. "Is that an existential question? I guess God made me like the rest of us."

Sharon chuckled.

"No," said Batya, shaking her head impatiently. "Why are you taking these classes? Are you planning to marry a Jew?"

"What?" That seemed so off the wall. "I'm not getting married anytime soon, if ever."

"So why?" Batya insisted.

Reb Jonathan raised a hand, starting to speak, but I beat him to it. "I think I'm supposed to be a Jew," I told her. "I'm studying for conversion."

Reb Jonathan looked a little surprised. "I was wondering if that was about to emerge," he said.

As far as I'd known when I arrived that night, it wasn't. But here it was. I gulped. "I wasn't planning to say it. The words said themselves." Actually, they jumped out of my mouth like a little green frog.

Batya bristled. "Did the words sign up for JDate?"

Jonathan's hand rose again, palm facing Batya. "We are forbidden," he told her, "to oppress the *ger*, the stranger."

'I'm sorry, Rabbi," she replied. But then she mumbled something under her breath. I heard "*shiksa*."

     Arlene Goldbard

When we debriefed over wine later on, Sharon explained to me that some people convert because they want to marry a Jew whose spouse must be Jewish. It might be about family acceptance. Potential grandparents might need assurance that children would be raised Jewish. But it could also be about a sincere spiritual awakening, a deep attraction. A *shiksa* was a non-Jewish female, Sharon said, but it wasn't exactly a term of endearment.

The next time I came to class, Reb Jonathan took me aside to apologize. "I should have stopped Batya right away," he told me. "Some people appoint themselves judges. I'm sorry to say she won't be the last one you'll meet."

The cat was out of the bag. I was becoming a Jew and all the Or Chadash regulars knew it. Anya, who was even-tempered and nice to everyone, was extra-nice to me, taking me aside to say I could call her anytime, whatever I needed. In every class, I learned something that added to that feeling of homecoming.

Pesach—Passover—was amazing. Some of the people at Sharon's Seder joked about having to slog through the *Manischewitz Haggadah* at family Seders. I'd never seen it, but I got the impression that it was long and maybe dull. Sharon used a bright, eclectic sort of booklet that drew not only on the traditional Jewish story of the exodus, but built on it, adding readings and stories that connected us to other peoples' enslavement and liberation. The Seder plate, sitting in the middle of the table surrounded by candles and wineglasses, was filled with the standard ritual foods, but also held an orange to call to mind all of the excluded, and a glistening dish of olives in solidarity with the Palestinians. I can't exactly explain it, but try to imagine: a meal that is a ceremony in which everything you eat and drink brings you closer to freedom.

What I loved most about Reb Jonathan's perspective was this: If someone asked how Jonah could have survived in the belly of a giant fish, his response was that the story was deep metaphor, not literal history. Jonah resisted God's call to go to the wicked city of Nineveh. He was trapped in the belly of his own fear. The story posed this question: what are we being called to do, and how we are responding?

I learned that the same framework applies to Passover or any other celebration or teaching or text. On Passover Jews avoid bread and other such foods, but it's not just a dietary rule or some kind of health cleanse. When we discard our leavening—*chametz,* whatever puffs things up—and eat only matzo for eight days, it's a signal to examine our lives at the halfway point in the Jewish year (halfway if you start counting on Rosh Hashanah, which isn't necessarily what everyone does), to notice what may be clogging or blocking us or inflating our egos. When we read about the escape from *Mitzrayim* (that's Hebrew for Egypt, but it also means straits or narrow places), we can think of it as a metaphor for the journey through the birth canal and be moved to inquire after our own constriction, our own desire for freedom. At Sharon's Seder, she invited everyone to ask themselves this question, and if they were willing, share their answers: "What is wanting to be born?"

Before I started on this path, I thought of time as a continuous ribbon, months and years stretching out in front and behind, counting off a life. Now my year is punctuated with special occasions, opportunities for reflection, connection, and growth. Each Shabbos and each holiday is an invitation. Each stretch of time is infused with its own qualities. I love it.

The plan was to continue through a whole year of study and practice, and at the end, Reb Jonathan would take me to a *Bet Din*, a panel of three Jews—usually rabbis—who would talk to me and if they approved, sign a certificate of conversion, and to a *mikveh*, a ritual bath where I would immerse and recite prayers. In addition to Reb Jonathan's classes and services, I would visit other congregations to get a taste of different ways of being Jewish. He and I would meet from time to time to discuss my questions and progress.

It was a busy stretch. So much to learn. Sharon was a huge help and a true friend. I enlisted her to go with me to services at other synagogues. She had her limits, though.

"You're not dragging me to anyplace with a *mechitza*," she said. I'd already heard that word in class. It was a kind of partition that Orthodox communities used to separate men from women. For the very observant in that world, there was a prohibition against *kol isha*—women's voices raised in song or prayer. Amazingly to me, people explained it as not appropriate for our voices to sound out in the presence of men. In the mild version, it would be distracting. The strict version flat-out said that it would lead to impure thoughts. Visiting old-style synagogues, you could see the balcony or fenced-off section where women sat and if they chanted, it was under their breath. In more modern settings, the *mechitza* might just be a curtain, but the women who prayed there did not sing out.

This is not the only Jewish law that creates different rules and conditions for women than men. The Orthodox women I've talked with who abide by these prohibitions say they exist to keep them safe. I have to accept that as their truth,

     Arlene Goldbard

but I couldn't believe it any more than I could believe the Southern Baptist preaching I'd sometimes heard back in South Carolina, declaring that the husband is the lord of the house, ruling over his family. Just like the Orthodox who prohibited women from serving as rabbis, the hard-core Baptists declared that the Bible prevented women from serving as elders or pastors.

Sharon was happy for me to see for myself how those attitudes shaped things. But she'd been there, done that, and wasn't buying any more of it. Listening to her talk about it was when I truly got that the different flavors of Judaism are just like Christianity: it would be nice to think it's all one happy family, but in truth, they don't necessarily like or even respect each other. When I said that, Sharon told me a joke:

Two Jews are shipwrecked on a tiny island. Years go by before they're rescued. When a rescuer does come, he notices three small buildings on the crest of the island, crafted from driftwood and palm leaves. "Is that where you live?" he asks. "Why three?" "No, those aren't houses," says one of the castaways, pointing. "That's the *shul* he goes to, that's the one I go to, and that's the *shul* neither of us would be caught dead in."

Sharon shrugged and said, "Two Jews, three opinions." I liked that too. It made me feel free.

She and I went one Saturday morning to a big Reform temple. The place was spacious and light-filled, with high ceilings and abstract stained glass windows. It looked like a midcentury modern church, but no crosses. We made our way to a back pew as streams of well-dressed people passed us. I whispered that I felt underdressed. "No," Sharon said, "you're fine. But I doubt anyone one minds if you feel that way." Then she shook her head and said, "Ignore my snark."

The service reminded me a little bit of a Presbyterian church I'd once visited back home. There was a choir. The rabbi felt familiar too, clean-cut and pleasant, peppering his sermon with quiet jokes that got quiet laughs. It was comfortable except for the feeling underdressed part. That was good to know because it made me realize comfortable wasn't necessarily what I was after. With Reb Jonathan, I felt stretched, always trying to learn and keep up. That was more like it.

I went to an Orthodox *shul* by myself. That took screwing up my courage. I put on a long skirt and a buttoned-up shirt and wore my one hat, which usually kept the sun out of my eyes when I hiked in the Berkeley hills. It was a warm day and as I climbed the stairs, I wondered what it would be like to have to be so covered up regardless of the weather. I could tell as I stood just inside the door that the place was smaller and fuller than the Reform temple. Noisier too. Folding chairs instead of pews. No stained glass in sight. No musicians. I didn't know what to expect except that there was a curtain of some kind I'd need to stay behind. I walked in and practically tripped over Batya, who looked me up and down and said, "A little spiritual tourism today?"

I was ready to turn right around and walk out when a much younger woman dressed pretty much like me slid between us, saying "Good Shabbos," and led me by the elbow to the women's section. "Have you *davened* here before?" she asked. I told her I was studying with Reb Jonathan and he had encouraged me to visit other congregations. "Welcome," she smiled, and showed me a seat. I did my best to follow the other women—when they stood up or sat down, opened their books or listened to someone speak. But the Hebrew prayers were said so fast I had to keep looking over someone's shoulder to know what page we were on. The women were friendly. They all seemed to know each other. And there didn't seem to be a competition to be best-dressed. Most of the women wore knit hats or scarves wrapped around their heads, long sleeves and long skirts. But I couldn't imagine ever fitting in.

I left right after the service, though most people stayed to eat. Batya stood on the stairs outside. "What do you think you're playing at?" she asked me.

My knees weakened. I took a deep breath and tried to stay upright. "I'm not playing," I said. "Reb Jonathan suggested I visit different synagogues. He told me he will ask other rabbis to be part of my *Bet Din*, and that I should see them lead services."

Batya laughed. "If you think an Orthodox rabbi is going to be part of a *Bet Din* with a Renewal rabbi like Jonathan, think again."

I couldn't summon anything to say. I grasped the railing and made my way down the stairs.

As August rolled around, we started preparing for the High Holy Days, *Rosh Hashanah* and *Yom Kippur* and the other holidays that follow each fall. These are the major spiritual cleansing opportunities built into the cycle of each new year. I was really looking forward to them. I'd heard umpteen stories about peak experiences. People do what is called a *cheshbon hanefesh*, a soul accounting, looking at places they have missed the mark in the past year, seeing if they have to apologize to anyone. Doing their work to get ready for the new

     Arlene Goldbard

year. A big part of the work is *t'shuvah*. If you look it up, it's usually translated as repentance or redemption, but the Renewal folks tend to think of it as turning, reorientation toward your own best self, to however you understand holiness.

There are some really cool guidelines associated with the apology and forgiveness process. For example, say the person who messed up was you and you attempt to apologize, acknowledging the harm and asking the person you'd harmed to forgive you. The tradition says that if you are refused, you should ask twice more. If someone says no three times, you are considered absolved. That seems so humane, not to be burdened forever.

I met with Reb Jonathan to talk about my own *t'shuvah* process. I pulled up a chair in front of his desk, as usual stacked with a mountain of books and papers. I cleared my throat and asked him if I had to forgive my parents.

"What for?" He looked very serious.

I told him that a few weeks before, anticipating the *Bet Din*, I'd told Momma and Daddy about my conversion. It was on a Zoom call. We did that a few times each year. Every call before then had been chitchat: *What are y'all up to? Nothing much, how 'bout you? Daddy got new tires for the truck and he's pleased as punch with them. The new kitchen curtains brighten everything up a treat.*

I was scared, but I screwed up my courage. I started with the dreams, because both my parents knew all about them and I was betting they had enough of an inkling of their meaning to connect with what I was about to say.

"Remember those dreams I used to have when I was little?"

Momma and Daddy sat side-by-side on the white couch, staring at the computer set up on the coffee table. I could see the top of a big bunch of gold chrysanthemums peeking into the frame.

"I surely do," Daddy said. "They scared the bejesus out of all of us." He took a sip from a blue coffee mug.

I bit my tongue to keep from making the obvious joke. "Well, I figured out what they mean, and it may be tough to believe, but I want to tell you."

"Okay, darlin,'" Momma said.

I explained about *HaGilgulim*, though I didn't use Hebrew words. I said I'd consulted some very wise people who knew all about that, and all the signs pointed to my being one of them, a Jewish soul reincarnated into a non-Jewish body. It made me see some things that had puzzled me for a very long time.

"I've been studying with a rabbi for nearly a year. I'll have my conversion ceremony soon. I'm becoming a Jew."

They both looked stunned, which wasn't exactly surprising. I tried to fill the silence with something that would soften it. "I know this is a stretch, and it might take some time to understand. But it is making me very happy, and I hope that will be enough to make you happy too."

"Well now, who are these wise people?" Daddy asked. "Is this some kind of cult?"

"No, Daddy, not at all. They're very well-educated and respectable." I felt about nine years old, trying to justify some childish misbehavior. "Reb Jonathan, he's the rabbi, he has his own congregation where I've been going to services." I left out the part where Or Chadash rented space from a Unitarian church because the community wasn't large or affluent enough to have its own building.

Momma's eyes filled. "So you're turning your back on Jesus?" I heard the soft scraping sound of tissues being pulled from a box.

"I wasn't exactly close to Jesus before, Momma. Remember how I never got baptized?"

She nodded, tearfully. "But I always thought you'd do that when you had little ones of your own. You'd have to for them to be baptized, or how else would they be saved?"

"I'm sorry to disappoint you," I told them. "The little ones aren't coming at this point. I'm pretty well past that time of life. Besides, I don't believe that. I need to live my truth."

Momma turned to Daddy. "What are we going to tell folks?" she asked. He shook his head.

Things drifted silently downhill from there. I wasn't surprised that *What would people think?* was the main question, but it still hurt. After what felt like a long time, I said goodbye and ended the call.

"It made me realize something," I told Reb Jonathan. "I know it hurt that I rejected their hopeful fantasies for me: coming home to Jesus toting a husband and a pair of kids. I hadn't said or done a single thing that would lead them to project that onto me, but that was who they wanted me to be. But they

   Arlene Goldbard

clearly had no clue how hurtful that was to me. I don't think they ever really saw themselves as hurting me. All my life, they'd done the expected parent things in a caring way: food, shelter, education. I'm grateful for that. But anything I said or did, anything that interested me that didn't fit the template they lived inside of, they just ignored. I'm sure they were just as relieved to have me leave home as I was to get out."

"And since that conversation?" he asked.

"Nothing."

"So they haven't asked for your forgiveness?"

I laughed out loud. "I could wait on that forever," I told him. "And every time I think about it, I come up with the same conclusion. If I told them I forgive them, they'd say 'What for?' and go right on doing the same things. It would be a blank check to do the same again."

"Then, problem solved. You aren't obliged to forgive someone who hasn't asked for it."

This was new.

Jonathan opened a desk drawer and rifled through a file. He fished out a piece of paper headed "*T'shuvah* Worksheet." "Here are the steps of *t'shuvah* according to Maimonides, the Rambam, a 12th-century sage," he said. "But put into plain English."

Recognize what you did and that it was wrong or hurtful.
Feel remorse about your actions.
Stop doing harm.
Remove the wrongdoing from your thoughts.
Resolve to never do it again.
Make restitution for damages you caused.
Appease the person you hurt.
Confess to G-d about your wrongdoing.
When faced with the same situation or opportunity, do not do the harm again. This is how you know your *t'shuvah* is complete.

I read the words and looked up.

"How can you forgive someone who hasn't even taken the first step?" Reb Jonathan asked.

The relief that washed over me wasn't a flood, more of a soft shower. But it was real.

"So how are you?" Jonathan asked. We were meeting in his space the day before the *mikveh* and *Bet Din*. It was a year almost to the day since Sharon first brought me to see him. The sun was setting, flooding the room with a warm light that made everything look sort of ancient.

Sharon sat beside me waiting for the answer.

"Terrified," I said.

"Tell me about it," said Reb Jonathan.

"I've got a long list in no particular order. Batya keeps turning up like a bad penny. What has she got against me? What did I ever do to her? She treats me like an imposter and I start feeling like one. Then I think about these rabbis at the *Bet Din* and what questions they will ask me...."

Sharon smiled. "It isn't some kind of citizenship test," she said, "where they're trying to trip you up. I know both these rabbis. They are kind people, and Jonathan's support for your conversion has convinced them to take part. They trust him, and that translates into trust for you."

"I know, I know," I said. "What about the *mikveh*? Someone told me the *mikveh* ladies are bossy and businesslike. If I get the words mixed up or don't do things exactly right, will that count against me?"

"They don't grade you on the *mikveh*," Reb Jonathan said, smiling. "Just do what they say and I guarantee you'll pass. When you immerse yourself three times in living water, you will feel something completely new. A new you."

"I know, I know. But I feel so puny and weak I could disappear right here, before I even get to the *mikveh*."

"Like a grasshopper," Sharon said.

"I guess so, like a grasshopper," I replied, "or even a fly. An ant."

"Grasshoppers play a very important role in Torah," Jonathan said. "Do you remember the story of the spies?"

"I think so."

"In *Shelach Lecha*, in Numbers, the people in their wandering reach the land that has been promised to them. Spies representing all the tribes are sent to scout out the land. They are supposed to bring back some of its produce and report on whether it looks hospitable. They're supposed to feel confident because they're on a God-given mission. But nearly all of them are frightened

       Arlene Goldbard

by what they find. Bunches of grapes are so large they need to be carried on a frame. There is an abundance of everything good. The land is inhabited by giants, *Nephilim*, and the scouts are scared. They feel small in all ways. 'We looked like grasshoppers to ourselves,' they say, 'and so we must have looked to them.'"

"Internalization of the oppressor," Sharon said. "When I read Paulo Freire's writing on education, that is what he called it. Look at the sequence in that sentence. The scouts are intimidated and diminished in their own sight, and even though they have tremendous power on their side, their fear dooms them to powerlessness. In our lives now, there are people who want to make us small so they feel big—your nemesis Batya, for one—and if we aren't careful, we find ourselves going along with them."

"Remember that story," said Jonathan. "Have it in your pocket at the *Bet Din*. Bring your whole self to your transformation, full-size."

So I did. And I was transformed. The *mikveh* was the last step. You showered in a dressing room, put on a loose white robe, entered a small, sparkling tiled room, then walked down seven steps into a small pool. The *mikveh* lady inspected my fingernails first, brushed a few stray hairs off my arms, smiled at me, and helped me settle into the water. I immersed three times, repeating the blessings. I'll never forget the exhilaration I felt when my head rose into the air that third time and every cell in my body knew that I was a Jew. I have the *Shtar Giur*, my certificate of conversion issued by the *Bet Din*, hanging on my wall. I look at it every day.

In our community, *tikkun olam*—repairing the world—is central to what it means to be a Jew. To some people that means perfecting spiritual practice. There's a folk saying that if every Jew everywhere observed Shabbos properly just once on the same day—I've also heard it as twice, two Shabbats—the world would be restored to true holiness. But we tend to understand it as social action, healing action, things you do to extend care to others and to all of creation.

I should thank Batya for where my life went next—but I haven't and don't plan to. After 20 or so years at the library, I decided I'd better live up to my commitment to *tikkun olam* in a very different way. I knew Jewish history well enough to understand that we had been othered and excluded many times. I knew what my dreams had meant. After the *mikveh,* I never had the dreams again, but I never forgot them. I also knew that it was all too human to turn some version of what had been done to you back onto others—the colorism some black people experience, the stories my young friend Iz has told me about mainland Japanese discriminating against his ancestors who came from Okinawa. I knew firsthand from my encounters with Batya that there were Jews who oppressed the *ger*, contrary to our teachings.

That's why I set up the Khegev Project (you guessed it, that means grasshopper in Hebrew) the year after my conversion, to promote full inclusion and participation in local Jewish communities. I still have blue eyes and a hint of my South Carolina accent, plus a genetic tendency to call people "honey" or "sugar," so I sometimes get challenged in Jewish spaces, though less and less, as the project has made me pretty well-known locally. We provide trainings in what it truly means to welcome the *ger*, and we come to the aid of people who've been made to feel excluded, perhaps as Jews by choice or Jews of color. Every Pesach, in the in-between days, we sponsor a community Seder that takes inclusion as our theme. Together, we pass through the narrow places of misplaced judgment into the freedom of belonging.

Sharon and I are still close friends after all these years. Family, really, as Reb Jonathan's will made us aunties to his daughter Sarah, who we both adore. So for the last couple of years, we two more or less spinsters have pottered around his big, book-filled house and made healthy meals for a growing girl. To tell the truth, it feels a little like living in the library, a fantasy I never thought could come true.

Now I'm sitting here wondering why I was so intimidated about telling this story. A slight case of internalization of the oppressor, Sharon would say. Some things take a long time to heal.

     Arlene Goldbard

RIVVY

Sam and I lingered over breakfast coffee at a table littered with bagel crumbs and orange peels. The sun was getting high enough to flood the table with morning light. My eyes were drawn to the way it made the bowl of oranges sparkle. Sam was listening to me obsess, and when I wrenched my gaze from the oranges, I could see it was taking him a lot of effort to hear what I was saying and offer no advice. That reminded me of a story that made me laugh.

"What's funny?" asked Sam.

"When my cousin Avi was little, he was a bundle of energy. He could barely sit still. Once my father, may he rest in peace, offered him a shiny half-dollar if he could stand still without moving for a full minute. Avi was doing a pretty good job, but just before the second hand reached the minute mark, Tateh looked down. Avi's foot was tapping the floor a mile a minute! I think my father gave him the coin anyway. That's what you just reminded me of, Avi trying with all his might not to do something. And you, my love, you are doing a very good job of not giving me advice."

"So do you want to hear the advice I'm not giving you?" asked Sam.

"In a minute, darling. Let me finish kvetching first," I told him.

I stared out the window. Trailing vines on the plants I'd hung in pots near the ceiling were threatening to block the light. I'd have to deal with that. But not right now.

"My problem is, I have a feeling. But maybe it's just one of those referred feelings—you know, you immediately don't like someone and it turns out to be because he reminds you of your annoying ex," I explained.

"Tell me the story. Go back to the beginning." Sam leaned back in his chair like someone settling in for a long stay. I loved Sam's solid presence. As he grew older, the lines and planes of his face seemed etched and carved. I could feel his sweet substantiality a mile away. It always reminded me of that line from Blake, "the lineaments of Gratified Desire." I was lucky to have him, and he said the same to me almost every day. I really wanted to walk around the table and sit in his lap. A hug and a good kiss would hit the spot. But I decided to wait. I picked up *Hintele*—that means "puppy" in Yiddish—our little poodle, a lapful of soft black curls. A hug from her was almost as good as one from Sam. She loved to have her tummy tickled, and doing it relaxed me as I talked.

Sam meant I should start at the beginning of my current dilemma. But maybe I should start a little earlier. I'm a rabbi, Rivkah Rosenblatt, but everyone calls me Rivvy or Reb Rivvy. You should too. I spent some years leading a congregation, but it turned out to be not my thing. Too much fundraising, too much negotiation with a board about whose authority stopped where, too little time for myself, my family, my friends.

On the eve of 2000, just before my 41st birthday, I woke up to yet another batch of emails about Y2K. If you weren't here for that, here's what happened: some people managed to stir up a tremendous panic around the idea that all of our computers would go crazy when the year changed at the millennium. This was because so much computer programming depended on dates, and somehow programmers hadn't anticipated what would happen when all four digits changed at midnight on New Year's Eve. Or something like that, anyway. Every time I heard any of that, I thought of those scenes on *Star Trek* where a computer talks itself into a standstill because it's been given contradictory instructions.

But that morning, I was thinking about turning 40. Our tradition gives tremendous significance to the number 40: 40 years of wandering in the wilderness, 40 weeks of human gestation, Moses spending 40 days on Mount Sinai, Noah's flood pouring down for 40 days—believe me, I'm just getting started. I was about to pass out of being 40. It was time to move on. But where? How?

I went to see Sharon Marks, a friend who is an investigator, mostly the Sam Spade kind. But she has a sideline as a *melitz yosher,* which is someone who intercedes with heavenly forces to help an individual with an illness, a problem, or a need. Sharon is good at it, which makes me *kvell* a little, since she first learned it from me. It's the kind of spiritual practice that a lot of people find too far-fetched: heavenly courts? Negotiating for your client? Carrying out an assignment? But it's an established practice rooted in 18th century writing by highly respected rabbi-scholars, and not some new age-y invention.

I have two things to say about that skepticism. First, the type of Judaism I'm most connected to, Renewal, is full of people who look at all such things as profound metaphor rather than literal truths. That can be true at the same time as believing that factors beyond our control can shape the course of our lives, and there is no harm in trying to influence them for the good. Even if you can't influence the course of events, you can change your perspective by trying. That's what I think, anyway.

     Arlene Goldbard

Second, living in Berkeley since the sixties dawned, I have encountered many advisors who consult an invisible guide or abide by an arcane system, and this is my conclusion: it's not the system, it's the advisor. If someone is perceptive, intuitive, compassionate, it may not matter if that person lays out Tarot cards or reads your palm, something useful to you may come through. What's wrong, of course, is that too many people who aren't perceptive, intuitive, and compassionate are willing to promise happiness in exchange for money, and often their clients get hurt by what doesn't happen or end up spending far too much to chase a hope into the ground.

Sharon cares. It isn't about money. And from everything I've seen, when she attempts to contact higher realms to help you find a job or the strength to fight a disease, the assignments she receives are never harmful or dangerous. An assignment could be reciting psalms, writing something, reading something, even singing, laughing, or dancing. You always get something out of doing them.

When I went to see Sharon as 1999 ended, I hoped for guidance as to my next move. You can intercede for yourself, but I didn't have the clarity to even know how to put the question. If I quit the congregation—with plenty of notice and goodwill, of course—what else would I do? Was it about the impact my choice might have on the congregation? What I needed most? What the Jewish community needed most?

The assignment that came through Sharon was to awaken each morning for 40 days (yes, 40) and on each day, write three questions that taken together sum up my outlook on life in that exact moment. If answers came to me, I was to write them down too. This reminded me of Rabbi Hillel's famous questions from *Pirke Avot* (Ethics of the Fathers), a compilation of wisdom:

> If I am not for myself, who will be for me? If I am for myself alone, what am I? And if not now, when?

On the first day, these are the questions I wrote down: Who am I now? What is my task? Where is my help?

The answers were full of surprises. Who am I now? Even though I don't have children, the answer that came to me was "mother." Anyone who knows me will tell you I have plenty of mothering energy. I like to take care of people, make them comfortable, help if I can. People always tell me I have that Earth Mother look—the long hair, full figure, scarves and shawls. So that fit, but also it was a brand-new answer, something I hadn't thought of before.

I will spare you the next 39 variations on the three questions theme. There was a lot of overlap, both in questions and answers. Right to the end, I was unsure they would add up to a new direction. But on the 40th day, I had a dream.

In the dream, I sat in a beautiful embroidered tent, many colors, filled with people lounging on cushions. They were talking about some of the challenges they'd faced as Jews in this society, where fewer than two percent of the population shares that identity but receives a much larger slice of attention, often suspicion or worse. It was dreamtime, so I caught snippets here and there, not the whole conversation. But the feeling came through very clearly: people trying to figure things out, sharing their feelings in a safe space where they would be understood, disagreeing without hostility. I like to say that one of the reasons I love being Jewish is that in our tradition, disputation is a form of worship. The dream embodied that.

That's when I realized that I had my mission. I would start a kind of retreat center focused on Jewish learning and dialogue. I asked a friend who is good at proposals to help me write it up. And by the time my six months' notice to the *shul* was up, I had seed funding for a space and programs. Twenty-plus years later, the Rachamim Center still stands. Its name means "compassion." I go there every morning when it's time to start work. My office door says "Reb Rivvy, *HaLev*," the heart. The sign was a gift on the Center's fifth anniversary.

That morning I told Sam that it all started when a visiting teacher came to the Center to lead a workshop. I'd never met Zach Levy before, but a glowing reputation preceded him. He'd published some popular books portraying Judaism as an ecstatic practice threaded through with eros. He had a bunch of DVDs (this was 2013) and a growing group of followers. The event was in the form of a Shabbaton: people would gather to bring in Shabbos on Friday evening, *daven*, chant, meditate, and rest on Saturday. From Saturday sunset through Sunday afternoon, Levy would teach.

"When he showed up Friday afternoon," I said, "I had that hit of not exactly dislike but skepticism that made me wonder if there was something I should check out myself. Was I instantly feeling aversion to someone who didn't warrant it? Was it because he reminded me of someone I wanted to forget?"

"So of course," said Sam, "you were extra welcoming and helpful to him."

"Of course," I smiled. "You know me so well, my darling."

"The first thing Levy did was say he wanted to change the schedule, which we'd worked out together beforehand—along with his beautiful young wife, Leah, who seems also to be his assistant. His approach rubbed me the wrong way. He has a boyish face despite his beard. He dropped his chin and looked at me with puppy eyes. He said he was so nervous, he needed to do some teaching during Shabbat dinner to ground himself. It would be short, he said, and in keeping with the occasion. He would consider it a great favor that would help calm him down. I didn't like being charmed quite so aggressively, but I ended up saying yes because it didn't make that much difference. Leah stood just behind him the whole time we talked, beaming me a pleading smile. She was small and delicate, and had the kind of charming English accent Americans love to hear. I started to wonder if she'd have to bear the consequences if I said no. So I said yes."

"So what's the dilemma?" Sam asked.

"The dilemma is that people adored him. Worshipped him. We'd made the space look great, full of color and light. We hung all the silk banners and put pots of flowers under each window. The room was set up in the usual way, with cushions up front for whoever wanted them, and curving rows of chairs behind. You know how some of the older people prefer the cushions even though getting up and down can be a little challenging?"

Sam nodded.

"The room was full. People were settled on chairs and cushions, waiting for Levy. He wanted everyone to stand as he entered the room. He got one of his longtime students to request that tribute once people were seated. I know that is a tradition in some practices, but I don't like it. If he had asked me, I would have mentioned the cushions and the elders and advised him to skip it. But he didn't ask. The core idea of the Rachamim Center is that we are all equal in the sight of *HaShem*, and maybe we can extend that to each other. I don't like to create a situation where everyone is hanging onto one charismatic person and all the others become nothing."

"I agree," said Sam, raking his fingers through gray curls.

"He had some messages about love that were worth hearing. But his style of teaching was to gradually assume power over his students. He would get them doing a call-and-response thing, which is fine, the liturgy has a lot of those. But it gradually morphed into everyone repeating things that were his words alone: 'I surrender to love. I embrace love. Fill me with love.' I watched him meet the eyes of every young woman in the room as he willed them to say these things. When the teaching ended, they formed a long line, patiently waiting to speak to him one-to-one. Somehow, he put his hands on each and every one of them."

"I'm beginning to understand," Sam told me. "Did you see him cross the line in an overt way?"

"Not exactly," I told him. "But all weekend, every time I saw him when his wife wasn't around, some other wide-eyed young woman was acting mesmerized by his every word. I didn't see inappropriate touching, but he always had a hand on a shoulder or an arm. To me, he was always too close. But no one complained, so I let it go. I told myself I was being hypersensitive."

"So we'll watch," said Sam. "Keep me posted, please. I want to know what you know so I can help if you need it." As he got up from the table, *Hintele* jumped off my lap. She loved him as much as I did.

I don't think I mentioned that Sam—his last name is Maimon—teaches philosophy at Berkeley. His approach isn't too obtuse or arcane, like the authors of that postmodern prose you need a translator to understand. His main work follows along in the lineage of John Rawls, what is needed for a truly good society. Ethics is a big part of it, obviously. I'm always glad I can rely on him to help me parse the ethics of any situation. But I was hoping this wouldn't turn out to be a situation at all.

I kept on thinking exactly that until two months later, when Sharon and I had coffee. "Did you see that thing about Zach Levy?" she asked.

Sharon sometimes likes to say she resembles Yoda: wide face, big eyes, small stature—and normal human ears, *baruch HaShem*. Princess Leia I'm not— maybe her somewhat *zaftig* mother. I'm not petite, but back in the day I did sometimes wear my dark hair in those braided things in the shape of a Danish over each ear. Right then, Sharon's eyes were as huge as Yoda's.

Sharon pulled out her phone and showed me an email. Someone had written a letter to *The Jewish Light*, a weekly newspaper in New York, accusing Levy of sexual misconduct. They said that when he was a teaching assistant during his time in rabbinical school, he had violated the rule against relationships with students. The young woman lodged a complaint, not accusing him of outright force, but of coercion. Because Levy had been a fellow student—with a somewhat ambiguous status since he also taught classes—he hadn't been formally disciplined. But he'd been warned. The paper interviewed the letter-

     Arlene Goldbard

writer, who said that he had solid evidence that Levy was at it again, but this time, the gap in age and status between teacher and student was much wider and more dangerous.

The paper talked to several well-known rabbis who'd had an association with Levy. All defended him strongly, saying there was no reason to suppose these charges were true. Ruth Kahn, a board member at one of the centers where Levy sometimes taught, speculated that people were envious of his success. She thought his expansive energy was prone to misinterpretation, but so far as she'd seen, he always observed proper boundaries.

"Oy," I said, "I don't know, Sharon. This smells. I feel complicit. I invited him to teach. He gave me references, but to be honest, I knew who they all are, so just reading their names felt like reassurance enough. Ruth Kahn was one of them. I didn't call anyone. Now Levy has the Rachamim Center on his resume. I feel like an idiot. How do these big-deal rabbis know how he behaves with women students, anyway?"

"They don't," said Sharon. "I once heard one of them say in response to a woman who had seen teachers mess with students that Renewal is a *ba'al t'shuvah* movement, meaning that these rabbis had sown their wild oats before they got *s'micha*, and we had to make space for repentance and redemption."

"I agree with that," I told her. "But I don't think there's total agreement on what *t'shuvah* is. You have to seek forgiveness from the person you wronged. And you have to stop doing it. If all of these stories about Levy are way in the past and he has actually made *t'shuvah*, fine. But the person whose letter triggered this piece said it was happening again. What if that's true?"

Sharon shrugged. "Let's find out," she said. "Give me the contact details for those references. I'll say I'm calling about future programming at the Rachamim Center. I won't be confrontational."

If anyone could find out, I knew it would be Sharon, who has made quite a success of her career as an investigator.

"Let's."

A week passed before Sharon was ready to share the results of her investigation. This time we sat behind closed doors at the Rachamim Center. My stomach held a flock of butterflies. I wanted to know, but I was afraid of what I might hear.

"Wel-l-l," said Sharon, dragging the word out. "I don't have anything absolutely definitive for you yet, but I wanted to update you on what I've learned so far. I called the references, saying that I was doing some programming on Jewish spirituality and I wanted to hear about their experience with Zach Levy as a teacher. It was pretty glowing, more or less what you said, that he attracted students who gave him high marks in their post-workshop evaluations. Then I hemmed and hawed a little and asked if they'd seen that article in *The Jewish Light,* that some of our staff were a little worried about boundaries. One got annoyed and said it was pure *lashon hara*, that I shouldn't gossip. The other two said very little, just that they hadn't had any problems. I decided to call one more place, a retreat center outside Chicago where a friend of mine works. With her, I could be a little more forthright, but still, I had to assure her our conversation was confidential.

"*Nu?*" I thought something was coming and I was impatient to hear it.

"You said you know Ruth Kahn, right?" Sharon asked. "She was the retreat center board member who told *The Light* that Levy always kept good boundaries."

"More like I know *of* her, but I did meet her once at a conference."

"Well, Ruth Kahn attended his workshop at my friend's retreat center, but she wasn't an ordinary student," Sharon said. "She behaved like a hostess, welcoming people and giving a little pitch to support Levy's project, Neshama Beit Midrash. I think she's on his board too. After dinner, my friend was rummaging through a linen closet in the hall to get someone an extra blanket. She heard a door open, some low voices, and when she peeked around the corner, Levy was hugging Ruth Kahn. But not just a hug. He was grabbing her tush with both hands. My friend says they didn't see her."

"Oy," I said. "So he's fooling around with the person who vouched for him to *The Light*?"

"Yes," Sharon said. But she's not a young student. She must be late 30s. I'd say he's 10 years older. Levy's wife wasn't there. Who knows? Maybe they have an understanding."

Who knew? I thought about it for a minute and made up my mind. "Keep digging," I told Sharon, "but quietly."

That turned out to be a pointless request, because less than a week later, I got a call from Zach Levy. He was furious.

     Arlene Goldbard

"I hear you're checking up on me," he said. "Why? I already did the Shabbaton and everything went well."

"I'm sure you've seen the article in *The Jewish Li...*," I started to say.

Levy interrupted. "That rag! I'm thinking of suing, but that would just invite more *lashon hara*. You know what they say: You can't put the feathers back in a pillow. But why would you do this to me? What have I done to you? If you want, I can promise I'll never teach at the Rachamim Center again. But what about my friends, the references I gave you? You called them just for the pleasure of slandering me?"

"You gave me their contact information as references," I told him. "Did you not expect us to contact them?

"To ask about my teaching!" He was yelling now.

"What we asked about was their experience with your teaching," I explained, keeping my voice level.

"I won't forget this! And neither will you!" With that, Levy hung up.

I felt wobbly. I had a sudden longing to see my mother, to be taken into her arms. That was a little bit nuts, since she'd passed so long ago. Jewish Renewal included so many who'd had troubled or worse relationships with their parents, I often felt like I should keep quiet about Mama and Tateh, their kindness and caring. Whatever capacity I have to love and be loved, I thank them. I miss them like it was yesterday. I closed my eyes and hugged myself. It helped a little.

I was still shaken when I talked to Sam about it that evening. We were sitting on the couch, sipping glasses of wine. The sun was setting, bathing the room in a beautiful warm light. I wanted to be able to sit back and enjoy it, but my stomach was grumbling and a headache was coming on. "It felt like a threat," I told my husband.

"I can understand that," said Sam, stroking his chin. "It's a little odd that he made that offer never to teach for you again, don't you think? It's like the opening salvo of a negotiation. But you don't negotiate unless there's something at stake. What he seems to be implying is that just asking about him is wrong, and he's making that offer to get you to stop. I could imagine myself in a situation where just asking about me could hurt me—'When did he stop beating his wife?' But then I'd do my best to convince the questioner that I'd never started, not put an offer on the table to bribe you to stop asking about it."

"That's true. I didn't see that till you pointed it out. What sticks with me, though, is him telling me that I'll never forget it. Like payback is coming. But what could it be? I can't think how he could condemn me for calling references without implicating himself in my reasons for calling. And everybody in Renewal has read that piece in *The Light* by now."

A few days later, Sharon came to see me with some new information.

"It's still pretty vague," she said. "Rumors. And I don't like to put too much faith in rumors."

"You are right about that," I told her. "Do you want to tell me about the rumors, or wait till you have something concrete?" I half-hoped she'd pick door number two. This made me feel very tired, and I had lots to do.

Sharon explained that "It's about Neshama Beit Midrash, his place in London. He spends just as much of his time in the U.S. these days—maybe more—but that place is the mother ship. It belongs to him and he's been able to make it whatever he wants. There was some back-and-forth in a counterculture-type newsletter in London about a superstar rabbi—no name, just a few adjectives— and a woman who'd posted accusations against him on a couple of social media sites. Sounded like seduced and abandoned. Apparently Levy mobilized some of his big-name supporters to denounce this, and the sites took the stuff down. I couldn't tell if it just kind of petered out, or it's still simmering. I've got to dig deeper."

"Keep digging," I said. Again.

This was late summer of 2015, seven years ago. In June, Donald Trump had announced his candidacy for the presidency. Everyone I know thought it was a joke till we woke up on November 9, 2016 and realized all the polls had gotten it wrong. But that summer, I was just the normal amount of too busy, with no major crises to handle unless you count the High Holy Days. Rosh Hashanah was starting on September 13th, which was definitely on the early side. We had an annual Yom Kippur retreat at the Center, led by people who were more into chant and meditation than doing every word of the traditional liturgy. But still it was a long stretch of fasting and praying from *Kol Nidre* at sundown one night through *Ne'ilah* at sundown the next. That didn't start until ten days after Rosh Hashanah, but we were already deep in final preparations.

Jonathan Fox would be leading. We have a big space and his congregation, Or Chadash, didn't, so it would be a joint service. I loved Reb Jonathan. He was deeply learned and deeply experimental. I knew he would find a way to integrate sacred silence and the high points of the services: *Kol Nidre*'s cancellation of vows, addressing the same Heavenly Court where Sharon pleads as a *melitz yosher*; *Avinu Malkeinu*, asking for forgiveness and compassion; *Unetanneh Tokef,* which conveys the utter seriousness of facing our own deaths; the collective confession of *Al Chet*. The *Avodah* service is beloved, because people imagine themselves in the Temple, and they really get into prostrating themselves as the high priests did in ancient times. And finally at *Ne'ilah*, as the gates of prayer are about to close and people are waiting for three stars to signal the end of the holiday, everyone is caught up in ecstatic song and dance, a tremendous release after a day of fasting and long silences. At the end, Jonathan liked to do a Rainbow Family song: "We are opening up in sweet surrender/ To the luminous love light of the One," chorus after chorus until everyone was floating off the ground. I looked forward to it each year.

I was humming that tune with a smile on my face, sitting at my desk charting out the Yom Kippur plan to discuss with Jonathan when the calls started coming. First came Ruth Kahn, who I barely knew.

"I apologize for calling about something upsetting, Rivvy, but it's the month of *Elul*, we're doing our *cheshbon hanefesh*, and I just have to talk to you," she said.

"Of course, Ruth. What is it?" I had a suspicion, of course.

"I'm hearing from all kinds of people that you are doing *lashon hara* to Reb Zach. I told the first couple of people that it couldn't be true. You and I don't know each other well, but everyone who knows you respects you, so I couldn't believe it. But now it's coming from so many sources, I don't know what to believe. I need you to tell me: why do you have it in for him?"

My first response was "Oy!" I caught my breath. "Ruth, I'm amazed to hear this. I don't have it in for him. He was here teaching a while back, and after *The Jewish Light* article came out, we had questions. I had someone call the references he gave me. And now you're saying there are accusations against me coming from multiple sources. Who are these people?"

"Of course I can't name names," Ruth told me. "But it's Renewal people from many parts of the country."

I steeled myself. "And what do these unnamed Renewal people say I'm doing?"

Ruth sighed. "They say you're jealous of Zach. That you aren't the teacher he is, that you can't draw people the way he can. They say you're trying to lift yourself up by putting him down."

"I'm very sad to hear that," I told her. "If I wanted to be a charismatic teacher, I would have tried walking that path. But I don't think I would have succeeded.

It's not my nature. I've put all my energy into creating a sanctuary, a safe space for others to teach and learn and debate. The Rachamim Center is my baby, not my platform. I'm its mother, not its star. I'm not trying to get gigs anywhere else."

We didn't get much further. With a lump in my throat, I thanked her for calling and hung up. Then I called Sharon and told her the whole story. That night, Sam did his best to console me. *Hintele* too. She stayed glued to me all evening. The three of us ate popcorn and watched an old movie—Judy Holliday in *Born Yesterday*—cuddling on the couch. I almost forgot about it for a minute or two. That was nice and distracting, but neither Sam nor I had any good ideas about what to do. By the time I took *Hintele* out to pee, I was obsessing again.

With Sam's help, I concluded that I couldn't fix it. But I didn't have to stay on the frontlines either. I decided it would be wise to step back a little. I didn't want to be a target, for one thing, and I didn't want to encourage this gossip. I declined an invitation to Rosh Hashanah dinner. Sam and I *davened* Erev Rosh Hashanah with Reb Jonathan, then ate at home with a few close friends. I hoped the whole bubbling *tzimmes* was quieting down.

A week and a half later, the Yom Kippur retreat was going very well. Jonathan always encouraged everyone to wear white. The tradition was to wear one's *kittel*, the white garment Orthodox Jews wear on certain occasions; it ultimately serves as a shroud. Here people dress in all sorts of flowy white outfits. When you gaze out at the assembled, you see them with the purity of new souls. White flowers filled the space with beauty and fragrance.

I breathed in the serenity, feeling truly present for the first time in weeks. Then one of the participants took me aside during the afternoon break, asking if we could have a word. This is common. People fill the long break after the *Mussaf* service by napping, chanting or learning in small groups, talking quietly.

D'vorah Klein was a visiting rabbi at another community in the East Bay. The liberal Jewish communities were all sort of allied, though we had our differences. The rabbis all knew each other. Quite a few people *davened* at one *shul* this week, another the next. There were times when we all came together, as for a community-wide Shavuot observance. Shavuot tradition is to teach something from every book of Torah, based on a practice of Isaac Luria and other 16th century kabbalists, who called it a *tikkun*, a repair. Everyone stayed up late to study together in an old school building, something different going on in each classroom. I often taught there. So that's how I knew D'vorah: to say hello to, to exchange pleasantries, nothing more.

D'vorah and I walked out into the small garden adjacent to the Center's main room. That time of year, the Japanese maples were dressed in shades of red, sunset, and wine. Normally, I loved being out there. Right then, I wasn't so sure. We sat on a bench in the shade.

The word she wanted to have with me had evidently been scripted by Ruth Kahn. "This is the time to mend what is broken," she told me. "Your attacks on Zach Levy are damaging our movement. I need you to understand how much you are hurting him. I think you should ask for his forgiveness."

I was shocked. I must have looked it. I felt the blood drain from my face. I tried to pull myself together and asked her what attacks.

"What do you mean, 'what attacks?'" she asked. "What do you call it when you're phoning people all over the country saying he can't hold sexual boundaries and offering yourself as a better teacher? The poor man is crushed. He can barely leave the house. Everyone is talking about it, and it all comes back to you."

I thought I was going to be sick. "So you've talked to many people about this and they all say the same thing about me, that I'm trying to destroy him to further my career as a teacher? How many people have told you these things?"

D'vorah paused. "I haven't talked to many people myself. But I trust Ruth Kahn, and she told me she has. She's on the board of Neshama Beit Midrash, and she called me as a friend to ask me to talk to you about the damage you're doing."

"Had you heard about this from anyone else before Ruth told you it was making the Renewal rounds all over the country?"

"Yes," said D'vorah. "One other person, and she was devastated."

Who would be devastated, I wondered? I took a chance. "Is that other person perhaps Zach's wife Leah?"

D'vorah blushed.

"D'vorah," I said, "we don't really know each other, but let me ask. Have you seen me promote myself as a teacher? Do I send out flyers and press clips and try to get your community to bring me in? Other than our communitywide Shavuot, have you seen any workshops or presentations by me? Have you seen my name on the programs of any of the retreat centers that book Renewal teachers?"

She hesitated. "No, now that you mention it."

"And am I known as a very ambitious person? Before this, did you hear about me slandering other teachers? I've been in this community a long time. Is this what people think of me?"

"No," she said, eyes a little downcast.

"So why is it so easy to believe that I'm not only pushing myself out but very willing to take someone else down in the process?"

"I guess because I know Ruth," she said, "and I think she's an honest person."

"Well, I don't really know her, so I have no way of judging. But I have a question for you: why is she doing this to me?"

To D'vorah's credit, she said that in the spirit of *t'shuvah*, she regretted believing gossip. She hoped I would forgive her.

"I will, D'vorah," I said, "I'll do it happily if you do me a favor. The next time you hear this *lashon hara*, will you please tell the person who's saying it about our conversation today?"

When I told Sam about it after the break-fast, I was still shaking my head. We were sitting at the kitchen table. I found myself pulling bits off a lump of raisin challah we'd toted home, and mindlessly putting them in my mouth. Hintele was begging at my feet, and even though it was against the rules, I gave her a few crumbs too. I took out the raisins first, though. Grapes aren't good for dogs.

"Levy's strategy seems so crude and obvious, "I said. "If you've done something blameworthy, and someone asks you about it, just make that person the villain. But I'm trying to wrap my head around the personality, the character, who chooses that strategy. I'd be afraid of it backfiring, wouldn't you?"

"Tough hypothetical," Sam said. "First, I'd have to want a whole raft of women to love and desire me, and I'd have to want it enough to come very close to the line in terms of public behavior. I'd have to go on wanting it even though some people had charged me with transgressing by seeking it, like that piece in *The Light*. That article would be enough for me, the actually existing Sam, to be scared straight, so to speak—unless it were all lies. But Levy has tried to explain away the earliest accusations by saying he and the young woman were in love, it was consensual, rather than denying it outright. So I ask myself, what would I want enough to risk becoming a scandal, especially when at least part of it seems to be known?"

     Arlene Goldbard

"That's true. You'd have to be driven."

Sam shook his head. He went to the refrigerator and asked me if I wanted a glass of seltzer. I did. "With lemon, please."

"And then you'd have to have a hyperinflated idea of your own powers and influence," he continued. "You'd have to think that people find you so wonderful and trustworthy that all you had to do was point the finger at someone else and you'd be saved. And—this is the cherry on the sundae—you'd have to not care about harming the person you chose as your scapegoat. What happens to them is of no importance."

I sighed, exhausted with thinking about it. I'd just spent 25 hours in community repenting for all the ways I'd missed the mark in the year gone by, and praying to be written in the book of life for another year. I was certain that Zach Levy had said all the same prayers. But how? It would be a challenge to take an erotic approach to Yom Kippur, an abstemious holy day on which we not only avoid work, food, and water, but also washing, sex, even leather shoes. The idea is not to suffer in penitence, but to rise above the needs of the body and concern ourselves with our souls. Did Levy ask *HaShem* for forgiveness for the lies he was spreading about me, or the way he was using Ruth Kahn and his wife Leah and who knows who else? I doubted it.

"I'm not in the psychology department," Sam said, "but I'm going with narcissistic personality disorder. That's got to be it."

Months went by. I heard quite a few whispers. So did Sharon, but the *tzimmes* never exactly boiled over until I had a meeting with one of our donors, the head of the Simcha Foundation. He requested that I come to his office. It wasn't grant deadline time or anything like that, but we had a cordial relationship, he was highly supportive of the Center's work, and I told myself he just wanted to check in. For some reason.

"Can I offer you coffee or tea, Rivvy?" Seated behind his large wooden desk in an office with an impressive collection of Judaica, mostly prints, books, and objects such as *kiddush* cups and candlesticks, Chaim Rubin seemed his usual self, polite and warm. Sandy hair, sandy goatee, bowtie, tweedy suit. I declined the drink. The rainy season had started, and I could hear the sweet sound of raindrops falling outside the window. Rain usually relaxed me, but not then.

"There's something I need to talk to you about, Rivvy, and it's delicate."

"Okay," I said, holding my breath.

"I've been contacted by a friend of Rabbi Zach Levy's, who has told me that you have been accusing him of misconduct, creating a hostile atmosphere around some of the centers and communities who've been working with him as a teacher. I know he's a bit of a controversial figure. These charismatic teachers often are. Of course I read that piece last year in *The Light*. But so many respected figures have come forward to defend him that I'm inclined to believe their denials, especially since the charges have to do with things that happened when he was very young, a student. I'm told that he denies wrongdoing, saying he and these young women were in love, and that he has apologized many times."

My heart sank. This again. "You've mentioned two things, Chaim. One is Levy's culpability and defenders. I'm in no position to confirm or deny that. And I've made no public statement about that. I've done exactly one thing in relation to the charges against him, and that's to have someone call his references after he'd led a Shabbaton at the Center. Having read the *Light* article, I wanted to know if it had been wise to have him, if it was safe to have him back. And even though Levy himself gave me those names and contacts, he called me in a rage and threatened me with retaliation for talking to his references. That was frightening. And hard to understand. Now it's a crime to call the references someone gives you?"

I stared out the window and took a breath. I liked looking at the stream of wet cars passing by. I wished I was in one of them. "The other thing is whether I have been defaming him, creating a hostile atmosphere, as you say. You know D'vorah Klein, right?"

Chaim nodded.

"D'vorah took me aside at the break on Yom Kippur to accuse me of masterminding this *lashon hara* campaign. She told me many people think I'm doing it, though it turned out she had heard that from one person, not from many. I asked her what reasons those people had for saying this about me. She reported that it was my ego and ambition, that I was jealous of his popularity and wanted people to have me teach in his place. Since she's observed me for a while, I asked her to say if she'd seen me exercising this ruthless ambition, trying to tear others down to get attention for myself. She said no. Now I ask you the same question. Please tell me the truth, whatever it is."

Chaim rubbed his eyes with one veined hand. "I can't see you doing this, Rivvy. But it was told to me by someone I respect. I had to ask. I don't understand what's happening."

"Neither do I," I told him. "All I can think of is Levy's threat to punish me for calling his references. I guess one way to try to discredit someone who questions you is to destroy that person, make it be about them. If I had to guess, that's what I'd say. But more than that, I'm sitting here worried that this will have consequences for the Rachamim Center. Your support is absolutely critical to our work."

"I believe you, Rivvy," Chaim said. "We've known each other a long time, and I've never seen you act in the way that's being described. But I have a board and donors and I need to talk to some people, because there is buzz, I have to be honest with you. But I can make one promise. As you know, your current grant is multi-year. It doesn't expire until a month before the High Holy Days in 2017. I'm not going to do anything to change that. But if board members have doubts, I can't promise you another renewal. We'll have to see."

I thanked him, we agreed to stay in touch. I walked out like a Zombie and phoned Sam the minute I could. He met me at our favorite coffee place, one with booths that ensured privacy. We sat on the same side of the booth. I was dripping—I hadn't thought to look at the weather forecast, so no umbrella. But I didn't care and neither did he. I hugged him so tight I doubt he could breathe. I knew I couldn't.

I had hoped that talking to D'vorah had stopped the feathers in this particular *lashon hara* pillow from traveling too far. I fantasized that she went back to Ruth to tell her about our conversation, because it seemed Ruth and Levy and Leah were the sources. But if Ruth had kept right on enlisting others like D'vorah to fight those she believed were Levy's enemies, then just stopping D'vorah wouldn't have had much impact. I didn't exactly forget about it. But I wasn't being confronted outright. I stayed stepped back, didn't go to many events, kept quietly to myself. I wasn't going to get involved in a public smear campaign.

By the time 2017 rolled around, I'd stopped looping about it every day— just sometimes, when I woke up in the middle of the night and couldn't get back to sleep. I stopped flinching every time the phone rang with an unknown number—now I only did it some of the time. I had at least six months until Chaim would let me know his board's decision on our future funding. I prayed every day that he hadn't been talking about it publicly. But if the Simcha Foundation decided to give us a pass (and if that happened, it would arrive packaged in that mealy funder language, *so many worthy applications, need to make room for new initiatives*, and so on, so there would be nothing we could protest), then I was pretty sure our other sources would start drying up.

In January, I went to a Renewal conference in St. Louis. This was an every-few-years kind of thing, rabbis and cantors and rabbinic students and chaplains and rabbinic pastors, and also organizational leaders and followers, teachers and writers, the whole *mishpacha,* the extended family. A lot of old friends would be there, and I was starting to feel that it might be welcoming for me, an experience I hadn't had in a while. I quietly asked a friend on the committee if Levy was coming, and was told no. That was a relief. Still, I imagined running into Ruth Kahn and D'vorah. I thought I could handle that. It was a large crowd, so fairly easy to avoid someone if need be. I hadn't yet decided if I would try.

The conference is kind of stellar: all the best-known and best-loved rabbis (not necessarily identical groups, but given the nature of celebrity...) led services and gave talks and workshops. The *davenen* was highest of the high, each prayer transporting you to other realms. The music was incredible. I was looking forward to all of that.

But I wasn't prepared for what happened. The first time, I was in a workshop on women in Renewal. The leader was a rabbi I knew slightly, Shoshanna Markowitz. As Sunny Mark, in a former life she'd been a singer and dancer in musicals. She was still given to big gestures and a booming voice, as if she were playing to the balconies. Only instead of a theater, we were in one of those rooms in a hotel that does a lot of conferences, where the walls move so you can adjust rooms' size or proportions. There were round tables and padded chairs. I always felt a little uncomfortable in these neutral spaces. Everything was gray-green and bland—no flowers, plants, art on the walls. But there were a few dozen women, perhaps half of whom I'd met before, and coffee bubbling away on a station at the back featuring little pastries and a half-dozen kinds of tea bags. "*Dayenu,*" I thought as I settled in my chair, "this will be enough for now."

We went around the table doing one of those icebreaker introduction things: "I'm Rivvy, I'm head of the Rachamim Center in Berkeley, and one thing you might not know about me is that my life changed in Y2K, when a spiritual practice I was doing with the help of a friend led me to leave my congregational rabbi job for a whole new direction."

We all offered our introductions, and then Shoshanna gave us a prompt: "What are the best things about being a woman in Jewish Renewal? What are the most challenging? Tell a first-person story that responds to one or both of these prompts."

 Arlene Goldbard

This was a story circle set-up, so we each had three minutes to talk while everyone else listened, no interruptions or comments. After we'd all taken a turn, there was time for discussion about what we'd observed—differences, commonalities, surprises.

My best things were easy, and they matched several other contributions. I told about the day I got *s'micha*, how thrilled I'd been to be part of a world in which women were truly understood as equal. Not that every person lived into that fully a hundred percent of the time; we were human, after all. But the institutions, ceremonies, and rituals were truly egalitarian. Then, describing a challenge, I told a story that took place a very long time ago, about learning that a teacher I greatly admired for his spiritual wisdom had enjoyed the boundary-crossing relationships with students that came easily to a person of his power, and how disillusioned I had been. I named no names or places, and Zach Levy having been a child at the time meant no one could think it was about him. I knew this was common to spiritual leaders—look at Dr. Martin Luther King of blessed memory—and by no means only a Renewal thing or even a Jewish thing. But I was still trying to find the best way to hold a disillusioning truth.

Both my stories opened the door to other stories too. That's how story circles work. One story sparks another and gives permission to tell it. But some of the women took completely different things from the prompts, talking about how the music, dance, visual art, poetry emerging from Renewal had helped open up all kinds of Jewish practice, so that more and more these other forms of expression were valued just as much as written and spoken prayer. One rabbi talked about how many of her congregants were what we called "sixties people," who tended to default to the idea that spiritual practice and money don't mix, objecting on those grounds to paying the dues that paid for the space, the rabbi's salary, and much more. In the final discussion, we discovered more commonalities than differences, and after the two years I'd had, that felt good to me.

I was glad I took part. As I was gathering my things to leave, a woman I didn't know approached me. She looked at my nametag.

"Rivvy, is it?" she asked.

"Yes," I said, extending my hand. "Rabbi Rivvy Rosenblatt, from the Rachamim Center in Berkeley. I don't think we've met." I expected her to introduce herself, but instead she looked at me with a wry smile.

"Oh," she said. "You're *that* Rivvy."

My heart sank. "*That* Rivvy?"

"Someone was telling me about your feud with Zach Levy."

Now I read her nametag: Beth Lazarus. "Feud?" I said. "You were misinformed, Beth." I saw that she was a cantor at a Renewal *shul* in Minnesota, far, far from Berkeley. "What did you hear?"

"That you tried to get him blackballed and get gigs for yourself."

"Oy! I have to sit down." I returned to my spot at the round table, motioned for her to sit. She did. "Beth, we've just met. We don't know each other from Adam. I'm grateful to you for telling me this *lashon hara* is making the rounds. I had no idea it had gone any further than a few people close to Levy. Remember that piece about him in *The Jewish Light*? It was more than a year ago, nearly two."

She nodded.

"He came to my center for a Shabbaton right before that came out. The article raised concerns. We called the references he'd given us to ask about their experience with him as a teacher. If there were issues, we needed to be alert for blowback, and that would affect whether or not we had him back. That's the entirety of my involvement with Zach Levy, except that he threatened me with harm for calling his references, something I couldn't understand at the time. But once the harm started coming in the form of this rumor making me the villain trying to get him canceled, I understood his threat. I don't know how much success he's had putting the attention on me rather than himself. Hearing from you today, someone two thousand miles away, makes me very scared. Would you be willing to tell me how you heard this story?"

"It's going around," Beth said. "I just heard two people talking in the ladies room. They said you talked about it in your story circle."

"No. I told a story about something that happened twenty years ago. Different time, place, person."

"Oh," Beth said.

I had three more such conversations in the course of the conference, all with people I'd never met before.

My good friend Anya Applebaum was at the conference too, so I texted her to meet me in the bar. Drinking an entire glass of wine is usually my limit, but Anya ordered us ladylike cocktails—mine was a Cosmopolitan, a pretty shade of pink—and by the time I finished recounting the conversations and sipping the cocktail, Anya's consoling words warmed me as much as the alcohol. She was a wonderful friend, Shomer of Or Chadash, Reb Jonatha's shul, enough older to have earned a reputation for wisdom—and to know which cocktail to order and look sophisticated drinking it. She told me a story about a time she'd come upon a much respected spiritual leader dallying at a retreat with a student half his age. She said she stood up straight and acted embarrassed, saying, "Oh, sorry, for interrupting. When I came around the corner I thought you looked just like Reb ___." He was Reb ___ and had to say so. She told me his face was the color of a ripe tomato. On the plane home, I spent half the flight making up mock-innocent things like that I could say if I ever encountered Levy again. But the whole time I was counting the minutes until we landed.

When I got home, there was a letter from the Jewish Federation. There were so many worthy applications, they were faced with the need to make room for new initiatives. They were sorry that they would not be supporting The Rachamim Center in the 2017-18 cycle.

We wouldn't run out of funds for months. We had a reserve, and there were a few donors I could call on to help in a pinch. But I started making plans to cut back on programming after the summer: more local teachers who didn't need major fees and travel expenses; a slight registration fee hike for those who could afford it; almost certainly fewer events overall. Our staff was lean, and I didn't want to let anyone down. I would try with all my might to keep jobs funded.

In the spring, I started going to local events again, but only if Sam would go with me. Luckily, he was obliging. I was asked to offer a workshop at the next community Shavuot gathering. I said yes and chose a fun practice that worked for Shavuot because it takes you through the whole Torah as appropriate to the holiday: birth *parshiot*. Having Hebrew calendars online makes it very easy to enter someone's secular or Jewish birthdate and discover the *parshah*, the Torah portion for that week. Every *parshah* is divided into seven *aliyot*, seven sections that each correspond to a reading from the Torah scroll. Because there are seven, they also match the days of the week. So the calendar instantly shows you which section corresponds to a person's birthday. In the workshop, we quickly do that research and then spend our time talking about what each person's birthday reading means. I love it. It's so simple and fun that anyone could learn it in the course of the workshop and go on to do it for their friends. A little like astrology, I guess (which is just beyond the limit of my woo-woo tolerance), but you didn't need to hire an astrologer or know a bunch of arcane stuff.

My workshop ended around 10 pm. The one Sam was in wouldn't be over till nearly eleven. I'm not a night owl, but the idea on Shavuot is to spend the night studying. Wimps like me try to make it to midnight, anyway. At the break, Sharon found me. She looked excited.

"I have an alert on my computer for Zach Levy's name," she said. Her big smile kept me from panicking. "Something has happened. It looks like a big something."

I gestured her over to an empty couch in a kind of open space off the corridor that led to the classrooms. "Let's sit here. More private." There was a jumble of background sound leaking through classroom doors: drumming, chanting, laughter, an emphatic point being made, not quite comprehensible at this distance.

"Levy is being sued by women here in the U.S. and in England," Sharon told me. They seem to be coordinating. After the alert arrived, I called and got an advance report from a journalist I know. The story is coming out tomorrow in *The Jewish Light*."

"Oy, *gevalt*! What for?"

"Sexual harassment and abuse," said Sharon. "Remember when we wondered if he and Leah had some kind of arrangement, an open marriage?"

"Yes."

"Well these four—or maybe it's five—women have stories, and each is a little different, but they come down to one thing, that he told every one of them that he loved her and wanted to divorce his wife and marry her, but they had to keep everything secret until he was free. In each case, the woman did a lot of work for Levy—at Neshama Beit Midrash in London or in connection with his teaching gigs in the U.S. They filed charges simultaneously in New York and London. The abuse charge is that he coerced them with lies and used them not just sexually, but as a source of free labor. One is a big donor who says he extorted a large sum of money from her, ostensibly as a loan, but he never repaid her. *The Light* will feature a quote from Levy saying he and Leah had an open marriage, that he long ago realized his nature was polyamorous and he couldn't force himself to be monogamous. He defends this as an unconventional but undeniable truth, something he's never hidden from anyone, including his wife. But then there's another quote from Leah denying that they had any such agreement. The leaders of the Beit Midrash have already put out a letter announcing that they are severing ties with Levy."

"Was one of the women Ruth Kahn?" I asked Sharon.

Arlene Goldbard

She nodded yes. I remembered my last conversation with Ruth. I'd asked her if her experience of me gibed with Levy's accusations, and she said no. But I never asked if the rumors about herself and Levy were true. Now I knew. If she was suing him, she must have awakened from the trance of Zach Levy. I wondered if Sharon knew anything about that.

"Not for sure," she said. "But there's evidently some part of the story where two of the women Levy promised to marry caught wind of each other. Maybe he texted one of them something meant for the other? My friend alluded to the women somehow discovering each other. But I only got snippets. We have to wait for the full story in *The Light* to come out."

When the story ran, it read like a comedy of errors, a French farce. Leah discovered that Levy was having an affair with one of the women, and she confronted him. Apparently it got very ugly, so much so that Leah, who had always displayed steadfast devotion to her husband, gave her own tell-all interview that—if believed—put him in a very bad light. Once Leah's interview was published, she was contacted by other women, Ruth Kahn and Levy's other paramours, who told more or less the same story of deception and exploitation, begging her forgiveness. They decided to join forces and filed suit.

The Light's reporter contacted all the respected figures who had vouched for Levy when the 2015 story ran. It had focused on transgressions that were said to have taken place years before, when he was a student. Now they couldn't hide behind understanding youthful indiscretions and Renewal being a *ba'al t'shuvah* movement. Though they didn't come right out and say so, I imagine they felt a little seduced and abandoned too. But most did say they were deceived and apologized for not taking the matter seriously enough. Those who had given him *s'micha* withdrew it.

Chaim from the Simcha Foundation called me the following day to say he was going to recommend multi-year funding again in the next round. I set up a meeting with the head of the Jewish Federation's grants program. The conversation was very subtle and allusive, but I got the strong impression we'd be back on the grants list. I'd like to say I got calls and emails from Renewal strangers all across America apologizing for defaming me, but no such luck.

Local folks were gracious, though. I was asked to take part in a ceremony of blessing and forgiveness. I wasn't sure about going. It seemed kind of easy, if you know what I mean. I conferred with Sam and Sharon, saying I was thinking about declining the invitation as nicely as possible. We were back at the kitchen table, but this time it was dark outside. I'd finally trimmed the runners on my hanging plants, so we could see a thick sliver of moon and a scattering of stars. Sharon and I each had a glass of white wine, and Sam was drinking his favorite, vodka tonic. *Hintele* was getting a banquet of belly rubs, changing laps each time one of us flagged. Sam had brought home a new Avishai Cohen album that I loved—the piano player, though he also likes the bass player with the same name—and he was bobbing a little to the music. Things felt lighter.

"So you no longer believe in *t'shuvah*?" Sharon asked.

"I do, of course I do."

"But what?" asked Sam, "just not for anyone who's harmed you?"

I had to laugh at that. Caught in the act. "How do I behave, though? Be super-gracious and start off saying all is forgiven? It feels like there's something for everyone to learn here. But what and how?"

Sam said "Lay it on us, then. What is the learning? I'll take notes."

"What a guy!" said Sharon.

We all laughed, but I knew her admiring look was genuine.

"Okay," I said. "First, and you've heard me say this before, we all need to understand that we can be deceived, that we can make a wrong judgment, that we are capable of misdeeds. The people who vouched for Levy were dazzled by his energy. They saw him as incapable of the things his accusers said. So they were very confident in declaring his innocence. We all know that both the *yetzer hatov* and the *yetzer hara* are present in every person's life. No one is immune. There are people you may truly know well enough to vouch for, but just meeting someone at a Shabbaton isn't a very firm foundation."

"Check," said Sam. "What else?"

"One of my favorite philosophers, Isaiah Berlin, famously said, 'Life is not worth living unless one can be indiscreet to intimate friends.' I doubt there's a person alive who hasn't gossiped. But it's one thing for two trusted friends to tell each other they've heard something about a third friend—a divorce or an illness, God forbid, or something good, a new romance. To then tell a stranger, or to be part of a chain that starts with you and ends up with strangers telling strangers—there's no way that can help anyone or make anything better. And the second level, where you hear something about a person you know, something that worries you, that could do harm to that person, and instead of talking privately to your friend, you spread it. I can't think of a single way that

     Arlene Goldbard

behavior can be seen as right conduct. So I would want to encourage everyone to think twice in such situations, and make the choice that could help to repair harm instead of worsen it."

"Check," said Sam and Sharon in unison.

"And then I think something about brokenness, because clearly Zach Levy is acting out some deep damage, some unquenchable desire to be loved. I wouldn't psychologize him. But I would tell the basic outlines of the story so they know what happened. And then make space for anything they want to ask about or add to what I hope will be a deep learning for all of us."

"Perfect," Sharon said. "I don't see why there wouldn't be room to give you a few minutes to say these things. Let's ask Jonathan what the plan is." Jonathan Fox had issued the invitation and would be leading the gathering.

"This deserves a *l'chaim*," Sam said, raising his glass. We all clicked, and I felt like something had been completed.

The gathering was lovely, really, even though I was nervous and didn't know what to with my hands. Or feet. Or anything. There were songs and blessings to start. Reb Jonathan of blessed memory introduced Nomi Riordan, who read a text of apology, asking in general terms for forgiveness for all of those in the community who saw themselves as guilty of *lashon hara*, and now understood the harm it had done. Nomi presented me with a beautiful papercut done by one of the artists of the Khegev Project, the organization she runs that is focused on inclusion in the Jewish community.

I thanked everyone and said that for me, this had to be a learning moment for all of us. Then I gave my teaching. And then we all had cake.

It's been five years now, and I don't know what became of Zach Levy. He disappeared shortly after the lawsuits were filed. There were outstanding rulings against him, damages levied but as far as I know, never collected. You can't get accountability from a ghost. I have a hunch he'll turn up again, though. Another name, place, religion. The longing for a loving guide who seems to recognize your unique specialness and promises to hold you in a lasting embrace—that seems hard-wired into a not-insignificant portion of the human race. I feel it myself sometimes. When they say to be careful what you want, we'd best take heed.

KEN

The first time I consulted Sharon Marks as an intercessor, I was desperate. That was a few years ago. I couldn't write and I didn't know why. I'd tried talking to my therapist. I tried all the techniques I'd learned from workshops and other writers, but I was dry. My best friend Lucy Perelman told me about this woman who was a private investigator by day, but also had a sort of mystical Jewish practice, pleading with higher powers to help someone who was in trouble, or sick—or like me, stuck. Lucy was much more involved in Jewish stuff than I was, but the main thing was that I trusted her.

Lucy knew I'd been blocked for something like two years by that time. She asked me if anything had happened to set it off. She looked like she had something in mind. I rifled through my mental database, and when I came to my mother's death in 2019, Lucy asked me if that could have something to do with it. It made no sense to me, but as I said, I was desperate. Lucy gave me Sharon's number and I made an appointment.

When I opened the door to Sharon's office that first time, I'd half-expected a cartoon fortune teller in a turban and many shawls who would read my tea leaves. But there were no props or costumes, just a neatly dressed short, slender woman with graying brown hair and huge eyes. I guessed she was a little younger than me. Her office looked like someplace occupied by an accountant or insurance broker, ordinary.

Sharon put me at ease in the funniest way. As she took me through the process, she kept saying, "I know you don't believe in this sort of thing." But it turned out I didn't need to believe for it to work. And man, did it work! The way Sharon's process goes—in Hebrew, it's called *melitz yosher*—the intercessor pleads for help, then receives an assignment to fix the problem. All she would say about how she receives it is that it arises in her mind. What arose when she first helped me was to write something addressed to my mother each day for thirty-six days. It had to represent my truth, how I felt, what I'd experienced.

I accepted the assignment thinking "What the hell." It all sounded like mumbo-jumbo to me, and I basically hated that shit. I wouldn't go so far as to say that religion was the opium of the people like Mr. Marx. For me it was more Groucho, not wanting to be a member of a club that would have me as a member. I now see it was some rejection of my upbringing masquerading as critical judgment. Back then, though, all I knew was that I wanted to be unblocked and was willing to try anything.

But the process of writing, carrying out my assignment, awakened something in me. Over time, my relationship with my mother and sister had become pretty pro forma. I sent money, they ignored me. Writing to my no longer living mother made me realize that I'd always wanted her to love and understand me, but had given up trying long ago. I asked her to see things from my side. I felt like an idiot, trying to get understanding from a dead person. But I did it, and the mind-blowing thing is that I got an answer! It led to a cross-country flight and a visit to the cemetery and learning that my sister had absconded with all the money I'd sent and hadn't even bothered to buy a marker for our mother's grave. It gave me a chance to put things right. I bought a marker and flew home to California. Ever since, the past has stayed past.

Now I felt blocked again. It was different, more political than personal. For the first time in a long life of writing, I felt daunted by the avalanche of words spilling out in print, online publications, social media. Everyone had an opinion (or a dozen). There was a big echo chamber reflecting back the most extreme positions, left and right. All this crap about canceling people for using the wrong words or having something good to say about the wrong group identity or whatever. Part of me was scared to put my neck out there. Part of me looked at myself in the mirror and asked what I had to say that could possibly help. Book ideas came to me, but every one of them petered out. The music that had always inspired me—Leonard Cohen and a raft of other singer-songwriters, electric guitar blues, even "Key to the Highway," even the Luther Allison version—left me cold. I felt my discouragement in my body, too, a sensation of weakness in my arms, a stomach that wasn't as reliable as it had been. When I looked in the mirror, I saw the usual things, gray crewcut, tortoiseshell glasses, black T-shirt, but my face had a haunted look I didn't like.

My first experience with Sharon had been mind-blowingly helpful. But it hadn't changed my thinking about spirituality. I put Sharon in a little box labeled "that was good." But all the rest was in a much larger vessel labeled "I don't really believe that bull."

"What could it hurt to make another appointment with Sharon?" Lucy asked. She had a knack for cutting through the shit. "If you don't like the assignment, all you have to do is say no. This is not like some movie where the sorcerer says you'll be cursed if you don't do his bidding. Sharon told you that you're free to refuse, no consequences."

Fuck it. I picked up the phone.

"This is different than last time," I told Sharon. "A loss of confidence, or purpose, or something I used to have. I'm a writer. Not a best-selling writer. My book on the commune where I lived in the seventies was my most successful, and that was published more than twenty years ago. But I've managed to get by with essays, stories, and books about culture or politics or history. I love to write—I'll never understand those people who say they hate every second of it and then win all the publishing prizes. This is the first time I remember not knowing *what* to write. My ideas have a half-life of a few days, and then they start looking weak and pointless. Maybe they are. Maybe I've just used up whatever small talent I had. But I want to write. I see myself sitting at the computer, fingers flying, and I have such a big yearning to be there. It's like being homesick." I swallowed hard. "And even though my last time with you was incredible, I'm still skeptical. I feel like I have to say that. So Is this the kind of thing you can help with?"

"Let's see," said Sharon. She's one of those small women who seem to hold a lot of compressed power, like a hand grenade, or one of those diamonds Superman made out of a lump of coal. Not that she's dramatic. Her businesslike manner clashed slightly with her elfin looks. I liked that about her. "Give me a few minutes," she said.

I sat back and looked around the room. There were some certificates mounted on the walls. Degrees, I thought, and maybe some kind of licensing thing for PIs. I heard Sharon mumbling softly, looking at a small leatherbound book. She'd told me last time I consulted her that she had to cleanse herself to do this work, to be sure the spirits responding to her pleas were the good kind. I'd been to a synagogue less than a dozen times since Lucy's kid Josh's bar mitzvah, and that was almost a decade ago. I couldn't really hear the words Sharon was saying, but I kind of got the tune. I thought she was chanting prayers.

"So tell me more," Sharon said at last.

I added as much detail as I could to my predicament.

She had a few questions. "The way you describe it, I see a kind of curtain or barrier between you and your writing. Do you have a felt sense of a barrier?"

I nodded. "It isn't like walking into a wall. Softer. But yes, it's like I see what I want and I can't reach it."

"All this noise on social media," she asked, "when did it start bothering you?"

I had to laugh. "When didn't it? But it's one thing to feel irritated at assholes on Twitter and another to just reel at the venom and nastiness and

 Arlene Goldbard

self-righteous cruelty that seems to have taken over those spaces. Definitely my feelings are Trump-related. I was always disgusted by the MAGA posts: Jewish space lasers, for shit's sake! These days I'm just as disgusted with parts of the left that seem equally righteous and intolerant, and equally eager to strike out at perceived enemies. Only now, the handiest enemies aren't actual fascists. They're what you'd call liberals. Like these leftists aren't going to trash Republican politicians for the stupid crazy shit they say, because that's what they expect from Republicans. But they're going to trash Democrats who are just a few words off from the progressive party line or who say they're willing to negotiate or cooperate or find a middle way. I've always thought of the left as the side I'm on. But so much of the time now, the left view is so fucking simplistic: the oppressed are clearly labeled and always right, the oppressor is everyone else and always wrong. Where is that going to get us?"

"So you don't know where you belong," said Sharon.

A big sigh escaped me. "Yes."

"And you feel a little bit exiled from your old community?"

"Yes. Maybe more than a little bit."

"And the way you're describing these feelings, everyone seems out for themselves. Everyone trying to win, not find solutions or make peace?"

"Yes," I said again. "And I feel worried about where the left has gone. The oppressed-oppressor thing is all about identity. That's not meaningless. Racism is real. But what about class, what about well-being? Beyoncé and the guy who camps out in a vacant lot down the block are both subject to prejudice by people who just see their skin. No argument there. But one has every privilege money can buy and the other one eats garbage. How does it help to pretend they're the same? It feels like the heart has gone out of politics."

Sharon asked me a few more questions, and then she said "Excuse me now" and went into—I don't know, a trance? Some subtly altered state.

When she opened her eyes, she was her businesslike self again. "Okay," said Sharon, "something came through very clearly. This is technical, Ken. You're going to have to read it for yourself, but I'll give you the high points.

"In *Parshat Behar*, starting in Leviticus 25, the people are told to observe two kinds of sabbatical year in which the land and animals are given a rest. There is an amnesty for debts, relatives can redeem people who are indentured or enslaved, and land is returned to its original owners. The *Shmita* or Sabbatical year comes every seven years; the *Yovel* or Jubilee year comes every 49. There are lots of associated details, 55 verses taking up all of Chapter 25. You'll probably need to read the whole thing a few times to get the context. But your specific assignment is to read the first half, Leviticus 25:1-24. Read it every day for 49 days and write whatever arises for you each day. The subject, the length, the form—those are all entirely up to you. You might feel like writing a sentence one day and ten pages the next." She paused for breath. Me too.

"Why don't you say the assignment back to me, Ken, so we're both clear that it's understood? And also if you want to do it—remember, saying yes and stopping can get you into trouble—not like an outbreak of boils or a plague of toads, but a spell of depression or free-floating anger, maybe, being visited by feelings that aren't exactly your own. But there's no penalty for saying no."

Half of me wanted to split. The text sounded like some arcane calendar thing. What would I learn from that? But then I remembered that I didn't have anywhere else to go for help. It did work last time, and like Lucy said, what could it hurt? So I repeated the assignment back and told Sharon I was in, wondering the whole time what it could mean. I didn't remember ever reading or hearing about these special years.

When I got home and sat down to read the text, I was blown away. It was some kind of revolutionary economics, but written down at least 2,500 years ago. Parts reminded me of Indigenous relationships to the land. The last line of verse 23 says "the land is Mine; you are but strangers resident with Me." The whole thing is like a great equalizer of social condition and position, because whatever land anyone acquired in the times between these special years was essentially canceled whenever one came around. You know that trite saying about leveling the playing field? They actually tried to do it.

That started me obsessing, and my obsessive thoughts filled many pages of my writing assignment. What if we had these...what could I call them? Customs? Policies? Lifeways? Imagine that the head of some corporate agribusiness would know as the year approached that the land he owned would have to be returned to those he bought—or took—it from. In the ordinary way of contemporary political bullshitting, of course, these ideas are laughable because there's absolutely no chance that those who've profited by exploiting others' labor would be willing to share the wealth, let alone surrender it. That set me to thinking about how our certainties—our ideas of what's possible—

  Arlene Goldbard

become embedded in our societies and our brains, and pretty soon we can't see around them or over or under them.

About the time I started Sharon's assignment, I had been reading this book that is hard to characterize, *The Dawn of Everything*. Sort of an alternative history/anthropology/archaeology. I'd been finding the book a struggle because those same certainties about the limits on possibility were in my brain too, getting in my way. Everything the book laid out seemed plausible, especially that the story of human societies that we in the West are mostly taught has an ideological slant that has become normalized. You know, life was nasty, brutish, and short until civilization arrived in the form of settlements and markets, after which we all progressed to enlightenment and the apex of civilization, capitalism. This book told very different stories. I loved reading them, but I was having trouble accepting some of them. My trouble felt like a kneejerk thing, not a considered opinion. I kept picking at it.

One section especially struck me and I had no difficulty believing it. I'd heard of Native Americans being brought to Europe a few centuries ago more or less as sideshow attractions, the same as certain Africans. You may have heard of the terrible fate that befell Sara Baartman, who they called "The Hottentot Venus." But the book said that some fluent and sophisticated Native American visitors were treated as honored guests, gave lectures, were presented at court, had a chance to observe European society at close range. Instead of falling to their knees in awe, they wound up horrified and incredulous at the cruelty they saw. The idea that people would let their neighbors starve, finding destitution fit retribution for whatever verdict they had concocted—the poor were lazy, shiftless, abandoned by God, deserving of punishment for their poverty— they found this appalling, unbelievable. And now I was reading a sacred text created eons before even the idea of European civilization emerged, and it was telling me that the Divine imperative was not only to love the neighbor and the stranger, but to ensure that that they were given every help to belong, to be free, to have enough, to stand side by side with everyone else.

Lucy and I met for dinner at this Korean place we both loved so I could debrief her on my consultation with Sharon. We both liked to eat, the hotter the better. When we sat down to order, Lucy told me she'd come to this place on a date and ordered her favorite, these incredibly messy chicken wings with a sticky hot red sauce, the kind that needs a dozen paper napkins. Then she felt horrified about eating this in front of a man she was trying to attract. Then she got sauce on her blouse and the evening ended in embarrassment. Licking her fingers, she said, "I'm glad I can eat them in front of you, Kenny."

We'd been friends for decades, ever since we'd met in a writers' group, the kind where you take turns bringing something you're writing to read aloud and have people respond. I should call it a critique group, because there was typically a lot more of that than compliments. It wasn't that I was looking for unadulterated approval. I just wanted people's responses to not be coming from a place of "If that were my book, I'd have written it completely differently." This is a problem I'd had with editors, many of whom seemed to be frustrated writers who wanted to impose their word choice or stylistic flourishes on my prose. I could never strike the right balance between saying yes, yes, yes to make them happy and rejecting their ideas outright until an older and more successful writer told me she never lets anyone edit her stuff. "I tell them to let me know if something is a problem and I'll fix it myself." That's been my policy ever since, and it works well. I don't mind tackling a problem, especially when it makes the work better. But at the time of the writers' group, I hadn't yet seen the light.

The writers' group included about eight very earnest people. Sometimes when the conversation flagged, I'd look around the circle and count off the markers of serious writerhood: hairdos that were shaved on one side and trimmed into steep geometric angles on the other; weirdly shaped glasses; all-black clothes (me too, though); Doc Martens. People were various ages and genders and races, but the gear was pretty much the same regardless. There was a backpack or messenger bag propped up behind every chair, ready to receive notebooks and laptops at the end of the session.

One night, a group member who'd taken notes all through my reading pressed me to change every reference to a person to conform to her idea of political correctness. This was before people were commonly asked to state their pronouns, so that wasn't part of it. But I was scolded for describing a teen-aged character as a girl rather than a woman, and so on. Lucy, who I didn't yet know, jumped to my defense, pointing out that the group existed to help us be better writers, not to bring us in line with a particular political vocabulary.

The discussion deteriorated into something like I remembered from the early seventies as crit/self-crit, a practice some leftists had picked up from accounts of life in revolutionary China. You were expected to criticize yourself for somehow not hewing to the party line. When I lived in the commune, I would usually start off confessing that I hadn't done my share of the dishes or something like that, just to inoculate myself against worse charges. Once you'd

     Arlene Goldbard

paid those dues, you were free to trash everyone else for their transgressions. Usually at least one person broke down in tears. In really hardcore groups like Weatherman, the only accurate description of this ritual would be bullying, as people piled charges that cut to the quick onto some dumb fool who'd thought he was among friends. Sometimes I was that fool.

The writers' group member whose critique Lucy and I resisted tried the same confessional tactic, patiently explaining how back in the dark ages she used to not understand how important it was to replace the default terms people use in the dominant society with words that expressed the values we want to live by. She'd made all the same mistakes, but since she woke up, she'd become a much better writer, and I could do the same. After which others picked up the theme of my retrograde vocabulary.

When time was up, I caught Lucy's eye as we filed out. It wasn't a flirtation. I had a type at the time and her energetic mop of dark curls wasn't it. We went for coffee and decided a writers' group of two would be much better in all ways, as neither of us would harass the other, and we'd both get to read every time. Since then, each of us has been the other's first reader, and over time also a shoulder to cry on, a plus-one to celebrate (or fulfill a social duty) with, a midnight texter when sleep eluded us. In short, I guess, best friend.

I told Lucy the whole story of my consultation with Sharon as we sat dawdling over a tableful of nearly empty plates and half-full cups of cold tea. I pushed some leftover tofu around in its puddle of red sauce, just to have something to do with my hands.

"Wow," she said. "I've never seen you so excited about a Torah portion. Come to think of it, I've never had a single conversation with you about a Torah portion."

Lucy was one of those East Bay Jews who alternated going to a bunch of different Jewish Renewal-ish services. She'd been a member of Jonathan Fox's community until COVID got him in 2020. Reb Rivvy Rosenblatt didn't really have a congregation, but Lucy spent a lot of time at her place, the Rachamim Center. I've gone to a few workshops there, but as Sharon kept affirming, my core attitude toward any organized Jewish community was that I didn't really believe in that sort of thing. Praying was Lucy's thing, not mine. I'd go to a Passover Seder at her house, eat latkes and light candles at Hanukkah, or come see her son Josh become a bar mitzvah. But sitting in a row of chairs holding a prayerbook, that had felt like being trapped in my seventh-grade classroom when I wanted to go outside and play ball.

"This is different," I told her. "I never read anything that spoke so directly to what our society is facing, the polarization of wealth, the entrenched privilege, the indifference to suffering."

"I'd like to say that is because you haven't read much Torah," she said, smiling. "There's a lot of stuff I tend to skip over or approach with my simultaneous translator on to reinterpret the parts where women are erased or non-Jews are treated like pest control treats cockroaches. But did I ever read you Isaiah 58?" She pulled out her phone and brought up a site that has all the Jewish sacred texts. "Listen to this."

> To be sure, they seek Me daily,
> Eager to learn My ways.
> Like a nation that does what is right,
> That has not abandoned the laws of its God,
> They ask Me for the right way,
> They are eager for the nearness of God:
>
> "Why, when we fasted, did You not see?
> When we starved our bodies, did You pay no heed?"
> Because on your fast day
> You see to your business
> And oppress all your laborers!
>
> Because you fast in strife and contention,
> And you strike with a wicked fist!
> Your fasting today is not such
> As to make your voice heard on high.

"You want political relevance?" Lucy asked. "Scorching criticism? Laying it out with no punches pulled? Read the prophets, Kenny."

"Show me that." I took the phone from her hand and scrolled down the list of books you could access at this site. "Every prophet has a separate book?"

She nodded. "Some of them are really intense. There's a whole body of writings beyond the prophets too. Have you ever read *Lamentations*?"

"No."

"It's recited to commemorate the destruction of the first Temple by Babylonians, the second Temple by Romans. It's a horror story, heartbroken, chilling, full of grief at God's abandonment of the city. Imagine Hiroshima and you come close."

I stared into the dregs of my tea. "I feel like I'm at war with myself. The 'I don't really believe' mantra is looping through my head as I look at this stuff. But these aren't exactly about belief. Angels aren't swooping down or anything. That makes me feel like kind of an asshole," I said. "All these years, I haven't bothered to even read what I rejected. It's such a superior attitude, like all of that is old hat and why do I need it? I'm not exactly an atheist, because who could be that certain and still respect themselves? I always thought atheism was another flavor of fundamentalism. But in the bits of Jewish text I've read before, quite a few things turned me off. I dismissed God as this massive ego demanding praise and obedience."

"I get that," said Lucy. "If I took everything literally I'd be that other kind of fundamentalist. But Reb Jonathan taught me that the texts aren't really their surface stories, they are full of symbolic meanings, of secrets and hints. He used to quote a friend of his, another rabbi: 'The God you don't believe in doesn't exist.' That feels so true to me, especially when it comes to the committed atheists. They adopt the most literal-minded, limited idea of God and then reject it on really stupid grounds like proving Samson couldn't have brought down the Philistines' temple with his bare hands. The God I do believe in exists inside all of us, in the human desire to repair, help, and care. I'm not going to waste my time with people who insist that if fables and parables aren't literally true in every detail, the whole notion of spirit is false. They're terrified to live into the mystery. I pity them. But they have the right to believe what they want."

Lucy worked herself into some kind of state saying this: bright cheeks, bright eyes, massive head of hair vibrating like an electrical current. I didn't see her like this often. Maybe never.

"So you want to hear a little bit of synchronicity?" she asked me while her hands made some kind of origami thing out of the paper wrapper from her chopsticks.

"You mean your fortune says 'you will enlighten a clueless friend?'"

"Very funny. No, the *parshah* you're reading, *Behar*, it's the Torah portion for this coming Shabbos," she said.

"You're shitting me!"

"I am not. You want to come to *shul* with me and hear what whoever's doing the *d'var Torah* has to say about it?"

To the amazement of my usual self, I did. I definitely did.

Or Chadash met in a borrowed space, a chapel in a local Unitarian church. It was a calm space, all shades of blue. No stained-glass Jesus windows or huge crosses on the wall. When I said something about that, Lucy told me Unitarians aren't Christians, which I guess I knew on some level, but not really. She steered us to the first row of chairs. "I'd rather skulk at the back," I told her. "Make a quick getaway if necessary."

"I want to sit up front," she replied. "Then I'm looking at whoever and whatever is up on the *bimah* leading the service instead of the back of someone's head. How about you go with my choice this time?"

"There may not be a next time," I said. I expected to be bored. "You could defer to me as your elder and hide in the back." I had eight years on her. She looked unmoved. "Okay," I said, "just this once."

Anya Applebaum made her way toward us as we were taking our front seats. She's Shomer of Or Chadash, something like president, I guess. She was here before Reb Jonathan passed and I think for a lot of people she represents continuity and whatever stability the community has managed to achieve. Anya and Lucy hugged. They were good friends, and we'd been at each other's tables many times. Anya turned to me with a complicated smile on her face, saying, "Fancy seeing you here, Ken." "Very fancy," I said, gesturing at my everyday black T-shirt uniform. I knew that's not what she meant, and she knew I knew it. Then someone else flagged her down.

Jewish Renewal services vary a lot. I understood that much from the few I'd attended. Some rabbis, such as the late and much lamented Jonathan Fox, came up very Orthodox, knew everything, and never tired of finding creative ways to turn and braid the tradition with something right up-to-the-minute. I had seen him chant Torah with the utmost spontaneity, switching as he chanted from Hebrew to English and back in a split second.

His scroll—which was Or Chadash's—was what they call a rescued Torah. There was a note about it in every newsletter. Lucy had a pile of newsletters stacked on a bookshelf in her living room in case anyone who happened to be waiting for her wanted a little light reading. The note said that hundreds of

     Arlene Goldbard

Torahs were plundered by the Nazis. After the war, more than a thousand of them were rescued from a repository in Prague. The Or Chadash scroll was old but intact. Torahs were written by hand without the vowels that make it easier to read modern Hebrew. But Jonathan read as fluently as a daily newspaper. Lucy told me that his translation was fresh, emerging in the moment, unique each time no matter how many times he'd read that passage before. That wasn't boring. But he wasn't here.

Most people who chanted would do it maybe once a year, painstakingly memorizing their Torah portions. If translation was provided, you could either read along or it would be read aloud afterwards. Certain Renewal rabbis had strong ideas about which prayers should be recited in which sequence, whether they should be offered in whole or in part. Some led long chants consisting of a few words or phrases repeated over and over again, each chant standing in for an entire prayer in the traditional liturgy. Familiar prayers were sometimes sung to the tune of popular songs or folk songs. Dancer-rabbis evolved sequences of movement that portrayed the meaning of a text while the words were sung. I'd been at a service when the traditional flow was paused so people could break into pairs to discuss a text or exchange blessings. When it was time for the Torah reading, Renewal communities did group *aliyot*, where instead of the traditional practice of one person being invited up the Torah to offer blessings as an honor, everyone who resonated with the reading was invited to stand together around the Torah table as the verses they connected with were chanted.

For people who liked variety and adaptation, relevance and participation, it could be wonderful. A lot of them were my generation, sixties and seventies people. It could also drive certain traditionalists crazy. I thought Lucy's father was going to have a fit at Josh's bar mitzvah. So all these levels were happening, but if you were like me all those times I'd made myself go for some reason, thinking about other things while waiting for it to be over, you weren't really there.

That Saturday morning, we did some singing and some chanting and some movement, and while I wasn't what I would call fully engaged, I was feeling kind of proud of myself for not ducking out. When it was time for the Torah service, the person who was leading—members took turns, as there was no official rabbi at that moment—called out the intentions for each of three group *aliyot*. She said that people who resonated with environmental healing should come up for the third *aliyah* to stand behind the Torah table as the blessings and reading unfolded. That text was the last part of my assignment from Sharon,

Leviticus 25:23-24: "But the land must not be sold beyond reclaim, for the land is Mine; you are but strangers resident with Me. Throughout the land that you hold, you must provide for the redemption of the land." I jumped up without really deciding to. My body led me.

"*Yasher koach*," said Lucy as I returned to my seat after I'd stood at the Torah table for the blessings and Torah reading. She reached out her hand as people usually do when they offer that expression, blessing you with strength. I took it as I slid into my seat. A handshake is normal, but this time, something else happened. It felt as if a bolt of electricity passed between us. It ran along the length of my arm, into my heart, and from there, to my surprise, straight into my cock. I crossed my legs and looked at Lucy, who was staring back at me with wide eyes, pupils dilated. "That was a surprise," she whispered. And it was.

Jesse Judah Tsosie, a member of the community, stood to offer the *d'var Torah* before they put the scroll away. He was half Indigenous—Navajo/Dine from out in New Mexico—and half Jewish. Jesse had long black hair in two braids trailing down the front of his shirt and disappearing under his *tallis*—the prayer shawl draped over his head and shoulders was made of Pendleton cloth decorated with Navajo designs.

He told us he was working with a movement called Land Back. He explained that this was a broad coalition of Indigenous people working for sovereignty, including return of lands that were stolen and restoration of treaties that were ignored or overturned. Jesse said that he had shared this *parshah* with other Land Back activists, to show them that the deep truths acknowledged by their people had been perceived by others many years and miles distant. He said that 2021-22, just a year ago, was a *Shmita* year, ending at Rosh Hashanah. I didn't know that! The next one would be 5789 in the Hebrew calendar, 2028-29. He said he hadn't known about it himself until recently, but with nearly six years to plan, he was dedicating himself to awakening Jewish communities to support the Land Back movement up to and throughout that year. He had lots of ideas. He figured we did too. He invited us to make *Behar* a story about today. And then he returned to his seat.

Without discussing it, Lucy and I didn't stay for the food offered after the service. We didn't say much as we walked along Ashby and turned down one of the side streets toward Lucy's place. We didn't hold hands, but it felt like we were; there was some kind of energy field connecting us. I held myself very carefully, conscious of every cell in my body. If I touched her, I thought, I might explode. Once inside the door, we faced each other. We both started to speak at

     Arlene Goldbard

once: "Do you want to talk about...." And then we fell into each other's arms for the first kiss of our long relationship and the best kiss of my long life.

Afterwards, we lay in the rumpled sheets smoking a joint. "I can't figure it out," I said. "I never thought of Shabbat services as an aphrodisiac."

"Though you do hear of the *frum* considering it a *mitzvah* to make love on Shabbos," Lucy said.

A big deal was made of Orthodox Jews' positivity toward sex, I think because it distinguished Jews from much of Christianity's negative feelings.

"Well," Lucy said, laughing, "you and I ignored that imperative for a couple of decades."

Each of us had relationships in the time we'd known each other, some of them serious but none, in the end, lasting. We kvetched to each other when things with someone went south, but we hadn't really gotten down into the weeds about how we'd felt, what we'd wanted. I think both of us—Lucy at 62 now, me at 70—had arrived quietly at the point of thinking we'd be single forever, neither a happy prospect nor a dire one. Lucy had told me that of her women friends who were divorced or widowed, most said they didn't want to marry again. Their reasons were practical: marrying in your sixties is likely to mean signing up to play nursemaid, what with both physical and mental ailments looming. Or they had money put aside and didn't want to negotiate a bunch of financial agreements that might have implications for their kids. Or they hadn't enjoyed being married all that much and prized their freedom more than whatever might come with a new spouse.

When Lucy told me that, though, she also said something poignant and revealing. She said the thing she missed was someone putting her first. I remember almost saying she came first with me, but it seemed inept. Did we list each other as our emergency contact? I usually wrote down my cousin's number. He and I weren't much involved in each other's lives, but he lived out here. Would I drop everything to care for Lucy if she had an accident? I'd like to think so, but it had never been tested and of course, I hope it never will be. I can't quite recall, but I have a strong hunch we did the usual and changed the subject, maybe with a joke.

But now, something had shifted. This wasn't old friends falling into bed out of boredom or intoxication or desperation. Lying together felt right. The amber light streaming through the bedroom curtains and illuminating every dust mote felt right. Lucy's long fingers stroking my arm felt right. I was thinking of a friend who did some research for me from time to time. Forty years younger, he'd let slip something about another writer my own age, that he'd loved women in his prime, but surely that was over now, the equipment couldn't possibly be working. I didn't say what about Picasso and Rupert Murdoch and Mick Jagger, because what's the point? The young believe youth is their special power, the apex of aliveness. I remember sex when I was young. I loved it, the pursuit, the challenge, the reward. But what I thought was amazing five decades ago turned out to be pretty meh compared to the gift my old body offered that day, time stretching out and appreciation building intensity. If I told him that Lucy and I, trusting our friendship, had entered the domain of the erotic together and had a life-changing experience, he'd probably laugh. But I couldn't imagine any reason to tell him.

"We did ignore it," I told Lucy. "But I now see that resistance is futile." I picked up the roach from the bedside table. Did I feel like smoking it?

"You will be assimilated?" she asked. "Like the Borg?" She'd begun to pull the sheet around her body, ready to get up. Then something changed. When I started to answer, she stopped and lay back on the rumpled pillows, listening to me. There was some ancient music in the background, Van Morrison's *Astral Weeks*. We'd both agreed it was our desert island album, even though digital music had made that idea obsolete, and Morrison had been an asshole about COVID vaccines.

"No," I said. "I've been thinking. Why did that electric current happen in services and not somewhere else? You know how you're always saying we exist simultaneously in four worlds—body, intellect, emotion, spirit? I never really got that. But that's what I experienced today after the *aliyah*. It felt like watching through a lens as everything suddenly comes into crisp, clear focus. I think my lifelong skepticism or aversion or whatever you call it put a kind of scrim over my vision. There were things I just couldn't see because they contradicted my story of reality. But when Sharon gave me the assignment of working with *Behar*, my vision started to clear. I started to see that I was part of this long, long line of Jews trying—sometimes failing, sometimes succeeding—to live into a kind of holiness. I can hardly believe I'm saying this, but encountering the description of the *Shmita* and *Yovel* years blew my mind.

"I remembered someone telling me that Shabbos was the first labor policy, that I should think how incredibly advanced it was to mandate that instead

     Arlene Goldbard

of working themselves like beasts twenty-four/seven, they believed humans should have a day of being instead of doing. I just blew him off. I thought he was stretching a point. I was wrong. Every day when I write my assignment, these ideas gather, and they're starting to take shape. I have quite a few of my forty-nine days left, so I'm not rushing it. But what I felt with you and for you today was a kind of awakening." I stared at her, taking in the familiar face, the dark eyes, the hair with a life of its own. "I'm a little scared to say this, but I don't want to go back to sleep, Lucy. What about you?"

She answered with a kiss. "The *shelshelot neshamot*," Lucy whispered. "The chain of souls—or you can say *shersheret*, necklace. Generations past, generations to come. You finally see yourself as one of the links," she said, stretching her arms above her head. "Welcome."

When I woke up the next morning, the air felt different. Not quite so relaxed. Lucy's bedroom was full of things to look at: silkscreen posters of Frida Kahlo and Rosa Luxemburg, a shelf of tiny figurines, a length of blue and green sari cloth pinned to the wall. But she was staring at the ceiling. I watched her for a minute. Then she felt me watching and turned my way.

"Good morning," I said.

"Good morning. I need to talk to you. Should we get coffee first?"

I had that sinking feeling, and then the feeling you get when you realize "Oh shit, I have that sinking feeling again." If I let myself go down that path, it usually takes me to punishing myself for getting my hopes up.

"Sure," I said.

We brought the coffee and bagels not back to bed, which I'd briefly imagined as the site of all-day pleasure, but to opposite ends of the worn brown leather couch.

Lucy looked me in the eye. "I don't want this to be one of those things where some kind of energy gathers for a minute and then our friendship is over. I depend on you. We've loved each other a long time, but not like this. Is this going to end us?"

"I can honestly say that hadn't occurred to me. When I woke up, I was imagining spending the day in bed." The image was fading fast.

"I don't want to be trite and say something like, 'Well, you're a man.' But you know how you're always talking about what you do and don't believe in?"

I nodded.

"The whole belief question is a puzzle to me. Most things, you don't have to get into belief. I don't have to believe in gravity; it proves itself every time I take a step and don't fly off the planet. I don't have to believe the literal words of bible stories about miracles and wonders to find something wise in them. I get how belief applies to ethics, like some fundamentalist Christian saying 'I don't believe in same-sex marriage.' They mean they don't endorse or accept it as right, but they aren't denying it exists. Sometimes it means possibility, like someone saying 'I don't believe in time travel.' So I need to ask you a question: do you believe in love? In any of those senses of belief?"

I had to smile. If you fall in love with a writer, get ready for a lot of wordplay. "I do believe in love, Lucy. I believe it's possible, I endorse and accept it. I've seen it for myself. I just didn't think it was coming to me—loving friendship, yes, but this thing I'm feeling right now, all four worlds lined up? I thought that time was past until yesterday opened my eyes."

"I keep having mental images of these movies from the forties," Lucy said. "Where Cary Grant or someone finally asks his coworker to remove her glasses and they live happily ever after. In those movies, the girl has always loved him but he never really saw her. And it's true, I have loved you a long time, but like a brother. I wasn't really looking for romance either. Not because I didn't want it, to be honest, but because I didn't want to torture myself by pining after what's never coming. So I think I'm feeling the same things as you, this awakening, pleasure, possibility. But I'm scared too. I don't have a lot of experiences of moving into a new reality without hitting potholes. I've fooled myself before. Am I doing it again?"

"I've loved you a long time too," I told her. "More than my sister by a mile. But I think we both put a shield around the relationship because it was so important to us. We'd seen affairs come and go. We wanted this to stay. I honestly don't know two people who've been as close as us for as long as us who never even flirted with it. Never even went off into 'What if?' after a few glasses of wine? I'm thinking how hard we kept that distance was a disguise for how intense it would be if we let it loose. I've never even had that thought before. I'm having it now because whatever we let loose when our hands touched after the Torah service obliterated all my careful self-protection."

     Arlene Goldbard

Lucy sighed and stretched. "A little bit of my careful self-protection is still wrapped around my heart," she said. "We can't know the future. But can we promise each other anything? What could it be?"

I reached for a piece of paper and a pen from the coffee table. "I hate the thought that we may be at the threshold of the greatest part of our lives and how shitty it would be if we let fear control us. Let's see what we can actually promise. I'm writing down 'truth.' After that, I'm putting 'to be truthful in all aspects of our relationship.' Can you go with that one?"

"Yes," said Lucy. "Put down 'kindness.' And maybe 'compassion' too. I hate those relationships where people do mean teasing, complain about each other in front of friends, fight in public, like that."

"Okay," I told her. "All that is good. It's what I want too. I'm putting 'communication.' If we don't stay connected, it won't work."

"Okay." Lucy laughed. "We've probably spoken about one billion words to each other since we met, so I don't see us getting reticent now. But, sure." She sighed. "Now I have a tough one. It scares me to say it. Put each other first."

"I remember when you told me you wished you had that. We were talking about your friends who didn't want to get married again, and you said that was your sorrow. I wanted to say you come first with me. Best friends, I was thinking. But I didn't say it. Instead I thought about who we have as our emergency contacts. I want that too, Lucy. I'm writing it now. And then I have a really tough one. I don't even know how to say it." I was getting choked up.

"C'mon. Let's practice everything on the list so far." Lucy picked up her coffee cup and held it with both hands in front of her mouth, as if she was planning to sip but not quite ready.

"Alright," I said. Deep breath. "We're not young, to state the all-too obvious. I'd like to think we'll die in our sleep on the same day, but the odds aren't great. One or both of us will have to take care of the other one sometime. I have an idea this might have come up even if our category stayed just friends. But it's a commitment I want to make out loud. If two people are going to join their lives at our age, that better be part of the deal. You have Josh, but Josh has his own life unfolding. I want you to know I'll be there."

Tears filled Lucy's eyes. "No fair," she said. "Of course I'll be there too. Friendship or lovers. But Kenny, which way will it be? Can we put our seal on this declaration after a one-night stand?"

"Plus twenty years of friendship where the worst breach we ever had was when you were thinking about moving back east and I was so hurt I didn't talk to you for a week. Do you remember my friends Peter and Joel?"

"Sure," Lucy said. "They're the ones that got married at City Hall after it became legal."

"Right. They told me they knew after three days they wanted to spend their lives together, but they decided to wait six months to move in on account of Joel's kids, who would think they were rash if they did it too soon. And then they waited another six months to get married even though they really wanted to do it on the first day they could. Again because of the kids. They figured at their age, they didn't have time to waste. They could tell the real thing from the false. Don't you think we have enough life experience to judge?"

"Is this a proposal?" she laughed.

"Kind of. Here's what I propose. I like the 49 days thing that Sharon gave me for my assignment, seven weeks. It's a solid amount of time. I propose we keep this list of agreements going and look at it regularly. I propose we use the same timeframe, trusting each other for 49 days, and at the end of that time, if we've kept the agreements and still feel the same, we move in together. I'd like us to get married. It kind of goes with that thing about taking care of each other. I want us to be each other's emergency contact. And I'd like to get some breakfast and go back to bed. What do you say?"

"I say yes to the last thing. And yes to the rest. But remember, we've got truth and communication and if I get scared again, as I'm pretty sure I will, I'm going to tell you, and I'll be banking on your kindness and compassion to pull me out of it."

I reached across the length of our legs to take her hand and shake it. "Deal. And I may need that from you too."

"Deal."

That was a sweet time. We started to spend just about every night together. Lucy's days were taken up with her own writing and her jobs as a freelance editor and writing coach. And I was working on my *melitz yosher* assignment with the same focus and excitement I usually brought to a new book. As the forty-ninth day of my assignment approached, I realized that what

     Arlene Goldbard

I'd been writing *was* notes for a new book. Lucy and I sat for hours on her sofa, feet stretched out, blues playing low in the background, facing each other, tossing around ideas, trying to find the structure and focus that would serve the subject best. This is something we'd done for years, each time either of us felt a new project coming on.

What kept coming back to me was that thing that had so impressed me in the book I was reading when I consulted Sharon, about Indigenous people visiting European courts where they were expected to marvel at the heights of progress and civilization, but instead were struck with disbelief at learning that Europeans found it perfectly acceptable to punish the poor for their poverty, to let their neighbors starve. That felt very close to my recent experience, how *Behar* had shown me that a far superior way to understand the land and the concepts of ownership, poverty, and status had been articulated many centuries before. The mealy-mouthed bureaucracies that so-called advanced societies use to separate the "undeserving poor" from the rest showed me with fresh shock how fully society's callous indifference had prevailed. I wanted to write a book that invited people to see and feel the same things, a book that gave them ideas anchored in the past that could release the grip of greed and indifference on their sense of the possible.

"Big project," said Lucy. "You may need help."

"Definitely. I need a researcher. It needs to be someone who knows Jewish history and texts a lot better than I do and who shares my desire to show this country the trap it's fallen into, carrying water for the people whose abundance depends on starving others."

"I know someone who'd be really good," Lucy told me, "but I don't know if he's available. Isamu Goodman."

"That sounds Japanese," I said.

"Close. Okinawan on his mother's side, Ashkenazi on his father's. He had a double major at Berkeley, Asian and Jewish studies. Rivvy introduced me to him about a month ago. He was thinking about taking a year off from his graduate studies. He was looking for editorial jobs—not an internship, but a part-time job. I can call him and see if he has the bandwidth for another project."

So she did. Isamu and I met up for coffee. He had a youthful, open face, an air of actual curiosity instead of what I encountered so often, someone waiting for your mouth to stop moving so they can say whatever they have queued up. He wore hipster horn-rimmed glasses which made him look like an Asian computer nerd from a tech startup, except that he also wore a Jewish Space Laser T-shirt, which didn't exactly fit the profile. I liked him at once.

I wondered if he'd been named for Noguchi the sculptor.

"Nailed it," he said. "Most people don't. My father always wanted to be an artist, he's a great admirer of Noguchi's work. Noguchi was hapa too."

"Hapa?"

"It means half. It's Hawaiian," Isamu explained. "Noguchi was half Japanese and half white American Protestant. I'm half Okinawan and half Jewish. Call me Iz. My Hebrew name is Isaiah, so it works both ways."

"So how do the halves get along?" I asked.

He laughed. "I think Lucy told you I had a double major, Asian and Jewish studies. Trying to keep the inner family together. My mom isn't particularly spiritual, but I got a bit of Shinto experience from my grandmother. It's very grounded in nature: every tree and rock, every force of nature, every living being has a Kami, a resident spirit. Definitely tilted me toward environmental stuff. You know that thing from *Midrash Rabba* about the blades of grass?"

I did not.

"The text goes 'R. Shimon said: There is not a single herb but has a *mazal*—a constellation—in the heavens which strikes it and says, Grow!' Around Renewal folks, that tends to morph a little sweeter: every blade of grass has an angel that watches over it and whispers 'Grow, grow.' The more I study, the more I find that we aren't so different in some ways. We just express things differently."

I was impressed. I told Iz the whole story: how I'd been blocked, met Sharon, got the assignment, was blown away by *Behar*, and had a ton of notes toward a book and an immediate need for a researcher and assistant.

Iz had questions. "So your main point is that we've lost this basic imperative to care for one another...."

"And the planet," I interjected.

"And the planet," Iz repeated, "and from there?"

"The project has a long way to go," I explained. "I think I have to look at it from many different angles, like social assistance programs that shame the people they are supposed to help. Like the social psychology of indifference to suffering, the focus on finding individual security instead of collective healing.

     Arlene Goldbard

It's all got to be in there, but I haven't got a structure yet. What I do know is that each sector I deal with will need research."

Iz pointed me toward a couple of things to read, mostly writings from Arthur Waskow, a Renewal rabbi who focused a lot climate and had also heavily promoted engaging in debt forgiveness in the last Jubilee year.

We talked a little about money and hours, shook hands, and went our separate ways. We'd begin work on Monday.

Every writer has a process. I was once at an artists' residency at the same time as Susan Sontag. At dinner one night, she told us that she'd spent three months writing the first few paragraphs of *The Volcano Lover*. Not her best book, but that would have made me cringe even if it had been. I couldn't imagine how to make my eyes fresh enough by the time month two rolled around to be sure I wasn't just rearranging furniture. My writing process was, first: talk it to death. Second: write it, a few drafts. Third: share it with people who could read and knew how to be honest. Fourth: revise and submit.

I usually talked it to death with Lucy. That was even easier since we had basically moved in together at both our places. Sometimes Iz joined us. I thought that if I could integrate whatever someone forty or so years our junior had to say alongside Lucy's and my perceptions, the resulting work might connect with more readers. I kept coming back to something that had been part of almost everything I'd written: connecting the small-scale story of my own life experience with something larger in the Zeitgeist. I knew I had to do that, but I kept circling around how without actually landing.

I'd been teaching Iz about my research methods and aims. He was a great learner, so much so that I began to think I could have skipped the lessons. Right around the time I had that thought, he stepped into the role of teacher.

"Let me try," Iz said. He was lying on my green couch, piled with pillows, a little beat-up but serviceable, definitely the best place in my apartment to stretch out. We'd been at it for about an hour, Lucy in one armchair, me in the other. We'd smoked a few hits. Elmore James' version of "It Hurts Me Too" was playing so softly in the background, I could barely make it out. But it added a vibe. Lucy and I each had a glass of not too bad red wine. Iz had a beer. A bowl of pretzels stood on the coffee table.

Iz sat up. "Ken," he said. "You had a moment of revelation." I nodded. It tickled me that this prophetic voice was emanating from someone wearing a

"Born to Kvetch" T-shirt, but he was right. I suppressed my smile and nodded. "Huge aha moment," Iz continued. I nodded again. "Not just what you read in *Behar* about *Shmita* and *Yovel,* but the way the whole experience showed you that a lifetime of saying 'I don't really believe in that sort of thing' hadn't actually served you."

"Yes," I said.

"In philosophy," Iz continued, "I studied this concept called 'potential consciousness.' One way to look at the idea is that if a belief becomes a fixed feature of your take on the world, then you will not be truly able to receive, understand, and accept something that contradicts it. A basic example is if a fundamentalist believes the world was created in six days, the idea of evolution is going to sail right over their head." He looked at me, waiting for a response.

But Lucy got there first. "Oh my God! Lucien Goldmann. Romanian Jew. Philosopher. I loved him and I completely forgot about him!"

Lucy and Iz enthused for a couple of minutes, and then Iz turned to me, serious again.

"So after a lifetime of rejecting any spiritual truth, one hits you over the head. Everything starts coming together. Not just being able to write again, but you and Lucy. Do you think that would have happened if you hadn't gotten stuck, if you hadn't gone to see Sharon, if you hadn't read *Behar*?"

Lucy and I shook our heads in unison.

"I'm not really into the idea that all of this was lined up for you by some superpower. I think revelations are everywhere but we can't necessarily see them through our present circumstances and belief systems. The Baal Shem Tov said it: 'The world is full of wonders and miracles but man takes his little hand and covers his eyes and sees nothing.' So what that tells me," Iz continued, "is that moments of revelation—of seeing something in a complete new way—can have epic impact *only if you let them.* Like you had this revelatory experience, and it catalyzed something very personal for you that plugged right into your understanding of the larger society. And that is what you'd like the book to do for anyone who reads it. Bridge from the very personal to the very political, like jumping a spark between two poles. Right?"

"Right!" Lucy and I chorused. We were both getting excited.

Picking up his beer, Iz reclined again. "So I think your structure has to be aha moments. Each chapter or section has to focus on some revelation and

     Arlene Goldbard

where it took you. I don't know what they all are. But for instance, Leviticus 19:15." Iz closed his eyes and spoke from memory. "'You shall not render an unfair decision: do not favor the poor or show deference to the rich; judge your kindred fairly.' Supreme Court much? You've been saying that when you read a text like that, you immediately think 'How did what was known so long ago get so lost?' That's what you want everyone to ask, right?"

Lucy and I looked at each other. I think an observer could have called our expressions parental, though we had no right to that when it came to Iz. But the mood was definitely one of kvelling. I looked at Lucy harder. "How did you find this fucking genius?" I asked her. "And how can I repay you?"

Lucy picked up a pretzel and started taking tiny mouselike bites, nibbling until the entire stick had disappeared. I could have picked up her hand and nibbled her fingers the same way, but we weren't alone.

"Thank Rivvy," Lucy laughed. "I'll take up your second question later."

The 49 days of my assignment from Sharon are up. I'm two weeks into drafting, two weeks into discovering the latest story or essay or research paper Iz has found for me, two weeks into reading a little bit out loud after dinner and not cringing. Two weeks into loving every minute of writing again.

I called Sharon to thank her. I didn't tell her everything, but I did talk about the book and express my gratitude. I probably sounded like an excited teenager at the thrill of it all. She was happy in her matter-of-fact way, and told me to get in touch anytime I needed her. I said to count on it.

It was also three weeks into the seven Lucy and I had marked off to try out our relationship agreements; four more weeks to go. Definitely so far, so good. But strange when your best friend is still your best friend, but so much more. Lucy's four worlds idea—it isn't hers, of course, a mystical *kabbalah* thing that says we live in four concentric worlds, greatly simplified for our purposes into body, emotions, intellect, and spirit—I'd told her I had no idea what it meant until that day at the Torah service, and that was true. But now I'm seeing that until that day, she and I built our friendship on just two of those worlds, intellect and emotion. Our bodies had been available in certain situations: eating, schlepping, doing yoga and all the rest. But they were not engaged in our relationship. And spirit, that was Lucy's department, with my role being the distantly wry observer of a part of her I couldn't quite take seriously.

Now we are consciously trying to show up for each other in all four realms. It's almost like one of those movies where everything is in black and white until the color comes on. *The Wizard of Oz*. Having almost the same conversation we might have had a few months ago, but wrapping it in the deliciousness of lying together as we talked, face-to-face, each propped on an elbow, legs entwined.

The cold feet moments have reared their heads, but not very often. We've each looked at ourselves in the mirror, peering closely instead of the usual cursory glance, and asked if the other will be able to stand us when the wrinkles overtake everything else, coming soon. Lucy pointed out that whether by divine design or accident, the thing that makes us need reading-glasses also adds a nice blur to each other's faces when we're only inches apart.

We've had late-night tears when disbelief comes calling: how can we be granted this happiness at long last? When will the other shoe drop? That reminded me of the time a friend and I put in for a big project grant. We got a call from the foundation telling us the money was coming through. After he put down the phone, my friend went dancing around the place exclaiming, "I can't believe it! I can't believe it!" Finally I said "If they'd called to say the application was rejected, would you have had any trouble believing it?" That's the story I keep thinking about. A lifetime of disappointments makes it hard to keep your hopes up. I think most of us dial them down out of self-defense. I hope Lucy and I have the strength not to go there.

Lucy just keeps repeating the famous mantra of Rabbi Hillel. "If I am not for myself, who will be for me? If I am only for myself, what am I? And if not now, when?"

"Good questions," I say, taking her in arms. "Twenty-eight days till we have our answers."

I know what I want them to be.

     Arlene Goldbard

IZ

I grew up with a double identity. Not in the more common flavor of, say, being an immigrant and becoming an American, but by being both Okinawan and Jewish. (American too, but that's kind of a base coat, if you know what I mean.)

My mom, Fumiko Eiko Kaneshiro, she's the Okinawan side. Everyone calls her by her English name, though: Eileen. She was born in Hawaii, and didn't come to the mainland till she went to college. Her grandparents had immigrated to work the plantations on Kauai, but fast forward a generation and her parents and the siblings and cousins in her family were destined for white collar jobs. "I want you to sit at a desk," her father used to say, "not dig ditches." She's a middle school teacher, so she has a desk, but she doesn't get to sit much.

College is where she met my dad, Simon Micah Goodman. Everyone calls him Shim, which is kind of an odd name, but not so odd if you consider it's short for the Hebrew pronunciation of his first name, Shimon. He's second-generation, the grandchild of a carpenter who left his family in Russia for greener pastures, and a mother they called a *balabusta*, which is like a super housekeeper who can cook and sew and clean like a demon. I only met my great-grandmother—Bubbe—a few times, but I still remember her rugelach and honey cake. Shim's parents moved to California when his father Joel got a job there in the sixties as a therapist, working with Jewish Family Service. His mother Laura was a weaver. Not exactly a job, but a vocation. They're both gone now, but her beautiful pillows are on every couch in my folks' house, reminders.

I look more like my mom than my dad. I guess Okinawan genes are stronger: black hair, dark eyes that are a little rounder than my mother's, a permanent tan. Shim is one of those rusty Jews, wiry hair that isn't really red but something close, doesn't do too well in the sun. I'm taller than both of them. If I have a trademark, it's funny T-shirts, most with a Jewish theme, but Eileen keeps reminding me I have to wear a jacket and tie sometimes. I just try to put that day off whenever I can.

In some ways, my parents' stories are similar, descended from immigrants working hard to make their children's lives better. People who came over not speaking the language and had to be fast learners. Missing the ones they left behind and would never see again. Life wasn't perfect: my dad's dad liked to gamble, my mom's dad liked to drink. But not so they couldn't pull off some version of the American dream.

One thing I've noticed is that when you ask some all-American person where they grew up or something like that, they almost always start the story with their own childhood. Ask the kids of immigrants and—if they know the story—it will start at least a couple generations back, like I just did.

Shim and Eileen are nothing if not fair-minded, so when I was born in 2000, they named me Isamu Joseph Kaneshiro-Goodman, which made my life, including filling out school forms and getting teachers to call on me, just as easy as you can imagine. I became Iz in kindergarten, and Iz is who I am today.

My first name is after the sculptor Isamu Noguchi, which is kind of cool. Ken Simon, this writer I'm helping with a project, asked me about it when we met. I told him I was hapa like Noguchi, then I had to explain hapa, which is basically half as it's said in Hawaii, where nearly everyone is part this and part that. When we first met, Ken asked me how the halves get along. I have a stock answer for that: "double major in Asian and Jewish studies, so obviously, my mission is trying to keep the family together." But that isn't strictly true. I mean who I am is who I am, double. But it was a long, strange trip to accept that fully, because in the messed-up world of contemporary cultural politics, there's a lot of pressure to choose a side. One side. One identity.

At Berkeley High, just wrapping their minds around Okinawa seemed to be a little much for most kids. They could call me Japanese and be more or less right, but the catch-all "Asian" was their preferred label, claiming a solidarity that confused me. I mean if you went back to the roots, the Chinese fucked over the Japanese who fucked over the Okinawans and the Koreans. Then they all got together in Hawaii to work the plantations with the Filipinos and Portuguese. Don't honestly know where the South Asians like Pakistanis and Indians come in, and then there's Vietnamese, Thai, Laotian, Cambodian...you get the picture. Eileen told me that her parents counseled her not to date *naichi* guys, mainland Japanese, because they looked down on us. The grandparents were gone before Shim came along, so no idea what they would have said about Jews.

High school is when I started my musical mission. I don't play, but I love to listen. I got the idea of digging into Asian musicians working in the zones other kids loved. Like Linkin Park. Did you know two Asians basically started it? Or the Slants, an all-Asian group that had to go to the Supreme Court to defend their name? Then I thought, why not work both sides? I liked that game of discovering Jews, who unlike many Asians, you couldn't necessarily spot right away. Joey Ramone, did you know he was Jewish? Of course I got to

    Arlene Goldbard

Dylan and Lou Reed that way. The whole thing was kind of retro, mostly rock and songwriter music that was almost as old as me, if not older. Then someone gave me Don Byron's Mickey Katz album, which was hilarious, and that led to Andy Statman's bluegrass-klezmer-jazz. By the time college rolled around, I was listening to more jazz—Jon Jang, Francis Wong—than anything else. I love Joshua Redman, go see him every chance I get. Looking back, though, I think my music thing launched my sense of identity, which was to open my arms wide and embrace it all. Now when people ask what kind of music I'm into, I skip the identities and genres, and just say "Music."

So many people at Berkeley High held confusing ideas about identity. Like I said, our great-grandparents wouldn't have seen themselves as part of one big happy ethnic family. What made people team up were two things. First because everyone who wasn't Asian themselves (and some who were) had trouble telling most of us apart and would never in a million years remember, let alone respect, what they saw as inconsequential details like whether you're Thai or Lao. So actually being seen as yourself was a losing battle. That led to the second thing, self-defense: wanting to have a big enough bloc on our team to earn a place among the five gross categories this country likes to sort people into: White, Black, Latino, Asian, Indigenous.

There are Jews that tick each of those five boxes, though again, since most people have no idea that Jews are anything but white, that truth isn't given much weight. I know two Black cantors and three Black rabbis; a bunch of so-called crypto-Jews in New Mexico who are learning Ladino and a rabbi in Mexico whose congregation is growing fast; a few artists who are hapa too, with one Jewish parent and the other Indigenous, Diné or Hopi or Lakota. All Jews are up against the same general ignorance, the default attitude that Judaism is a religion like Christianity and can be viewed through the same lens. Jewish Studies helped me understand how that idea caught on in the twentieth century to counter the Nazis' assertion that Jews are a race. Fair enough. But everything our texts and prophets and scholars tell us points to one thing, that in all our difference, regardless of the many places we come from and now live, Jews are a people. Instead of dogma we have a centuries-long debate about how to understand existence and live. Instead of the Christian God who fathers children, our idea of the Divine does not have a body except as metaphor. No beginning, no end: that's my favorite chant these days, *B'li reishit, b'li tachlit* in Hebrew.

That doesn't mean we have to clump together and throw our weight around like a nation, though some people think so. The Christian Zionists seem the most convinced. I think of their viewpoint as roundup theory: they put a lot of lobbying into the idea that Jews must return to the Holy Land to hasten the second coming of their false messiah, Jesus. They usually neglect to mention that it's an efficiency move, making it easy to eliminate all of us while the righteous Christians are raptured up.

If you're getting the impression that I'm a little tired of the simplistic ways identity is used, especially Jewish identity, you're right.

My parents have their doubts about identity too. If I came home from school and told my parents I was supposed to pick a racial category and stay in it, they would patiently explain that our family belonged to several categories and we were against being slotted into one identity box for some bureaucrat's convenience. I liked the way they expressed that when I was growing up. Both Shim and Eileen like to cook, so we had all the delicacies of both cultures, Okinawan-Hawaiian and Ashkenazi Jew. We did not keep kosher, because to be Okinawan is to eat pork. My mom told me they used to call us "pig-eaters." Pig's feet soup with chunks of daikon and greens was a big favorite. Also sashimi. My dad didn't love raw fish, but he didn't really have any problem with all that as long as Eileen would eat chopped liver and gefilte fish and matzo brei. He did tell me that the first time he fixed matzo ball soup for her she practically paved the surface with hot peppers, so some compromise was involved on both sides.

When I lived at home, we lit candles on Shabbos and celebrated all the holidays. I still do. We went to services sometimes at Jonathan Fox's place. He was a mensch, my dad always said, welcoming everyone with his whole heart. He definitely welcomed me. Shim and Eileen and I went to the Okinawan *bon* and *eisa* dances during the Obon festival every summer, where I got a tummy ache from eating too many *ondagi*, dense little donuts that Shim used to say shared a lot of characteristics with certain Jewish foods: brown, fried, liking to hang out in your stomach for a long time after they're ingested. We had a little shrine in the house where we lit incense to the ancestors, leaving fruit and flowers sometimes, asking for their help.

So yeah, I'm hapa, but the two halves dance with each other so closely entwined it's sometimes hard to tell where one ends and the other starts.

It's not like all Jews are warm and welcoming, either. I definitely give the ultra-Orthodox a wide berth, but I don't really need to because I doubt they see me as a member of the tribe.

     Arlene Goldbard

It comes down to this: I'm just really pissed at the way the gross identity categories have messed it up for everybody.

Case in point. We did this virtual Pesach second-night Seder three years ago, in 2021, COVID putting the kibosh on actually getting together. In the section of the Seder when you traditionally do the *Magid*, retelling the Exodus, we ask everyone to share a story of their own freedom or struggle to be free.

My mom's friend Susie talked about her challenges trying to organize with the diverse communities of her city. "The whole walking on eggs, internal disagreements thing makes me feel unfree. We have to be so careful. I wish everybody could get it together on what they want, it's all over the map, Central Americans want this, African Americans want that, Asian Americans some other thing. Getting the Straits Chinese and the Taiwanese to agree on anything, it's exhausting."

Then Sarah Fox—Reb Jonathan's daughter, she was 17 then—said, "Yeah, I know what you mean. White people are the worst—they cannot agree on a common agenda!"

Everybody laughed, because everyone knows that the category "white people" includes a lot of different people wanting a lot of different things. Nobody expects them to all agree. Then everybody looked sheepish. I DM'd Sarah: "And we are supposed to be the liberal, pro-diversity camp." She sent me a poop emoji.

I am a big fan of Nomi Riordan, who heads the Khegev Project, which is all about inclusion in Jewish communities. My bar mitzvah project supported Khegev—we did a garage sale for it. I also did an internship there one summer during undergrad. Nomi was at that Seder too, along with Sharon Marks—they've been Sarah's guardians since her dad died. A lot more energy is needed to give Nomi's work the impact it deserves. But I have to confess, the hardest work for me so far has not been outward, but inward, in community, responding to barriers and prejudices. It's been internal, finding my way to a full embracing and representing of my own identities. That's my story.

One part of my ecumenical upbringing was going to Reb Jonathan Fox's Sunday School starting when I was six or seven. His wife Judy did most of the teaching for the younger kids: learning Hebrew, songs, holidays, stories, little craft and cooking projects like making hamantaschen. It was fun. Right about when I turned 11, I switched to the b'nai mitzvah prep class, where kids went to grownup services. We learned the parts of the service and practiced some of the liturgy. We studied the *parshah* and *haftorah* assigned for our birthdays, learned how to *leyn*—to read Torah—thought about what our community service project would be, and planned our *divrei Torah,* our speeches.

My birthday *parshah* was *Balak.* It features a talking donkey, which right there is all a growing boy could want for his bar mitzvah. There's a short bit at the end about having sex with Midianites and a plague coming from that, but almost the whole *parshah* turns on one story. It's about Balaam, a prophet, but not an Israelite. He is invited by Balak, a king in Moab, on behalf of his own people and the Midianites, to come curse the Israelites, who have become numerous and strong, defeating everyone in battle. God tells Balaam not to go despite major enticements, gifts and like that. Finally, God gives permission on the condition that Balaam does only what God instructs, and the prophet sets out to meet Balak. Along the way, his donkey balks and swerves off the road. She backs Balaam into a wall and finally lies down, refusing to go farther. Balaam is furious and beats the donkey. That's when the donkey talks:

"The jenny said to Balaam, 'Look, I am the jenny that you have been riding all along until this day! Have I been in the habit of doing thus to you?' And he answered, 'No.'"

It turns out an angel has been sent to block the way. The donkey sees the angel, but Balaam can't see it until God opens his eyes.

From there it's a long story with altars and sacrifices and Balaam being unable to curse the Israelites. He climbs to different vantage points to try, but each time he ends up blessing them instead, frustrating Balak. One of his blessings is part of the liturgy we sing first thing in the morning service: How fair are your tents, O Jacob, Your dwellings, O Israel!/*Ma tovu ohalecha Yaacov, mishkenotecha, Yisrael.*

I don't know if I can do justice to how I felt finding out at 11 that this is my birth *parshah.* It made me want more than anything to have a bar mitzvah. I read *Balak* as portraying how adults always think they know everything, like Balaam starts beating the donkey for disobeying him. What else could be going on? What could a stupid animal know better than a wise prophet? And then it turns out that the stupid animal can plainly see an angel blocking his way, and all Balaam can see is his own anger. At that age, this was the perfect revenge for every time someone said "My dear child" or something like that to shut me up. I'm not exaggerating when I say it became a mantra for me: *what are you not seeing?* And it still is.

When I got ready to write the *d'var Torah* I would deliver on my bar mitzvah, I focused on the argument between Balaam and the donkey, using the concept of *machloket l'shem shamayim,* argument for the sake of heaven, not to defeat your opponent, but to find truth.

It was a good choice, even though I didn't get all its implications at the time. It was clear that Jews love debate. It is so foundational to our identity that our texts are arguments. Each page of Talmud, for instance, the main text of rabbinic Judaism, is divided into blocks. Every page contains a central block of text, and all around it are opinions, disputes, elaborations attributed to different rabbis. None of them is the "right" answer. When years after my bar mitzvah I got interested in studying Talmud, I told Reb Jonathan I was loving it. He smiled at me. "Iz," he asked, "knowing you, how could you not love a practice in which disputation is a form of worship?" Then he told me Reb Rivvy said that. Jews have a big thing about giving credit. *Yikhes,* they call it, meaning something like pedigree. Whoever said that thing first, it turned out to be the key to my life. And the answer was that I did love it, despite whatever pushback I got.

Once I discovered Balak, I started talking with Shim and Eileen about my bar mitzvah. I was excited. But they didn't seem excited. They exchanged looks that meant a serious conversation was about to happen. We sat at the kitchen table with glasses of iced tea and a bunch of snacks; the little varnished Japanese rice crackers called arare and another kind that has a peanut in the middle, kosher pickles, a little bowl of chopped liver and some slices of tiny rye bread, humus and some pita wedges. I got the impression they were expecting a long talk. We munched a little, listening to the refrigerator hum. The sun was going down, and the only light was a cone-shaped one that hung over the white kitchen table. Our old cat, *Shachor-Lavan*—meaning black-white in Hebrew, which describes her perfectly—strolled into the room and settled herself on my feet. I called her Shak. I miss her.

Finally, Shim said, "According to Jewish law—the *Mishnah Torah*—if your mother is not Jewish, you are not Jewish. The original idea was that if the child entered this world through a Jewish mother's body, there could be no controversy about the birth. Before DNA tests, how could you prove who the father was? Nowadays, Reform Jews and some other liberal Jews accept patrilineal descent."

"Patri-what?" I didn't think I'd heard that word before.

"Where the father is Jewish, but not the mother," Shim said. "Patrilineal, the father's line."

"So do we?" I asked. "Recognize patrilineal descent?"

"Reb Jonathan says he will do whatever we want. The important thing is you want to be a bar mitzvah. Nobody's pushing you. But he knows Jewish law, *halacha*, and knowing Jonathan, I'm guessing he'd like it to be kosher, an official conversion before your bar mitzvah. That's a little bit complicated." Shim looked over at Eileen. She rolled her eyes, but smiled while she did it.

"Your dad explained it to me," my mother said. "If someone converts before bar mitzvah age—that is the age of consent—the conversion is considered provisional. The person who converted as a child can renounce it later if they want to."

I was really confused. "I've always been Jewish. And Okinawan. Everybody knows that. And now I'm starting to feel like people will think I was trying to fool them or something. But how can I be fooling them by being me? And why would I want to stop being me later on?"

"I don't think you will, son." Shim looked very serious. "So we have an idea. To be converted, you need a *mikveh* and a *Bet Din*. You know what those are, right?"

I did. A ritual bath and a panel of three Jews, usually three rabbis. We learned those words in Sunday School.

"So it's simple," said Shim. If you want this, you will be 13 already when the bar mitzvah happens. A day or two before, we go to the *mikveh*, the *Bet Din* members talk to you, they sign the certificate, and you are officially Jewish when you go up to the Torah on the big day. Two of the *Bet Din* rabbis can be Reb Jonathan and Reb Rivvy. They can easily line up the third person. There's only one hitch, and we hope it works for you. You were circumcised by a doctor, not a *mohel*. So to be truly official, you need the *brit dam*. A *mohel* takes a single drop of blood from the place where you were circumcised, and that would probably happen a week or so before."

My hands flew to my crotch.

"I know some people who've done it," my father said. "They were nervous, but it didn't hurt and it healed quickly."

     Arlene Goldbard

He told the truth. But man, was I anxious until the day of the *mohel*.

Reb Jonathan told me the big, fancy bar mitzvah thing is an American idea. He said that traditionally, all you had to do was make an *aliyah*: come up to the Torah for blessings and reading. The huge party, the gifts, the community projects and speeches and all the relatives flying in, that was extra. I told my parents that I wanted to just do the service, the *d'var*, the *aliyah*, and have some food afterwards at the *oneg* or at our house with some friends, and maybe we could use some of the money we saved to contribute to the Khegev Project, which I'd already chosen as my community project. I knew I didn't want the big deal thing like some of my friends had, a dress-up party with a band and all that. Shim and Eileen definitely wanted something that relatives and friends could join in, but it wasn't necessarily their style to rent some hotel ballroom. Finding the sweet spot between my bare-bones idea and their modest approach, well, that was my first *machloket l'shem shamayim*.

Looking back, I wonder if that was when I became a textual Jew. My friend David and I joke about it now. We are *chavruta*, more or less, which means we study Torah together every week. Just between the two of us we call it "textual healing." "When I get that feeling, I need textual healing."

Jonathan used to say there are *davenen*—praying—Jews, Torah study Jews, singing Jews, etc., etc., meaning everyone has their own way into the practice and tradition, their own approach that aligns with their character and needs. "When the student is ready," he used to say, "the teacher will arrive." But the teacher didn't necessarily have to be a person. At going on 12, I was determined to have the bar mitzvah I wanted. My idea was to sift through whatever texts I could to find evidence to support my case. Another kid might have found his calling as a lawyer in this moment. That could have been me: after all, Shim's a lawyer, the public-interest kind. But it wasn't the law that drew me. It was the argument.

My need for textual citations happened to arrive at a moment in time when the entire Jewish textual armory was easily available online, fully searchable in English and Hebrew. Back then, my Hebrew wasn't good enough for that, so I stuck with English. I'd heard that the prophet Isaiah was a scorcher. It was lucky I started there, because it didn't take much time to find my text in chapter 58. Isaiah voices *HaShem*'s anger at people who perform outward rituals without awareness of the deeper intentions:

Is such the fast I desire,
A day for people to starve their bodies?
Is it bowing the head like a bulrush
And lying in sackcloth and ashes?
Do you call that a fast,
A day whenYHVH is favorable?

No, this is the fast I desire:
To unlock fetters of wickedness,
And untie the cords of the yoke
To let the oppressed go free;
To break off every yoke.

It is to share your bread with the hungry,
And to take the wretched poor into your home;
When you see the naked, to clothe them,
And not to ignore your own kin.

It expanded on something I was going to chant at the bar mitzvah anyway, the *haftarah* for *Balak,* which is from *Micah,* and contains this passage:

Would YHVH be pleased with thousands of rams,
With myriads of streams of oil?
Shall I give my first-born for my transgression,
The fruit of my body for my sins?

"You have been told, O mortal, what is good,
And what YHVH requires of you:
Only to do justice
And to love goodness,
And to walk modestly with your God....

My parents are somewhat countercultural: longtime Californians of a certain generation and all that. But at that time, their hopes for me were pretty conventional. That meant we didn't start out on totally opposite sides, with them wanting a Hollywood-style bar mitzvah and me wanting to avoid all glitz. But there was still a gap to close.

I got home from Sunday school with printouts in hand and told them I wanted to talk. The kitchen table again, but this time no snacks, just a bunch of cabinets and appliances doing their thing. I read them the *Micah* part, and

     Arlene Goldbard

then the *Isaiah*. I said that one of the messages of my *parshah* was that all kinds of riches and power were nothing against the truth of what is holy, and I just didn't feel right making a spectacle out of something that was supposed to be holy. I wanted to celebrate, but modestly. That was a new word for me, straight out of *Micah*. I'm pretty sure I pronounced it moe-destly, but they got the point.

It turned out Shim was ready to negotiate. "Good point, son. So what would that look like?"

I didn't really have a plan. I hadn't thought past the argument. That was a good lesson in being prepared. I punted. "I can say what I don't want: a band, a fancy lunch, a million presents, a big performance with every relative I don't know up on the *bimah*."

"Okay," said Eileen. "Your dad and I want some relatives there, and they will be proud of you, so they will want to express that somehow. Maybe a group *aliyah* with a few extra words for you from a few people."

I nodded and tried to keep my sigh invisible.

"No problem about the band," my mom said, "and we do need to feed people. We can't control who gives you a present, but you can decide what to do with them. As long as you write thank-you notes, you can give all the money to the Khegev Project or wherever you want."

"What about renting the Rachamim Center?" Shim asked. It's a great space, they have room for the service and food after."

"But we're not doing a potluck," Eileen said in that putting her foot down tone of voice.

I knew what she was going to say next. My dad and I said it in unison: "I can't handle all-brown food." Jewish Renewal potlucks tended to lean heavily into brown rice, kasha, vegetarian stews and like that.

Machloket l'shem shamayim. Argument for the sake of heaven. Everybody happy. Even me.

Most of the kids I knew then, I'd gone to school with since kindergarten. I was hapa, but I wasn't the only one: Black and White, Black and Latino, Asian and Latino, and on and on. Fewer hapa kids in Sunday school, but there were some, and also a couple of kids who'd been adopted by parents who weren't the same color. I didn't really stick out anywhere.

But by the time I got to Berkeley High in the fall of 2014, I was one of thousands of students, majority kids of color, maybe 10 percent Asian. I can't say how many Jewish kids there were. They don't keep those demographics. But the overall numbers for the Bay Area say that about one-third of its Jewish population lives in the East Bay. That adds up to a larger percentage of Jews than nationally, about four percent, double the number for the U.S. as a whole. At Berkeley High, just like at any institution that isn't specifically Jewish, we Jews were definitely a minority. Quite a few were totally secular, so we didn't even necessarily have Jewishness in common or hang together in or out of school.

If you live in America and don't fit the WASP profile or most of the other big sorting categories, there's one question you are likely to be asked a lot: *What are you?* I hate that question. It just feels like the people who ask it want to fit you into some slot so they can stop getting to actually know you. My Okinawan half is pretty visible in the sense of othering me, but mostly we don't look like *naichi* Japanese from the mainland, pale and smooth. We *unchinanchu* can be darker, we have thicker beards and more hair in general, our features may be more pronounced, but most people have no idea about any of that. Being hapa makes me even harder to peg. So a lot of the "what are you?" questions are followed by guesses: Filipino, Thai, what have you. When I visited New Mexico, people started talking to me in Spanish or asking which pueblo I was from. The whole thing makes me wonder what kind of ethnicity maps people carry around in their heads. And you know what's funny? If someone just told me where their people are from and asked where mine come from, that would feel like an interesting and neutral conversation. But not one you can have with a single word: Japanese, Jewish.

So freshman year, from kids I hadn't met before, I got a lot of "what are you?" And a lot of not knowing what to say back when I answered "Half Okinawan, half Ashkenazi Jewish." I was both, and I wanted to stay both, and I wanted that to be okay with other Jews and Asians and everybody else. Fat chance.

Sometimes it actually was okay, though. Junior year, I started going out with Cynthia Chen, who I'd met in Sunday School. Her dad was Chinese, her mom Jewish, so she was bona fide. We kind of bonded around the weirdness of being unidentifiable Asian and Jewish, more than some great love. It was good having someone to go to parties with, even Jewish holidays. We understood what each of us was up against. We enjoyed laughing at the kids who laughed at us. Kissing was exciting. But kissing was Cynthia's limit, and I wasn't the type of guy to push it. In the end, making a united front wasn't enough to sustain our connection after we graduated. Last I heard, she was headed for med school.

I met my best friend—my *chavruta*, study partner—David Rojas the last year of high school, when his family moved from New Mexico. That's how I came to visit there the last summer after I graduated. They have this thing there called Conversos or crypto-Jews (nothing to do with Bitcoin). They are descendants of Spanish Jews who were forced to convert under pain of torture or death during the Inquisition, some exiled, some escaped. More and more in recent years, some descendants are looking into what that means and pursuing Jewish identity. David's grandmother was Catholic, like everyone around them, but she had these customs her neighbors found odd, like lighting candles on Friday night or separating meat and milk.

When his mom married a Jew a few years after his father died, things started to make sense. Then his grandmother passed, and the three of them moved to Berkeley, the idea being to prepare David for the kind of world he'd encounter in college. I met him the first day of senior year. We definitely bonded around being uncategorizable. He didn't know anything about Okinawan culture, and I didn't know anything about New Mexican. But both of us were really interested in learning, and that made it okay. When I told him about Reb Jonathan and everything, he was curious. Fast forward: *chavruta*!

Sometimes school wasn't okay, though. If I brought some inarizushi—fried tofu pouches stuffed with sushi rice, with a pickled plum in the middle—some of the Jewish kids would make stupid jokes, "Look, Iz has stuffed balls for lunch again today!" If I brought chopped liver on rye, it would be "Iz is eating that green liver again!" from Asian kids. When we studied World War II in history class, there were a few stupid jokes about which side I was on, which were actually beyond stupid because somehow they had the idea that I would have supported Japan. I guess they hadn't heard of the Shoah. Mostly little shit like that, but enough to feel I wasn't allowed to belong. A different kind of hapa, half-in and half-out.

When I think about it now, I see two sides. One is that feeling of permanent alienation, not completely belonging. I had this undergrad class where the professor asked "Who here feels like a real American?" and only two students out of 20 raised their hands, a blonde girl from Iowa and a white guy who appeared to be some kind of jock. Everybody else from another race or ethnicity or religion just sat there. That's when I realized that the we-are-all-Americans-together thing felt fraudulent because it was the "real Americans" who owned the right to invite the rest in. Or not. So yeah, I know what it is to be outside. But I wouldn't trade that for belonging. For me, outsiderness breeds empathy. I doubt David and I would have discovered each other if we'd each fit perfectly into some familiar identity. He was a deep thinker and a huge *Matrix* fan. He told me "Everyone I like is an alienated weirdo like us, man. That's just how it is unless you take the blue pill and wallow in default reality." I understood exactly what he meant. When I registered for Berkeley and declared my double major, Jewish Studies and East Asian Religion, Thought, and Culture (I usually just say Asian Studies because that is such a mouthful, even though a few people get mixed up because there's an M.A. program called Asian Studies), I got a lot of questions from professors and students that suggested I was giving off an alienated weirdo vibe. But I guess my answers were acceptable, because they let me in.

It wasn't until late in the two years of graduate work I did for my M.A. that I started thinking about becoming a rabbi. It was a strange time. When COVID hit in 2020, I was exactly halfway through my undergrad, and suddenly everything went virtual. That didn't start to change back until I began my grad studies. When Reb Jonathan died that first year of the pandemic, the whole community mourned bigtime, each in our own little square of the Zoom window. Jonathan's death seemed so unfair and stupid and made a hole in so many lives. We were all furious over the murder of George Floyd, halfway across the country from where that happened. Nobody was doing in-person Shabbos services. People tended to find different virtual services on YouTube or whatever, and we all became serial *daveners*, which was a Berkeley tradition anyway, though it used to mean driving from *shul* to *shul* rather than changing the channel.

Then in 2023, halfway into my grad work, October 7th came, the paragliders flying into a concert and slaughtering a bunch of kids and kibbutzniks, and people went different kinds of crazy.

The first sign was when some people I knew were trashed for posting to social media on October 8th about friends and family they'd lost in Israel. October 8th! Before Israel even talked about retaliation. Some Asian Studies students retweeted academics celebrating the thrilling revolutionary violence of Hamas' long-overdue vengeance for the Occupation. "Exhilarating" was the adjective of choice.

     Arlene Goldbard

On November 3rd, less than a month later, the Association for Asian American Studies put out a statement that could have been assembled from a glossary provided by what David calls the paraglider left: genocide, Zionist settler colonialism, praising terrorism, yada, yada. Folks in Jewish Studies knew about my double major. They asked me what I was going to do about the statement. I made a few jokes about changing into my Superman outfit or mobilizing the Jewish space lasers, but nobody laughed. Everybody—all kinds of groups that had nothing to do with the region or foreign policy and had never issued such a thing before—had to put out a statement or find themselves on a list of Zionist enemies to be blackballed. At least in Jewish Studies, there was a range of opinion, from Israel can do no wrong to I'm going to put on my keffiyah and join the encampment. But when two conflicting opinions met, it wasn't any easier in that program than elsewhere on campus.

Let me be clear. The better part of a year into that war now, and there must be something wrong with me because I still have room in my heart and mind for all of the terrible suffering, the parents and children of hostages, the parents and children killed and displaced in Gaza, the people of Israel who seem unable to dislodge their corrupt and brutal leaders, the people of Gaza facing the same powerlessness. I'll make it short: Hamas is evil, Netanyahu and his far-right racist buddies are evil, both are pursuing some idea of victory that makes massive death tolls easy to shrug off. Hamas, having spent decades of relief money on tunnels and arms, is happy to use its own people as human shields. Netanyahu is willing to mete out mass death and risk his own people to maintain his political power. It should have stopped a long time ago. The U.S. should have lined up on the side of peace and used everything in its power to stop it. Trump has proclaimed himself a presidential candidate and enough progressives are declaring their unwillingness to vote for Biden over Gaza that—added to the RFK bullshit and all that—he might actually win. What a nightmare.

This didn't start on October 7th. Many Renewal Jews have been advocates for peace and justice in Israel-Palestine for years. For decades. Just like they've advocated for every campaign for racial, economic, and environmental justice supported by the so-called progressives who now tell us we don't have the right to mourn. And maybe not the right to exist. In those circles, the price of admission for Jews, regardless of how long and hard they'd worked side by side in all kinds of movements, was to praise Hamas, step back, and swallow whatever was shoved down our throats. Obviously, I'm not one of those long-term activists who felt betrayed by so-called allies on October 8th. I've dabbled a bit here and there, showing up for Black Lives Matter, for Sunrise, for debt forgiveness and like that. But I'm 24, not 60. Shim and Eileen were gobsmacked, and so were a bunch of their friends. They felt duped, all those solidarity pledges down the toilet, suddenly realizing that "ally" actually meant flunky or even lackey.

Israel was never the center of my world. I didn't go on one of those birthright trips. To me, it was another faraway place with some long-term connections, like Okinawa. But if you want to hear them, I have all kinds of opinions about places I've never been where I have no actual skin in the game. The difference being that on this one, everyone's an expert, and in academia and environs, there's a pretty big consensus that of all the places on this planet where people are being murdered and starved, Israel is the worst perpetrator of all and the only nation that by collegiate consensus has no right to exist. That pisses me off. Does the U.S. have a right to exist? Who is authorized to say? Another difference being that on this one, friends and family members no longer speak to each other. The world isn't big enough to hold different perspectives anymore, at least when it comes to Israel and Palestine.

You can imagine the arguments I got into with classmates. You don't have to imagine, just listen to this one with Mike Takahashi, who I thought was a reasonable guy and a friend:

Me: "So you're saying we don't have a right to mourn the 1200 murdered and taken hostage?"

Mike: "It was a token compared to the harm Israel has done with the Occupation. How can you mourn when a small retaliation comes to the Zionist settler colonialist Occupation? You should rejoice!"

Me: "So if one of the many groups the U.S. has harmed paraglided into Coachella and killed 1200 concert-goers, some Asian, you'd celebrate in solidarity with the oppressed? Actually, wait, the numbers are off. Israel has nine million people, so 1200 there would be the equivalent of about 40,000 in the U.S. I'm thinking of how many people would know someone who was killed, raped, or captured. And you'd be out there telling folks not to mourn and expecting the U.S. government not to retaliate?"

Mike: "I'm done with whataboutism. It's not the same situation."

Me: "But similar. Or take another example. You're *naichi*, right? A hundred and fifty thousand Okinawans were killed in World War II by the mainland Japanese using them as shock troops, forcing them into suicide attacks, or

     Arlene Goldbard

failing to protect them. They gave out hand grenades and told people to use them if they were going to be captured by American troops. The *naichi* were cool with that, because they didn't see the Okinawans as really Japanese. Or human."

Mike: "I never heard that. But it's just more whataboutism."

Me: "Really? Is the U.S. a settler colonialist society? Thought I'd heard you say that more than once."

Mike: "Yes. Europeans came here and wiped out a massive number of Indigenous."

Me: "True. And Israelis displaced 700,000 Palestinians and Arabs. Nothing close to matching our 55 million Indigenous, but still a huge catastrophe. Do you know anything besides that about Israel's history and population? Did you know that 20% of Israeli citizens are Arab or Palestinian? Did you know the majority of the Jewish population is Sephardic and Mizrachi Jews whose people were expelled from Iraq, Morocco, other North African countries that seized their homes and exiled them with nothing? Did you know that unlike Europeans coming into North America for the first time, there's a strong archaeological record of Jews living on that land for many, many centuries? Did you know the Al-Aqsa mosque is built on top of the first and second Temples in Jerusalem? You can hate the Occupation and all the policies that support it. I do. You can oppose Israel's actions. I do. But you can't erase history. And unless you're advocating genocide, you can't erase a whole country's worth of Jews—seven million—any more than you can banish all the people like you and me who are living right here on stolen land."

Mike: "So what do you think should happen?"

Me: "Not that anyone gives a shit what I think, but from what I see, no one in Israel-Palestine is leaving. I support the peace groups with Jewish and Palestinian shared leadership working for shared land, human rights, a shared or two-state solution. But since we don't actually have a major peace movement, just two massive warmongers, I doubt what I think matters."

I'd like to say Mike had second thoughts based on my very persuasive argument, but not long after that I saw his picture. He was standing on the fringes of a campus encampment. He had on a T-shirt with a Hezbollah flag. I guess he confused supporting an Iran-funded, Holocaust-denying Shia nationalist party with liberating Palestine.

I stuck out the nine months till the school year ended. Went to class, tried to avoid pointless arguments, turned in my papers, did my research, even though the passion had leaked out of my topic, the Jews of Harbin, China, in the late 19th and earlier 20th centuries.

But mostly, I found myself searching Jewish texts for consolation, especially for reminders that we don't have to create a hierarchy of oppressions. We don't have to divide the world into victims who can do no wrong and oppressors who deserve no human rights. We can argue as long as it's *machloket l'shem shamayim*, a way of seeking truth. But there's not a lot of interest in that these days. It's about winning, demolishing your opponent, plain and simple. It's just a really, really bad moment for people with open hearts and minds. Most days, I've felt even more other, even less belonging, than in high school.

David found the best textual reference in the *Talmud, Megillah 10b*. After the waters closed over the Egyptians who pursued the fleeing Israelites they'd enslaved, it says this happened:

> The ministering angels wanted to sing their song, for the angels would sing songs to each other, as it states: "And they called out to each other and said" (Isaiah 6:3), but the Holy One, Blessed be He, said: The work of My hands, the Egyptians, are drowning at sea, and you wish to say songs? This indicates that God does not rejoice over the downfall of the wicked.

There's a ton of commentary on this, of course. People keep pointing out that it was okay for the Israelites to rejoice, as they had just escaped slavery and their pursuers wanted to kill them or return them to slavery. But not the angels, who must see the biggest picture, the holiness of all creation. I buy that, and not just for angels.

I found myself wishing even harder than usual that Reb Jonathan were still with us. It felt like a spiritual crisis as much as a political one, this energy that was driving everything else offscreen and everyone to choose up sides like some demented video game. All kinds of crappy and pointless lines kept popping into my mind: "Where were you when the U.S. presided over the killing of 300,000 Iraqis to avenge Bush the elder's reputation?" I did my best to suppress them, to avoid contributing to the mounting *mishegas*. I could control what I said out loud, but I couldn't get any of it out of my head.

By midsummer I was deep into helping Ken Simon with his book—a political book that had been inspired by biblical texts—and I'd started thinking about going to rabbinical school. The cons included whether I could really take

    Arlene Goldbard

more school after 18 years; that the Renewal rabbinic program was hard and strict because in the way of countercultures, the people who designed it felt they had to be more hard-nosed and diligent than everyone else to prove they weren't just a bunch of hippies; and that I didn't have a clear idea what I'd do afterwards. Be a congregational rabbi? Maybe in the way Jonathan did, small community, time for writing, room for creativity. But truth be told, Jonathan had married Judy and Judy had come from money, the kind of money that was willing to support a rabbi's work. With my dating luck I'd never wind up with someone like Judy, even though Shim keeps reminding me that my Grandma Laura used to say "It's just as easy to love a rich girl as a poor one." I didn't think for a second I could ever be a great soul like Jonathan. But maybe I could be guided by his example and help people like he did. Maybe I could help make some space for compassion and nuance and possibility.

I prayed on it. I turned it over with anyone who would listen to me. I went to see my parents. Every time I walked into the house, I expected to see Shak purring her way to me, but she went to the next cat world not long after I moved out. I was hoping for a *Whatever you want, son* from the parents, but instead, I got major pushback.

We didn't spend much time in the living room unless there was company, but here we were, sitting on couches and easy chairs, propped up by Grandma Laura's beautiful woven pillows, watching the sunset through the picture window. Everyone had a glass of something, beer for me, wine for Shim and Eileen.

"Before you got this idea," Eileen asked, "what did you think you'd do for a living?"

"Academia, I guess."

"Which area?" Shim asked.

"Well, wherever I'd go, all of me would be there. But I guess I thought Jewish Studies would be the most welcoming, as I'd be ticking a person of color box in addition to what I was bringing from my academic work, my work on Ken's book, the Khegev Project, all that."

"Not much call in Asian Studies for the Jewish angle, hm?" asked Shim.

"Maybe my Harbin research would be enough."

"So the idea would be to go for your PhD and then try to get a job?" Eileen looked a little puzzled. "Or try to be a T.A. or something next year and finish your terminal degree while that was happening?"

I started to feel exasperated. "I haven't thought it all the way through, Mom. I was going to write up the Harbin research, see if it could be a book maybe, then start putting out feelers. But then everything changed."

"Everything?" Shim waited for an explanation.

"Okay, not everything. But COVID was still going first year of grad studies, things have been staying a little rocky since 2020. Then Jonathan dying, and last year, October 7th and all the shit around that. I started thinking I should be able to secure a place in academia that could give me a certain amount of personal comfort and stability. Start paying off my student loans. But all I could think is that it wouldn't do a damn thing about what I see happening all around me, which is people demonizing each other, doing anything to triumph over each other, lying freely, slandering freely, celebrating the suffering of others.... I think you get my drift."

"This isn't the first time people have gone to extremes in this country," Shim said. "The McCarthy era, the witch hunts, the bombings and shootings in the sixties. But somehow reason reasserts itself and then no matter how appalled people are at what happened, they still have to pay the bills, put a roof over their families' heads, find a way to live through it all. What will you do as a rabbi? Serve some suburban congregation that can afford to pay decently? Become an administrator and fundraiser like Rivvy? I know Reb Jonathan is your hero, but what would he have done without help from Judy's family? At least in academia they still have tenure."

I couldn't refute any of it. But I also couldn't turn off the voice in my head, and it was getting louder.

David was home when I got back from my parents' place.

"Just about to open this," he said, holding up a bottle of beer. He looked like a beer commercial: clean-cut young Latino in a white T-shirt, a huge smile inviting you to partake.

"Sure." I took a beer and we trooped out to the living room, which was uncharacteristically tidy. Video games and controls stacked neatly on the shelf below the TV. The pillows were all squared up on the gray corduroy couch. Shoes lined up by the front door. Books in neat piles on the coffee table. I guessed David's girlfriend Teresa had been over earlier. He definitely didn't want her to think we were slobs.

"Eileen and Shim grilled me to a crisp, dude," I told him.

David was sympathetic. He listened to my whole story, nodding like mad. Then he threw my core question back at me. *What are you not seeing, Iz?*"

"Shit, man, probably a whole lot. I wish Jonathan were here," I said. "I keep trying to think what he would say. I actually think if he were alive he would support me in becoming a rabbi, like he supported me all along. But a lot has changed in a few years."

David thought for a minute. "Is there anyone who knew him real well you could talk to? Maybe someone has insight like that."

I didn't have to think about it. The answer popped right up. "Duh. Anya!" Anya Applebaum, the Shomer of Or Chadash. She was Reb Jonathan's right hand all those years, and she'd been the glue that held the community together since he'd been gone. I called her right away, told her my dilemma. I fantasized that she might say something like "Well, Jonathan would have said...." But that would have been pretty *chutzpahdik.* Instead, she surprised me by suggesting I go see Sharon Marks. Anya told me Sharon had helped her with some tight decisions. That sounded good.

I knew Sharon, of course. We'd hung out at her and Nomi's and Sarah's place a fair amount. I knew how much she'd helped Ken. I knew how Nomi felt about her. I'd never gone to her for help before, but clearly, it was time.

"*Izzie!*" Sharon was the only one who called me that. It made me feel like a little kid, but I didn't really mind.

We hugged. She gave me one of those post-hug looks where you hold the person by the shoulders at arm's length and stare searchingly at their face.

"Oy, Iz," Sharon said after a long minute. "Come sit. Tell me what's wrong."

I sat in one of those desk chairs that swivels, which was good, because moving around helped with my nerves. I felt like I was in a walk-in lawyer's office, something like that. I guess Sharon likes things plain.

It took ages to get the whole story out, but Sharon was patient. Every time I flagged, she offered encouragement.

"So your question is whether to pursue rabbinic studies?" she asked.

"That's the bottom line, but I can't settle either way. Every time I get excited by the idea, I think of Shim and Eileen bringing up all the practical objections, and they're right, those are real. And every time I start to imagine myself staying in academia, my heart shrinks."

"Let me ask you some questions," Sharon said. "Just so I understand the whole situation."

"Sure."

"So are your parents supporting you?"

"No," I said. "They helped me through undergrad, but less as I got jobs. I did a lot of stuff for Reb Rivvy, you know, computer stuff, PR, helping her with systems for registering people and accepting payment. Tech isn't really my favorite thing, but I'm good with numbers and systems and even at a nonprofit, it pays better than being a barista. David and I lucked out finding a two-bedroom place we could afford. I'm working with Ken Simon now, you know, on his book." Then I remembered. "For sure you know! I don't think Ken and his book and Ken and Lucy and therefore me and Ken would have happened without him asking you for help." Somehow I'd forgotten about that.

Sharon gave that modest little Yoda smile. "So it's really up to you," she said. "It's not your parents' decision, but you don't want to upset them."

"Yeah, yeah. But if it's between upsetting them and living for someone else, I have to go with upsetting."

"And this yearning to be a rabbi," Sharon asked, "why?"

"I have a bunch of reasons," I told her. "I love studying and I love connecting what I study to whatever we face right here, right now. I've definitely heard folks from more conservative, traditional Jewish spaces complain that not everything has to have a moral for our times, that we're twisting things to make them relevant. That kind of cracks me up because how could we twist a text more than, say, *gematria*? So Jewish numerology is perfectly acceptable to them, and to believe that the Source of Life talks to us through these texts is bullshit? But whatever anyone says, for me, the mega-question is always this: "How should we live now?" I think lots of people are interested in that question."

So that was reason number one.

Arlene Goldbard

"Also," I said, counting off a second finger, "things seem really fucked up right now. It's July before the 2024 election and Biden passed the baton to Harris after that disastrous debate, even though some are calling him insane for doing that. The Supreme Court just told Trump he could do whatever he wanted and be immune from prosecution. Israeli generals are calling for a ceasefire and Netanyahu seems to be stoking the fires of war with Hezbollah. Everyone I know is terrified. Rebbe Nachman told us that to be alive is to cross a narrow bridge, that the important thing is not to scare ourselves. I don't think he was saying that we can switch off fear like pressing a button. But it's one thing to fear a very real danger, and another to feed it and multiply it in our own minds until we can't think straight. Spiritual practice is one of the ways we can calm our reptile brains. No matter how bad things are, that helps. And me wanting to be a rabbi is all about that."

I paused for a moment. "I'll just name one more. I know you're familiar with Heschel, with radical amazement."

Sharon nodded.

"It's a mindfuck, right? We're on this rock spinning through space, scientists are measuring everything, we have tremendous understanding of *how* things work, but we don't have a single clue as to *why* anything exists. The way Rabbi Heschel tells it, letting our minds be blown by the fact that we *are*, that all beings *are*, that all things *are* is our true state of being. Take a look around, though. In general, the people we meet take everything for granted. There's a huge pressure to act like it's all no big deal, science has almost everything figured out, and wonder is just a cute phase for kids to go through. A lot of people need to hear the truth of radical amazement, really take it in and let it rattle around for a while. So that's reason three, to be one of the people who tells that story."

"Eloquent, Izzie." Sharon smiled, a little like I was a cute kid. "If it were up to me, I'd say you have good reasons. But I'm just a channel. Let me ask you another question. You've put so much into your academic work, and I think it was pretty important to you. Is it still important?"

"Good question, Sharon. It is, no doubt. But it's important inside a particular frame, opening academia up to more sources of knowledge and more ways of being than would usually be reflected in the canon. So higher ed is one box, it has social importance, but most people are never going to intersect with it, let alone climb in and look around."

Sharon raised a finger, signaling me to pause. "You know Jews are maybe two percent of the U.S. population, right? And fewer of them go to *shul* than college. So the vast majority of your fellow Americans are unlikely to climb into either box—the one marked grad school or the one marked Jewish community." Sharon waited for me to think this over.

"True," I said. "But Jonathan used to say that each people has a particular role to play here on Planet Earth. I'm not going to say 'a light unto the nations.' It's a great aspiration, but sadly, we're as messed up as the rest of the humans. How much light is being shed in Israel and Gaza right now? How much in Washington, DC? But for me the core thing we have to offer is *machloket l'shem shamayim...*"

"Argument for the sake of heaven?" Sharon asked.

"Yes, I believe enough of us are still capable of that and still committed to that and engaged in that. Maybe we'll be one of those pebbles that gets dropped in a lake and ripples out. Maybe our ultimate contribution will be that some of us kept asking questions and refused to settle for pat answers. That's not too shabby, is it?"

"Let's see what they have to say upstairs," Sharon said. "I'm going to chant a few things to cleanse the pathway, Psalm 91, and *Emet v'Yatziv*. You can join me if you want."

I did, but very quietly, under my breath. When Sharon fell silent, eyes closed, I sat and waited, feeling peaceful for the first time in ages.

"I got a very clear assignment for you, Izzie," Sharon said. "But I don't know if you will like it."

I took a breath and held it for a while before exhaling slowly. "Fire away."

"I'm sure you know this section of *Pirke Avot*," she told me. "The first time I read it, I was younger than you by a lot. Someone showed it to me as a kind of antidote to the optimism of sixties radicalism. It offers a reason for doing the work other than getting a big prize at the end."

Then she read me *Pirke Avot* 2:16:

> Rabbi Tarfon said: the day is short, and the work is plentiful, and the laborers are indolent, and the reward is great, and the master of the house is insistent.

     Arlene Goldbard

He [Rabbi Tarfon] used to say: It is not your duty to finish the work, but neither are you at liberty to neglect it....

"Here's how I read this as it pertains to you, Izzie. That becoming a rabbi is a great work you are being encouraged to take on. But you will work very hard and never feel finished. A friend of mine once told me that all essential things are always in the process of becoming: love, democracy, belonging, care. If we ever treat them like 'Yay! It's done!' they will be gone in a flash. I think that's part of what the text is saying."

Her words hit me pretty hard in a soft place just under my breastbone. I felt tears and laughter bubbling up together. I felt elated and disappointed. It felt right.

"So that's the text," said Sharon. "And the assignment is a doozy. It says you're supposed to have eighteen conversations that start with the same question: 'Let's say you're doing work you really believe in, working hard and steady, but without any huge victory to celebrate, just little advances and setbacks. Would it be worth it? Would sticking be your choice? Can you imagine looking back after many years and feeling satisfied?' After each conversation, make notes on how it felt, what rang true to you, what questions people asked in return. You can interview anyone you want. You need to be done by mid-August, which is a good deadline because that will give you a month to get your application together if you want to apply to start next spring."

"That is very detailed," I said.

"I know!" Sharon looked surprised. "I think that's the most detailed and elaborate assignment I've ever gotten." She took a breath. "Think about it, Izzie. Do you want to accept it? You are completely free to make up your mind, no pressure. The only hitch is that if you do accept it, you have to follow through and complete it. It's not like lightning will strike you if you don't—or at least no one has actually been injured that I know of. But it's suggested that some sort of bad luck may result. So think hard."

I tried to make myself think about it. But I was already making a mental list of who to interview. I was going to text David as soon as I left Sharon's office. He said he'd be home tonight. He could be first.

"Yes!" I smiled at Sharon, one of those ear-to-ear grins you can't wipe off. "Absolutely yes."

ANYA

My personal ah-ha moment came in the early eighties. I was at a big Jewish Renewal gathering. I'm not really sure what made me decide to attend, but a friend showed me the program and there were classes that appealed to me. I needed a vacation. Besides classes, there were many types of Shabbat services—chanting, movement, traditional, and more. The one I chose that first Saturday morning was held in the enormous tent used for the opening and closing ceremonies and evening events.

My mother had died a few months earlier. Freida and I were not close at the best of times. Long story. But the last part of her life had been far from the best of times. She hadn't spoken to me in over a year because I'd expressed concern for her well-being at the hands of her husband, who had been less and less patient with her lapses in memory each time I visited. I called and wrote and got no reply. Before long, I learned that Freida was gone.

Back then, I would not have seen myself as observant. Probably not now, either, to tell the truth. Let's just say I'm immersed. But in those days I worked for a nonprofit focused on domestic violence, and if I went to *shul*, it was probably Rosh Hashanah or Yom Kippur or someone's wedding. Still, I wanted to say *Kaddish* for Freida. Maybe I thought it would mend something, I don't know. Or saying the prayer would just be a way of structuring my grief and regret, which had as much to do with the mothering I'd never received as the mother I'd lost. Traditionally, for a period of 11 months, you say *Kaddish* three times a day for a parent. People who belong to Orthodox or Conservative *shuls* that have a *minyan* three times a day could just pop in to do it—unless they were women, because some of the Orthodox *shuls* still don't count women in the ten people it takes to make a *minyan* and say the prayer. Nowadays you can easily find a minyan online. But forty years ago, contrary to tradition—and to Jewish law for anyone more observant—I mostly said it all by myself.

By the time of the gathering I'd been saying the words by rote, not thinking much about Freida or anything else. Doing a duty. But as a hundred or so people rose from their folding chairs to say *Kaddish*, I felt an energy passing through my body, head to toes, making me shiver in the heat of the summer day. High above my head, where the spokes of the tent came together, I saw a small cherubic figure reclining on a cloud. This was the chubby baby that often appeared in the background of Renaissance paintings, head resting on one hand. Only this baby was Freida, gray curls and light-blue cat's-eye glasses, and a delicate string of pearls she always wore. She floated happily over the

     Arlene Goldbard

bimah, carried aloft on the prayer. I felt something soft settle inside me. She looked so happy. "I am released," whispered a voice I knew no one else could hear. I watched Freida float until she drifted out of sight as the service ended.

What happened to me that day wasn't usual or expected or otherwise recognized as part of Jewish spiritual practice. I seldom tell the story, because it sounds like something out of a movie. Nor do I believe that my dead mother literally morphed into a floating baby. But I saw something, and what I saw changed me. That day in the tent, I realized two things. First, that the ancients knew something about the human spirit and its healing, and it would be foolish to pretend otherwise. I needed to learn. And second, that beyond all that is known in this world is a mystery than can never be solved, and I wanted to honor it.

My life took a turn. From that day, everything I did was colored by those two truths.

I am Anya Applebaum (I went by Appletree for a while in the sixties, but reverted right after Reagan's first election). I am Shomer of Or Chadash, the Jewish Renewal *shul* founded by Reb Jonathan Fox of blessed memory. "Or Chadash" means "new light." "Shomer" means guardian, a countercultural word subbing for "president," which is what most people in comparable positions are called.

At 77, I do not feel young, but I am still fully able to get around, express, and care for myself. My memory isn't terrible. I do all kinds of exercises. The fear of decrepitude is a great motivator, inspiring me to maintain a full range of motion. Occasionally, I pass someone younger going upstairs. We'll see how long that lasts.

Why this *apologia pro vita sua*, you ask? Well, you probably didn't ask unless you've crossed paths with Cardinal Newman, but you get the gist. Because I've endured months of controversy about President Biden's fitness as a presidential candidate. I was on the "pass the torch" side that won that debate, but it was because of his behavior, not his number. Endless commentators and reporters described Biden's 81 and—less often, go figure—Trump's 77 as unimaginably old, a prima facie argument for disqualification, as if it were impossible to imagine that an 80 year-old could walk and chew gum—not even necessarily at the same time. I agree younger candidates would be preferable, and surely, after whoever's elected next, they'll continue coming right up. But I think using age as a cutoff point for sentience is bullshit. Who else is 80 or older? Mick Jagger, Jane Fonda, Harrison Ford, the Dalai Lama, Herbie Hancock, and my personal favorites, R. Crumb and Margaret Atwood.

So yes, I am old, but neither down nor out.

Since Jonathan passed in 2020, the community has been moving forward with visiting rabbis and teachers, plus a group of very experienced lay leaders. For a long time, people didn't think we could ever replace Reb Jonathan, but the fact that the pandemic kept us from meeting in person for a few years made that a less urgent question. We weren't going to spend the effort and money to find someone who would appear once or twice a week in a Zoom window.

But now it's 2024 and we're ready, which means a world of hope and almost certainly a world of problems. When a community like ours sets out to find a rabbi, things are a little more complicated and ad hoc than when the synagogue in question belongs to the Union for Reform Judaism or United Synagogue of Conservative Judaism, where their dues entitle them to assistance in selecting from a roster of rabbis: consultants, technical assistance materials, the whole ball of wax.

That isn't really an impediment, though, because, as with most things, we like to do things ourselves. Why? Let me count the ways. Our roots are countercultural. The folks who started our communities are mostly my age or older (or gone). If Reb Jonathan, who came into it when he was pretty young, were still with us, he'd be 67. It's not an old-age thing, though. These days some new communities are being started by younger folks. We've also got quite a few younger members now. While they aren't exactly in the mold of their forebears, they also tend to like making their own path through the tradition, borrowing and adapting and inventing rather than following. Back in the day, countercultural meant politically progressive, egalitarian, creative, experimental. Most of that still applies, but there's a whole lot layered on: gender fluidity, personal pronouns, polyamory, ancestral healing, priestesses....

I can imagine an element of satire being read between these lines, and I'll own up right now. It's kind of hilarious (to me, anyway) to sometimes find ourselves—we, who dared to carve a new Judaism out of the crooked timber of tradition, nay-sayers be damned!—on the other side of the generation gap. But I want to say something about us first, which is to let you know that what

     Arlene Goldbard

draws people to Or Chadash and other communities like ours is the depth and seriousness of spiritual practice, and that is no joke.

Some members grew up in the type of Orthodox households where they felt forced into studies and practices that seemed harsh, some even punishing. When the sixties dawned, many of those kids ran headlong into an amorphous hippie spirituality that mixed boundary-dissolving drugs with all sorts of meditation, fasting, chanting, and dancing and had few if any rules about sex or dress or food. At the other end of the spectrum, some grew up in assimilated suburbs where the children of immigrants blended into an all-American stew. That was my family. If we did go to services, it felt more like a social gathering than a spiritual practice. We knew we were different—we didn't have the Christmas tree almost everyone else on the block displayed in their front windows, we didn't go to church with our neighbors, there was an edge of otherness—but compared to our parents' parents, not all that different.

Whichever path people took to Renewal, what kept them coming back were experiences of awakening, like my cherubic vision of Freida at the Jewish Renewal gathering. The Jewish life they'd previously experienced prepared them to be bored or antagonistic, to spend their occasional time in a *shul* they disliked picking a fight with concepts that never sat right—Lord, King, the expressions of power they'd rejected in other realms. Now they were encouraged to find their own language, to discover for themselves the seed of possibility embedded in the Torah portion, to meditate their way through the *Amidah*—the standing prayer—and discover, waiting for them in the silence, something that filled a hollow place in their hearts.

When Reb Jonathan led services, sometimes he would be on the *bimah* reading from that week's *parshah*, dancing back and forth between Hebrew and English, and he would pause to invite everybody to turn to the person next to us and respond to a prompt, for instance how the story we'd just heard connects with our lives in the here and now. That was one of my favorite things, because while I listened to him *leyn*, the story was *out there*, engaging but separate from me. But as soon as I thought about Jonathan's question, it was as if a camera zoomed in for a closeup. The distance collapsed, and I was Rebecca at the well, facing a moment when my whole life depended on taking a huge chance, or Nahshon, stepping up to his nose into the Sea of Reeds before the water would part and allow the people to cross to safety. It wasn't the same for everyone, of course. The melody that wound itself around my heart might leave the next person cold. Many times I'd read the passage about the Jubilee year that changed Ken Simon's life and birthed his last book, but it hadn't sung to me as it did to him. So while it wasn't the same thing for everyone, there was something that drew each of us along the path.

Some people, especially fundamentalists, like to put out the sense that Jewish tradition is carved in stone (no pun intended). This is absurd on the face of it, considering that the foremothers and forefathers we read about in Torah were the antecedents and then the practitioners of Temple-based Judaism. Not my favorite, very complicated rules and lots of bloodshed. A priestly class presided over endless rituals of animal sacrifice and sacred offerings of grain and oil and other food to expiate sin, celebrate blessings, consecrate roles and relationships and objects. When the first Temple, Solomon's Temple, was destroyed by the Babylonians half a millenium before the common era, it was rebuilt, becoming the destination for countless pilgrimages, then destroyed by the Romans a couple of thousand years ago. Believe it or not, there are some *haredim* out there breeding a spotless red heifer in the hope of returning to sacrifice. How much chance is there that this happens? I'd say zero, but go figure. People want what they want.

Without the sacred space of the Temple and the practices it housed, Judaism had to completely retool. We call its next chapters rabbinic Judaism. The rabbis asked a question that still seems relevant today: how is it possible to live in alignment with the holy and to approach a state of ritual purity under current conditions? The Talmud and a vast amount of other rabbinic writings take up this question. We put out so many possibilities that we became the people of the book. What these writings offer isn't dogma—a set of settled and final answers—but more and more questions and disputes. In place of physical spaces, fire, and matter, we have words.

Now, I am not a Talmud scholar. Nothing like it. But I know this much about the history of Judaism, that it has been an evolving process of inquiry and practice. It is foolish to try to say anything simple about these developments. But fool that I am, I will just note that at key points this process has given birth to something new. To me, the biggies are the ecstatic mysticism of the kabbalists coming to light in medieval times, and the formation of Hasidism a few centuries later.

Many people think of Jewish Renewal as a kind of neo-Hasidism, influenced by the Baal Shem Tov's call to connect directly with the Divine, and his great-grandson Rebbe Nachman's further development of the idea of God as a friend

    Arlene Goldbard

we may speak with directly, going out into nature to open our hearts. To put it in a super-reductive way, you could see it as studying and following the rules versus seeking a heart connection to the truth in which they are rooted. You can do both, of course. They did.

Why this mini-tour of Jewish history? Only to say that when sixty years ago the first inklings of Renewal arose, the people who sparked it saw no harm in integrating today's music and movement, in reaching back to the 13th century to study and incorporate the radical meditation practices of Abraham Abulafia and others, in fully honoring women as teachers and leaders, contrary to tradition. They saw all this as needed to renew and revitalize Judaism, especially for the young people who were being attracted in droves to Yoga and Buddhism and other Eastern spiritual practices. Most of those practices had counterparts in Jewish history that had been forgotten or erased. Maybe they could be reborn. And they have been.

Have I succeeded in portraying us as boldly going along a new path that connects the personal with the political and spiritual? Okay, then, but now the reality-check. The thing is, everyone can be holy and still have bugs in their ears around ordinary differences of perspective or custom. For instance, every time I sit down for a chat with folks my age, the pronoun thing comes up. People have a trans kid or their kid's best friend is non-binary. They do their best to change the habit of a lifetime and start calling the person who used to be their little girl "they."

I have a take on it, needless to say. It's both an opening out, a reminder that gender isn't only a two-party system, and a power move, as youngers demand the right to control their elders and to take umbrage when said elders slip. Things change. What can I say? We'll get used to this. "*Gam zu l'tovah*," they say, "this too is for good."

Writing up our search criteria for a new rabbi involved a few generation gaps too.

We were in agreement about the progressive, egalitarian, creative, and experimental parts. Also about the person being welcoming and respectful to all, working well with the board, collaborating with members who were part of lay leadership, working with people to adapt *minhaggim*—customs—instead of unilaterally imposing new ones.

Other things were controversial.

The Rabbinic Search Committee had a heavy-duty negotiation about money. I had an idea it was coming and tried to prepare. I got a good night's sleep. I put a Patti Smith compilation on the minute I got up. Her big heart and persistence always inspired me, especially now that we were both grayheads. When I looked in the mirror before I left my place, I thought my short gray hair went nicely with the blue sweater I'd chosen. I wasn't as au natural as Patti, but I didn't go in for heavy makeup—my personal fear was looking like Colette or some other ancient personage who favored pancake makeup, many coats of mascara, and a blood-red mouth. I was tastefully understated, I told myself, as I put on my favorite earrings, long silver and lapis drops. It's amazing what a boost feeling put-together can be.

I made sure the food and water bowls were full and the cat door was unlocked for Mickey Katz, my Siamese. I scratched him behind the ears till he purred, then left for work.

Money was a countercultural challenge. I remember it always frustrated Reb Jonathan that people would say spirituality should be free, they didn't want money to be the price of admission. No one was ever turned away for lack of payment, but they didn't want to have to even think about it. He told me he was tempted to fling that back at them: "I feel the same way about (medicine, legal help, food…fill in the blank with the speaker's profession)." But he was a *mensch*; he never did that.

We had people who've been here for decades but never became members because "it would make me feel obligated." Some would make gifts on *yahrtzeits* or in tribute to something, but those weren't reliable in the same way as annual dues. The conscientious objectors to money were mostly in the sixties people cohort, my age group; the youngers mostly wanted to get paid and didn't see why everyone didn't deserve that. Setting a salary range, benefits, and so on took us two long meetings. It wasn't as if we had a brawl. It was just an endless rehashing of the same points. My challenge wasn't enduring loud voices or angry statements. It was keeping myself in my seat wearing a pleasant expression and thanking speakers instead of what I felt like doing, ordering everyone to stop behaving like children and get it done.

Everybody knew that the salary range for a more standard congregation could easily be twice what we offered. The hippie legacy was a factor, to be sure, but also that we never had more than 100 households in the membership and dues were low. We expected a rabbi to do what Reb Jonathan had done, supplement congregational income with writing or teaching or speaking or all

     Arlene Goldbard

of the above. You couldn't really call it a fulltime job in terms of required hours, but needs arose at all hours: someone was ill, passed away, needed to plan a wedding or face a divorce. From a rabbi's perspective, being a congregational rabbi was a neverending job. But the board tended to add up the required hours into a part-time position: so many services, so much prep for each, etc. At the second Search Committee discussion, which we all agreed had to produce a final decision, I started with the figure we'd been paying Reb Jonathan—$75,000. The predictable response unfolded.

"It's been nearly four years since Reb Jonathan, *alav ha-shalom*, passed on," I said to the committee members assembled around a long worktable. "We all know that since COVID, everything has gotten more expensive, so the $75,000 we were paying him has less purchasing power now. We all listened to each other's points at the last meeting, and now we need to make a move. Should we up the offer when we let candidates know the salary range. What do you think?"

I reached for one of the tangerines in a bowl on the table, right next to a bowl of nuts and raisins. We were on a healthy snacks kick, not wanting our many Search Committee meetings to add ten pounds to each member. Healthy snacks were messier, I realized. The table was already littered with tangerine peels. I'd get them later.

Eve Rappaport was first out of the gate. A large, formidable woman who had been one of the founders of Or Chadash, she felt a strong ownership of the community. She could rub people the wrong way. It was hard to honor the entirety of her effort and investment at the same time as you were wishing she didn't feel the need to speak every single thing she thought, usually in commanding tones. "Hah!" Eve laughed, shaking the scarves and shawls draping her shoulders. "I've never made $75,000 a year in my whole life!" Eve had been a social worker but was now retired. It seemed self-evident to her that her earning power ought to be a benchmark for the new rabbi's compensation.

Alon Friedman—our newest board member, mid-twenties, uses they pronouns, has a day job in a tech startup, has the appearance of a very tidy and well-dressed schoolboy—said, "Starting salaries in tech are around $100K and that's for someone just beginning a career. If we're looking for a rabbi with experience and maybe a family or something like that, don't we need to pay them enough to live around here?"

I could see Jacob Adler's lips moving. I figured he was planning what to say next. I expected a history lesson, and that's what we got. "Let me fill in some of the blanks," he said, adjusting his rainbow *kippah* and stroking his long gray beard. "Renewal rabbis aren't really going to be in it for the money like in Silicon Valley. They know a lot of us live pretty close to the bone. They'll be attracted to the spiritual level they'll find here. We know this from experience."

"What experience?" Alon asked. "I thought Reb Jonathan was here at the start of Or Chadash. Haven't you only had one rabbi?"

"Yes," said Jacob, "technically. But we've been deeply involved in the Renewal world for years, so we have a good idea of how other small communities make it work."

Ya'el Berg spoke up. She was kind of an in-betweener, forties, a gig worker, but her gigs tended to come from the Jewish community: editorial work, PR, event planning. She volunteered quite a bit of time for our community. She had a no-nonsense look that tended to inspire confidence: even features, thick brown hair pinned up with a clip, black-framed glasses, buttoned-up cardigan. "Conditions have changed. We do a ton of stuff online since COVID. Cheaper and easier to produce. A lot of it wouldn't demand a rabbi's time. But it's also true that the money Reb Jonathan got is worth less now. If you list a salary range, everyone wants to be at the top of it. But if we switch to just asking people what their needs are, you don't know what they'll say. What if someone needs $125K?"

Rachel Gold was the administrator, keeping memberships updated, paying the bills, editing the newsletter, working with vendors. A halftime job, as the entire congregational budget was less than $300,000. (I'm one of those nut cases who considers my Social Security a government supplement for volunteer work. Dedication or compulsion? You decide.) Rachel looked as efficient as she was, and truth be told, a little uptight: hair pulled back from a pale face into a high, straight ponytail, given to full skirts and neat little collared sweaters that evoked the fifties. "Do you want to hire someone who has to raise the money to pay his or her own salary?" she asked. "Because I don't see us raising that much ourselves."

There was a spacey moment as people gazed toward the ceiling, thinking about Rachel's question. No doubt everyone harbored the fantasy of a rabbi with easy access to major donors, solving two problems with one hire. No doubt everyone knew it was a fantasy. We finally hit on this language: "Compensation $75K for 30 hours a week. If you are interested, but your needs exceed that, please send us a note of explanation." I thought that might be a turnoff for

     Arlene Goldbard

someone who didn't believe in "to each according to his (her, their) need."
We'd see.

Other things were less explicit but still hard to work out. Or Chadash as
a whole was pretty loose about *halacha*, Jewish law. We did same-sex weddings
out of the gate. Also weddings between Jews and non-Jews. There were a few
parents who hadn't wanted their boys circumcised, and we decided to look the
other way. But some longtime members were much more stringent in their own
observance, and searching for a rabbi would offer them a chance to find an ally.
So while most of the board members were fine with our policy of *eco-kashrut*
for potlucks, choosing wholesome and sustainably produced vegetarian food,
an influential few were stricter and wanted to pick a rabbi who wanted every
food to be hechshered, stamped with a rabbinic certification. This was a major
controversy, because many hechshered foods were ultra-processed, while most
Or Chadash folks were not so inclined.

The *kashrut* question showed up when we invited a rabbinic candidate
to lunch. It was at Eve's small, light-filled house crammed with the bits and
pieces she collected: salt and pepper shakers, tiny ceramic animals, a shelf of
souvenir teaspoons she'd developed a passion for on a trip to England. She was
a vegetarian, which usually finessed the question of keeping kosher, as no meat
was prepared in her kitchen. But when she brought out dessert, she happened
to mention that she'd just found the pretty blue ceramic pie plate that held it in
a nearby thrift shop.

"So you don't know who used this pie plate before you owned it?" asked the
candidate. He was young, earnest, and we now understood, *glatt* kosher. He
took off his wire-rimmed glasses and polished them on a corner of his napkin,
waiting for an answer.

"That's true," Eve said. "But it's a pie plate, so it held pie."

"There are meat pies," said the candidate, "and ceramics can't be kashered."

During the ensuing silence, I wondered where he stood on issues such
as interfaith marriage or circumcision. And whether Eve was going to say
anything about the provenance of the lunch dishes that had just been cleared. I
was pretty sure that thrift shops were her go-to for almost everything: recycling
and saving money.

Eve sprung up from the table, saying "I'll get some fruit from the kitchen."

She brought a few apples and oranges in a glass bowl and a stack of glass saucers to eat them on.

Jacob looked thrilled. He would love to have a rabbi who wanted to engage with him on minute questions of *halacha*. They could pull out volumes of Talmud and talk into the night. "If it was a glass pie plate, rabbi, purchased secondhand, what would you say?" He stroked his beard and waited.

"It depends," said the candidate. "Sephardim say glass doesn't absorb, so it doesn't need to be kashered. Some Ashkenazim say that delicate materials such as glass theoretically can be kashered, but since immersion in boiling water is likely to break them, they shouldn't be. What is your community's *minhag*?

"Good pie," said Alon. "So sorry you don't get to taste it."

We took a vote after the interview, just to be punctilious. Only Jacob voted to advance the candidate to the next step, which would be an invitation to lead a service. He could be a fine rabbi for an Orthodox congregation, but not for us. No one disputed the right of Jacob and others to keep strictly kosher; neither did anyone want to drive out members whose personal observance was looser. I always thought our motto on such questions was live and let live. Now I exhaled with relief and silently thanked God that I wasn't the only one who wanted to avoid a hair-splitting contest that would likely rupture the congregation.

The search process was lengthy: review written applications and select promising candidates; do a Zoom call with the Search Committee, a subset of the board; contact references; hold either an in-person meeting or a larger Zoom call with the full board; then a tryout with the community including services, meeting with lay leaders, the parents' group, and our administrator, Rachel. At each point, people were invited to submit comments, and these were shared with the Committee. If all the steps felt right, the board would move to negotiation, and if that worked, hiring. We used the process a lot in those few months, getting all the way to a tryout three times.

To me, the process told a larger story: the values of Berkeley progressives like most of Or Chadash's members versus the top-down culture of the right. Rightists knew where power lay, and people lined up behind the boss, putting a premium on doing what the top guy wanted. Our side was all process, making room for each person to be heard as much as desired, which typically took forever and seldom entirely satisfied everyone. Multiply Renewal *shul* politics by millions and you get the American left. On the other hand I don't think I've

     Arlene Goldbard

ever obediently lined up behind a leader in my life, though I willingly voted for some. So who am I to talk?

The High Holy Days in the fall are the start of the Jewish year for congregations: The biggest services, the most engagement, dues, and contributions, setting out on the right foot. So there was a lot of pressure to hire by August at the very, very latest, leaving some time to prepare.

I can't know exactly what it was like for candidates to visit the community for tryouts, but I'm pretty sure it was a mixed blessing. Beyond the usual pressures an applicant faces, everyone still missed Reb Jonathan. He felt irreplaceable. If things went well, at some point in the general schmooze—at the *oneg* after Shabbat services, for instance—one member after another would engage the candidate in a conversation that quickly wound its way from joy to oy.

Congregation member, grasping candidate by the arm and locking eyes: "That was lovely. I especially enjoyed the way you called us up for the group *aliyot*. The way you asked us to align our attentions with a specific part of the *parshah* reminded me a little of Reb Jonathan. Did you know him?"

Candidate: "Yes, I had the pleasure of learning with him a few times. He was a great soul and a great teacher."

Member, wiping a tear: "We were lucky to have him."

Candidate: "You were. I bless you that the right match comes to your community soon."

At which point I'd swoop in and take the candidate by the elbow, saying "Come, let me make you a plate. You must be starving."

On one particular Shabbos, I found myself praying that the candidate wasn't feeling as if she were on a first date with a widower.

Debora Weiss was vivid: early thirties, long dark hair and large eyes, bright cheeks and lips, a strong singing voice, a trim figure and a bouncy energy that kept her in motion. Her application looked good. She wanted to move to the west coast to be closer to her parents who'd retired to a senior community about an hour away. The board and Search Committee members had enjoyed their time with her. Her references had been positive, and we'd called a couple of extra people, such as the head of the rabbinic program where she'd received ordination. If she were hired, this would be her first congregational rabbi post. She'd done graduate work before starting rabbinic school, then taken a job at a

Jewish organization devoted to adult education, where she planned events and led classes and workshops.

After her services, members kept pulling me aside to say they liked her enthusiasm. She met with some parents and kids after the *oneg*, and it was easy to see she connected with the little ones. I felt myself getting excited. As it turned out, so did the rest of the Search Committee members and the board. The contract negotiation was easy—Rabbi Debora wanted an extra week of vacation, and we happily agreed. She said she wanted to spend time with her parents, so 30 hours a week for the salary made sense. We were thrilled. She arrived around the first of August and with the help of community members found a little place to live right away.

As Shomer, my job was to make things as easy as possible for Debora. We had weekly meetings, with Rachel joining us every other time. We talked about how everything worked. At first, it was mostly acquainting her with who and what she needed to know, and preparing for the High Holy Days. The weekend before Rosh Hashanah would feature *Kabbalat HaRav*, a ritual some Renewal communities did to welcome a new rabbi.

Less than a month out from Rosh Hashanah, one of the lay leaders came to see me. Joni Bindler had been part of the community longer than I had. She'd been brought up Orthodox back east, and her *davenen* skills and knowledge were strong, an asset to the community. She had a personal aim, to bring all she knew and loved of the tradition to people who hadn't necessarily experienced it for themselves. She wasn't hidebound, not in the least. She was lovely, and seemingly without vanity. I think she cut her hair with a bowl. Everything about her was modest and sweet. So to see her upset was jarring.

"Anya," she said, "there's something I want to talk to you about. In confidence. I don't want to do *lashon hara* but I'm worried about something. Can we talk?"

"Of course. This is between you and me." Half the people I know tell you the secret first, then ask you to keep it confidential. One thing I liked about Joni was her ethics. I got us a cup of tea, and when I brought it out, Joni was stroking Mickey Katz, who was curled up on her lap.

She exhaled and cast her eyes down. "It's about Rabbi Debora."

"Okay." Once your spirit starts to droop, it's difficult to stop it, but I tried to just be there and listen.

     Arlene Goldbard

"We're planning High Holy Day services—you know that."

I nodded.

"Rosh Hashanah plans went well. We showed her everything from last year as a starting-point. She had some great suggestions, and she was open to ours. I think it will be good."

I nodded again.

"But when we got to Yom Kippur, we hit some snags. She wanted to cut parts of the service that everyone else wants to keep—*Al Chet*, for instance. We don't usually do it the full ten times, maybe once the first night, and then three or four times on Yom Kippur day. I love that it's a collective confession of sins, we all take responsibility for the community. Rabbi Debora said that it oppresses and depresses people to ask them to confess to sins they haven't actually committed. And the custom of beating our chests with each sin—no one really pounds, we just touch—she said that could easily bring up the trauma of being abused. We told her why we value the prayer, but she was pretty adamant. In the end, she said we'd do *Al Chet* once and Jacob would lead, not her." Joni folded her hands in her lap. "She gave the impression that was the last word she wanted to hear."

"How do the others feel?" I asked. Reb Jonathan had his share of heated negotiations with the lay leaders, though things settled into a groove over time. You have four people up on the *bimah*, one of them being the rabbi, first among equals, the other three jockeying for airtime; it could get tense.

"Miri is worried that it's going to be Yom Kippur lite. She told me she was waiting for Debora to suggest snacks during the afternoon break. It was a joke, but I guess that's the feeling, that she doesn't want anyone to be uncomfortable, she wants it all to be up and bright, but what about *t'shuvah*?" Joni paused. "I was asked to come see you on behalf of the three of us."

"Thank you, Joni," I said. "I know it wasn't easy to come to me with this. Please tell everyone I hear your concerns and understand them. I also understand that when a new rabbi comes, there can be tension around change. I don't want you to feel things are taking a wrong turn. And I don't want Debora to feel there's no room for her to lead. Give me some time to think about it, okay?"

Rosh Hashanah went well. The space looked beautiful. The Unitarians were always welcoming, they put out wonderful flowers and let us hang our banners wherever we wanted. Joy had been in short supply since Reb Jonathan passed, and people were ready to embrace it. When they greeted each other in the traditional manner, *"L'shana tovah u'metukah,"* "for a good and sweet year," the sweetness seemed palpable. When we shared apples and honey during the break, the mood was happy and relaxed.

I didn't exactly forget about Joni's concerns, but neither did I bring them up. When I inventory all the ways I missed the mark this past year, that will go at the top of my list, because Joni was right and I was a coward.

Yom Kippur lite wasn't a huge exaggeration. *Unetaneh Tokef* was missing; instead, Rabbi Debora sang the Leonard Cohen version, "Who by Fire?" which is a powerful song but far more oblique than the prayer, lacking the solemn weight of judgment of the first paragraph:

> "And the great shofar will be sounded and a still, thin voice will be heard. Angels will be frenzied, a trembling and terror will seize them—and they will say, 'Behold, it is the Day of Judgment, to muster the heavenly host for judgment!'—for even they are not guiltless in Your eyes in judgment."

There was only one *Al Chet* that Yom Kippur, as Joni warned. Debora prefaced it with the same message Joni had conveyed about not needing to feel responsible for sins you have not committed. The whole day had a sort of pop-psych feeling, with the message being not to be hard on ourselves. It's not that this was entirely new. Every Yom Kippur service I've attended starts with a warning that the purpose of fasting is not to afflict yourself, but to rise above the body, that people should listen to their bodies and not punish them. But that's the body. This was the spirit.

The really bad moment came when people reconvened for *Mincha,* the afternoon service. Or Chadash has a tradition called "Torah Truth." Anyone who wishes can take a turn sitting in a chair off to the side on the *bimah* and hold a Torah for a few minutes, whether or not they want to speak.

Chana Fuentes, a longtime member, often took advantage of this opportunity. She cradled the Torah and brushed the thick coils of her gray hair away from her face before she spoke. "I came here to cry," she said. "I believe it is our sacred duty to come together on Yom Kippur and acknowledge the ways we and our society have missed the mark, leaving so many to suffer. The rest of the year, people tend to sweep it under the rug. During the High Holy Days, we take responsibility. Every year, I open myself to *Kol Nidre, Unetanneh Tokef, Avinu Malkeinu, Al Chet,* and more. And every year, my tears join thousands who live into this tradition and weep to heal the world. This year, I did not cry, because we did not fully embrace the prayers that have always unlocked my tears. I ask that they be returned to our services next year."

That was an incentive for half a dozen others to take their turns at Torah Truth, speaking their own similar feelings and wishes. While Chana talked, Rabbi Debora composed her face into a stiff half-smile. By the time Torah Truth finished, she looked beyond distressed. I wasn't sure if what I saw on her face was hurt, anger, agitation, depression, or a mix of all. She spoke briefly to Joni, then left the *bimah* before that segment of services ended. Joni came forward to lead *Yizkor*, and services continued through the closing *Ne'ilah* service without Debora. *Ne'ilah* was a time for everyone to dance and sing until three stars appeared in the sky. It overflowed with the high that fasting produced: energetic, intense, ecstatic, a powerful release.

There was a buzz of questions as we continued outside for *havdalah*, marking the end of the holiday, but Joni said Debora had a bad headache, and that seemed to suffice.

I looked for Debora at the break-fast, but I didn't see her. The room was packed with people talking and eating, helping themselves from a buffet of bagels and lox, cold salmon, salads, cakes and cookies. Usually I headed straight to the dessert table. But now I was worried and somehow not hungry. I asked Rachel to check in with Debora and let me know. She came back and told me Debora had answered the phone, saying she was already sleeping and would talk tomorrow.

I decided to let it lie until our next regular meeting, two days later. Debora showed up looking not quite her vivacious self. I told myself that High Holy Days are tiring for leaders.

"I'd like to understand what happpened on Yom Kippur," I said. "I didn't see you again after Torah Truth. I understand you were to lead *Yizkor* and *Ne'ilah*, but the rest of the team stepped in at the last minute. After the meeting, Rachel told me she checked in on you that evening and you were okay, but you had me worried."

"I'm so sorry," Debora said. "I'm sure you can understand that this has been challenging for me, new rabbi, High Holy Days. When Torah Truth started," she made air quotes as she said the name, "and was it Chava?"

"Chana," I said.

"Chana criticized the service, I admit, and what with the hunger, the thirst, the fatigue, I got triggered. I needed to take myself for a break. I told Joni I had a headache and she said she'd hold things down. I wandered into one of the classrooms that had a couch, thinking I'd lay down for a few minutes. I'm embarassed to say I fell asleep. When I woke up, I realized it must have been hours later. I could hear that the break-fast was happening, lots of voices laughing and talking. I didn't want to reappear while everyone was eating. I ducked out. I slept for twelve hours."

"What do you think about what Chana and the others said?" I asked.

"I thought they were missing the way things used to be."

"I'm sure that's part of it, but the specific point was that they hadn't felt the depth the services usually brought. Leonard Cohen instead of *Unetanneh Tokef*, only one *Al Chet*...." I trailed off, waiting for her answer.

"The *Mishnah* describes Yom Kippur as one of the happiest days of the year," Debora said. "The Talmud says that is because it is a day of forgiveness. I wanted to bring that out."

"But before forgiveness comes facing the past, acknowledging wrongdoing, making *t'shuvah*, no?"

Debora sat up a little straighter. "I understood that as rabbi I would have room to bring my own skills and outlook to services. I didn't think that was a board responsibility."

"You're right. But the understanding is that you will work with the lay leadership team, and that anyone in the community is free to speak their truth. The rabbi isn't a monarch here, but a *shaliach tzibbur*, messenger of the community. We're all in it together. I'm asking you to stay connected to that, not exit if something happens that you don't like."

"And I'm asking you to see it from my viewpoint. I was on the *bimah*, working hard, feeling a little weak, and surprised to learn than anyone who wanted could come up and attack me." Debora's face had hardened.

"Chana said what felt missing to her, what she would like next year. How is that an attack?"

"I hear you, Anya. Can you give me some grace for not knowing everything about how this community works?

That seemed like a reasonable request. "Of course," I said. Then we went over plans for Sukkot and Simchat Torah—not liturgy, just dates, times, what to expect. The conversation didn't leave me satisfied, but Debora's apology

     Arlene Goldbard

seemed sincere. I understood she was in a stressful situation as a newcomer. I told myself I had to give it time.

Or Chadash doesn't have a fulltime *hazzan*. Lay leaders sing and lead chanting most of the time, but for the High Holy Days, a member who is not officially a cantor (a more conventional *shul* would call him a cantatorial soloist or something like that) fills that role and receives modest compensation. Avi Silverman has a soulful voice, knows the liturgy, and people find him easy to work with. Avi's day job is for an organic winery, so he also gets us discounts, a nice twofer. I knew he was going through a lot, including a divorce, and I appreciated and respected that he had shown up as usual for all the work that went into High Holy Days services.

But I was surprised to see Avi standing next to Rabbi Debora, a protective hand on her back, as I opened the door for my weekly meeting with Debora. Rachel was already here, sipping tea.

"Avi!" I said. "I didn't expect to see you this morning. Come on in, both of you."

"Good morning," the pair said in unison. They took seats side-by-side on the couch, a little closer than I would have anticipated. Debora wore a cobalt blue sleeveless dress. She looked brighter than the last time I saw her, her dark curls pulled back with a woven band. I hoped that was a good sign.

"Debora, I wasn't expecting anyone but you this morning. Is there anything relating to Avi's role you wanted to discuss?" I asked.

"No," she said, giving Avi a quick smile. "But Avi was kind enough to offer to accompany me after I talked to him about Yom Kippur."

Avi is a solid, substantial-looking person. He almost always wears a white shirt and a dark vest. Graying curls frame his round face and blue eyes. But that day, his mouth was uncharacteristically set in a tight smile. He nodded and cleared his throat. "I'm just concerned, Anya, that Reb Jonathan is a hard act to follow, and I'd like to see Debora get a fair chance here." When he said Debora's name, he touched her hand, just fleetingly.

"And you think she's not?" I asked.

Avi and Debora looked at each other. Debora spoke first. "I'm worried that my feeling tired toward the end of Yom Kippur was taken as a failing."

"I understand your being tired," I told her. "Believe me. I was tired and I wasn't on the *bimah* all day. But you said you were attacked, and that did concern me."

"Chana," said Avi, raising his eyebrows. "She can come on a little strong."

"Maybe," I said. "But she didn't say anything about Debora. She just said she missed some of the things that helped her *t'shuvah* in past years. If you feel responsible for omitting those parts of the service," I turned to Debora, "I can understand how that might have felt directed at you. But Chana had no way of knowing that. For all she knew, the lay leaders may have seen this year as their chance to make changes."

Avi and Debora exchanged a look that to me read as "See, she doesn't get it." I told myself I can't read minds. I should have given myself some credit for reading faces, though. I kept thinking about it after the meeting. I liked Avi. I'd always found him trustworthy. But if he'd been falling into the gap between divorce and the future, and a beautiful woman came asking him to be her protector, would he question her motives? Rachel told me a buzz was building around them, people seeing them out and about together, arms around each other. The community is pretty open to all types of relationships, so I doubted there'd be scandal, but that kind of attention to a new rabbi, not ideal. Would Avi show up for my next meeting with Debora? Would I somehow find myself on the other side of a united front?

I was worried. I was torn. I didn't know who to talk to. I didn't want to raise questions that would upset congregation members. But that started to become moot when people began coming to talk to me. I'll mention a few.

First was Sarah Fox. Everyone knew and loved Reb Jonathan's daughter. She'd been through some very dark places, her mother dying and then her father, the family of her partner Yasmin trying to separate them when the Israel-Gaza war broke out. Nomi and Sharon had become her aunties when Jonathan left them in charge as guardians. Under their loving care, she'd been healing and growing. This year she was teaching the children, a role her mother had filled for many years. She was loving it. They sang, learned a little Hebrew, talked about history and holidays, made drawings to give their parents, told stories.

The next holiday coming up was Hanukkah, and Sarah had the bright idea of making paper dreidls, spinning tops that were used in a holiday game. The body of the dreidl was a cube with a small handle on top, tapering to a point at the bottom that allowed them to be spun. They were easy to make out of

     Arlene Goldbard

cardboard and popsicle sticks. The four letters inscribed on their sides had two meanings. First, *nun* stands for *nisht*, meaning "nothing," *gimel* for *gantz*, "all," *hei* for *halb*, "half," and *shin* for *shtel arayn*, "put in." Kids usually played with candy or nuts and raisins. Where the dreidl stopped and fell told them whether to take half of the pot, put one in, take all, or do nothing. The letters also stand for *nes gadól hayáh sham*, "a great miracle happened there," alluding to the Hanukkah story in which a small amount of oil left after the Romans sacked the Temple miraculously kept the eternal flame alight for eight days.

When Sarah came to see me, she was distraught. She and the children were happily making their dreidls and talking about the Hanukkah story when Rabbi Debora came into the room. Debora said "Hi, kids!" and they greeted her in return: "Hi, Rabbi Debora!" Then Debora began talking very fast about the holiday. She had no way of knowing she was repeating information that Sarah had shared earlier, but the kids looked confused and frustrated about having their project interrupted. Some started to call out, "Sarah told us!" This evidently pushed Debora into high gear, as she began talking louder and faster. Sarah tapped her on the shoulder. "Thank you for visiting us, Rabbi Debora," she said quietly. "Now that the children have heard the Hanukkah story, they're making their dreidls. Nice, hm?"

Sarah said that Debora turned on her, looking furious and saying something Sarah found terribly hurtful: "Just because everybody around here thinks your father was a saint doesn't give you the right to tell me what to do!" Sarah was shocked. It must have shown, because Debora suddenly went quiet and left the room. Sarah told me she went home after class and told Nomi and Sharon all about it, and they advised her to come to me.

"Oy, I'm sorry, Sarah." I said. "This is very upsetting, and I'm glad you told me."

"Really?" she asked. "I wasn't sure if I should. She seemed nice before. I couldn't think what set her off. Maybe something terrible happened."

"Maybe," I said. "I need to investigate further, but I want to assure you that this is not okay. Can you give me some time to figure it out and get clear about what to do?"

"Yes, sure. But whatever happens, can you explain to Rabbi Debora that she has to talk to me if she wants to come into class? It's the same for every class. People can't just barge in and disrupt things."

"I absolutely understand and I will," I told her.

The very next day Ken Simon came to see me. He'd been more and more involved in the congregation since he had the experience that inspired his new book. He'd done a book event for the community that Sunday night, on Zoom and in person. Rabbi Debora had introduced him by reading the "about the author" copy on the book jacket. Then Ken talked a bit about how the book came to be, read a few excerpts, and invited questions. The book was inspired by the two special years—the sabbatical year and the Jubilee—the Torah set aside to rest the land, forgive debts, restore things to their rightful owners. That led Ken to other commandments about fairness, justice, and caring that had been ignored by modern society. His focus was what we, facing climate crisis and debt crisis, could learn from ancient wisdom.

He'd planned to field questions himself, but Debora strode to the front of the room as soon as he stopped reading. What she said annoyed him: "Well, that was controversial, wasn't it? What do you think our ancestors would have made of being enlisted as social justice warriors?" She smiled brightly and waited for a reply.

Jacob raised his hand. "I wouldn't say 'enlisted.' The original text makes it clear that these years are necessary to set things right, especially for those who have been dispossessed or enslaved. It states that if we do these things, we will be blessed and flourish, but we'll be cursed if we don't. I admire Ken's book. It shows how we need to bring ourselves in line with what is good for the earth and all who live here. Let me read you a few words...." He pulled a tiny *Tanakh* out of his pocket and began to squint his way to the *parshah* in question, *Behar*.

Debora cut him off. Now she looked stricken. "You're like a bunch of clones! It's sad. No one sees it differently?"

Ken told me that the room subsided into silence. People looked uneasy. Debora just stood there. After a few minutes, he said "There are refreshments back at the table. Lucy will sell you a book at a special Or Chadash discount, and I'll be happy to sign it. Thanks for coming." When he turned around, Debora was gone.

I had to talk to the board, but I didn't feel on solid ground. I needed trustworthy advice from someone who wouldn't spread this around. I called Rivvy, a good friend who had lots of experience dealing with conflict in her role as head of the Rachamim Center. She said to come on over right away.

          Arlene Goldbard

When I sat down in her office, one of those big "ooof!" sounds escaped my mouth. That was embarrassing. Maybe I was getting too old for this. Rivvy was dressed all in black today, with bangles stacked on both wrists. I barely noticed the garden outside her window, which usually mesmerized me. I refused the proffered tea and cookies and the whole story gushed out.

"Let me ask you a few questions," Rivvy said when I'd finished. I liked that she was thoughtful. Too many people blurted their immediate reactions, but Rivvy always asked first.

"Sure."

"This sounds like a disorder: PTSD, or bipolar, or something. For a person to be so defensive and attacking, to switch from anger to sleeping twelve hours. There's got to be some history. Did you get an inkling when you contacted her references?" Rivvy asked.

"No. Everyone was positive: she's knowledgeable, a good service leader, everything we asked." That word "asked" suddenly stood out for me. "But we didn't ask whether she has a history of emotional problems," I said.

"Oy," said Rivvy, smacking her cheek. "The *lashon hara* barrier."

I wasn't completely getting it; I'm sure she saw that written on my face.

"Remember that whole sordid Zach Levy business?" she continued, "how I was reprimanded for being a gossip by asking questions relating to the safety of people who came to his workshops? How he turned it around on me, telling everyone I was undermining him out of envy. It was terrible. We almost lost all our funding. We would have had to shut down. But thank God it ended with solid proof, followed by him disappearing and people apologizing. I'm thinking you ran into the same thing. The people you asked for references didn't want to do *lashon hara*, so they stayed quiet, even though the Chofetz Hayyim says there's a duty to warn rather that surpasses the desire to withhold, which people do out of tact or delicacy or fear. I don't know if there is anything in Debora's history that connects with these incidents, but if there is, people didn't tell you."

"*Oy gevalt*," I said. "I see it now. I always thought it was much of a muchness that there's one path in the tradition that says that even praising someone can be understood as evil speech because it might lead someone else to challenge your assessment. Or attract the evil eye. If there was something to tell and they didn't say it, I'm guessing some of them probably thought 'let's give her a chance.' Some might have wanted to be extra-scrupulous about not committing *lashon hara* themselves. Some wouldn't want to be responsible for her not getting the job. But from where I sit, all of them forgot to consider what impact it could have had on Or Chadash to withhold that information. High-mindedness backfires as often as not. Go figure."

"And there you have it," said Rivvy. "The classic ethical dilemma. Is it better to be fastidious in avoiding even the appearance of wrongdoing, so you stay clean, or risk being a little less pure to help someone else? It reminds me of that teaching about charity: Is it better to give one coin with a full heart or ten coins grudgingly? When I put that question, many people choose one coin, because they are thinking of their own virtue and satisfaction, how they would feel. But the value of charity is to the receiver, who can buy more food with ten coins than one, so that's the right answer. This is the same. Protecting a whole community should come before keeping yourself clean."

"So what do I do?" I asked. "Should I go back to the same references and tell them what's happened and dig deeper? That sounds like a *lashon hara* opportunity if there ever was one, especially if they have nothing to add."

Rivvy hesitated. "I have some thoughts. But what keeps coming into my mind is for you to consult Sharon. This is a spiritual challenge as well as a practical one. Get her advice before you go further."

I'm glad I did. Sharon too told me to come right over. As soon as I sat down in her boring office, I started to breathe more freely. It was no problem swearing Sharon to secrecy. As a private investigator and a *melitz yosher*, confidentiality was her stock-in-trade. It was a relief to tell her the whole story, all the details. We chanted *Emet v'Yatzav* together and read Psalm 130: "Out of the depths I call You." Then I waited while Sharon went "upstairs" to seek guidance. She came out of her trance looking surprised.

"Well that was different," she said. "This is the first midrashic reference I've ever gotten, as opposed to something direct from Torah or a prayer. I had to stop and look it up afterwards. *Talmud, Sotah* 37a. Standing at the Sea of Reeds with Pharoah's army in pursuit, none of the tribes wanted to step first into the water. 'Then, in jumped the prince of Judah, Nahshon ben Amminadab, and descended into the sea first, accompanied by his entire tribe....' and the waters parted, allowing the people to escape over dry land."

"I tell that story all the time, Sharon," I said. "He's some type of avatar of selfless courage I'll never live up to, but he inspires me."

"I didn't get a more specific assignment like doing something for a certain number of days. But there was a secondary text, what Yitro says to Moses in

      Arlene Goldbard

Exodus 18, advising him to delegate, not to try to do everything himself. That aspect of the assignment came through clearly," Sharon told me. "Talk with the leaders and find a way to jointly act as Nahshon for the community."

Sharon helped me see something I'd been hiding from myself: that every time Debora behaved in a way that troubled me, I'd told myself to wait and see. How was that different from the people we asked for references who withheld the truth for fear of doing *lashon hara*? Standing back from necessary action didn't seem noble or discerning in that light. I'd told myself that I wanted to spare others involvement in this mess. Well and good, but since I couldn't handle it all by myself, that led to inaction. I realized that my fear of starting some public brouhaha that could hurt the community was controlling me. There was no ethical alternative to bringing other leaders into it, facing it together. It was overdue, and I'd been wrong to hesitate. I went back to my office and texted the other Search Committee members. It was time for a meeting.

Eve, Alon, Jacob, and Ya'el sat around my dining room table. It was dark outside, but I'd turned on the overhead light and left lamps lit in the living room that connected through a wide archway.

Rachel was there taking notes. She brought out tea and mandelbrot, arranging the teapot, cups, and plates on the yellow tablecloth. But no one reached for anything. You know it's a crisis when Jews refuse food. I opened the meeting with the blessing that had become our tradition: "May we think with care, speak with lovingkindness, treat everyone with respect, and may the highest possible wisdom infuse our deliberations and decisions. And let us say *ameyn*." Everyone chorused a heartfelt *ameyn*.

"Is this about Avi and Debora?" asked Eve, adjusting her scarves. "People are seeing them everywhere with their hands all over each other. It's not such a good look, with Avi's divorce not being final yet, but is it our business?"

The question struck me as a little odd from the person who'd evidently been tracking the gossip, but regardless of the source, it was legitimate to ask.

Mickey Katz was sitting in Alon's lap, allowing himself to be petted. Alon raised their eyes from the cat, looking puzzled. "What about Avi and Debora?"

"They seem to be in a relationship," I said, "and it's a little dicey to some because Avi isn't all the way divorced yet, and it's a fairly public statement for Debora to be making so soon after she arrived."

"Are there some kind of HR guidelines about not being in a relationship?" Alon wanted to know.

"You've seen the manual," I told Alon. It was actually a looseleaf binder of all the policies and guidelines we'd adopted over the years, a little funky but useful. I made sure it was frequently consulted and updated, because people had a habit of making policy up as they went along. "It's not like we're a corporation with hundreds of employees. It doesn't cover the lay cantor having a relationship with the rabbi. That may not be optimal, but neither is it scandalous." I took a breath. "But that doesn't matter. I asked you here to talk about Debora. Avi is pretty tangential."

All eyes turned to me. I quickly narrated the incidents: the conflicts with lay leadership, the Torah Truth episode that sent Debora off the *bimah* and home to sleep for a day, Debora and Avi showing up together at the weekly Shomer-Rabbi meeting, Debora barging into Sarah Fox's Sunday School class, Debora making people uncomfortable at Ken's reading, and a few more. "Acting out this way suggests a disturbance. It appears that ordinary things are triggering her a lot. I spent too long thinking about this on my own, wanting to protect everybody. I apologize for that. I started to realize that the references we contacted may have been withholding relevant information, not wanting to do *lashon hara*. I want us as a Search Committee to dig into this a little, but do it confidentially so we don't create a huge fuss with the community."

Ya'el spoke next. "You mean go back to references and ask them if there's anything they didn't tell us?"

"Yes, at least go back to whichever of them we agree would be best. This is not unheard-of. Sometimes references don't want to tell the whole truth because they think the person deserves a chance to start fresh, or they don't want to be responsible for the person not getting the job. Or they put a fence around *lashon hara*, not wanting to say anything that could possibly be construed as gossip. Or like me, a voice inside tells them to wait till there's more evidence. We'd have to find a careful way to ask, strictly confidential. What do you think?"

"Have you asked Debora?" That was Jacob.

"Debora had explanations for some things: she was tired on Yom Kippur. She's new, she doesn't know all the rules yet. But I didn't ask about her past and she didn't volunteer anything."

"So what you want to know," said Eve, "is if she's been diagnosed with some kind of trauma or condition or had difficulty in other jobs because of emotional

     Arlene Goldbard

challenges. You know I was a social worker, right? People have no obligation to answer questions like that. So if we ask, we should be sure it's people where there's some trust and connection already built up. And where everyone agrees to keep it confidential. Who fits that?"

We started to look at the list of references we'd called. I asked committee members to speak up if they had a relationship with anyone. But after a few moments, Alon interrupted. "This doesn't sound great to me," they said. "If anyone withheld information, it was Rabbi Debora. I think we should be straight with her and say we've been asking ourselves this question given her recent behavior, and rather than return to her references out of the gate, we are coming to her."

"Thank you, Nahshon Friedman!" I said to Alon. We'd all been wading in the shallows, but Alon stepped right into the deep water. We composed a note to the rest of the board members explaining our recommendation and suggesting a couple of dates for a meeting with Debora. I offered to call each of the others—there were only four members who hadn't been on the Search Committee—to brief them and find out if they could make the meeting.

I didn't enjoy telling the story of the whole insane *balagan* over and over again, but it had to be done. Debora would know beforehand that the board had concerns based on a number of incidents that had been brought to our attention, and that we wanted to discuss them with her. I was assigned to summarize the situation at the outset, and to ask if she neglected to tell us about similar problems in her past, things that might have influenced our hiring decision. Then she would have time to respond, and everyone else could pose questions or comment.

We met at my place again. The board members came half an hour early. We were already prepared, so mostly we schmoozed a little, made tea, tried to relax. Debora arrived with Avi in tow. They both insisted he stay, even though I hadn't said he shouldn't.. He sat next to her, holding hands.

I offered the opening as planned, detailing our worries and ending by saying we were concerned both for her well-being and the community's. "We are trying to understand why this is happening, Debora," I said. "And our first question is whether you have faced challenges like these before. We know this is your first job as a congregational rabbi, but definitely not the first time you've had a major organizational role. How have these problems come up before?"

"I'd like to say something before I answer that," Debora said. "I think you're overreacting, and I'm starting to feel unsafe here. I think you're pathologizing behavior that doesn't deserve it."

"If that is your perspective," said Ya'el, "then another way to look at this is that we have very different ideas of acceptable behavior, and need to deal with that."

"Possibly," said Avi. People didn't look thrilled to hear from him. He left it at that.

I asked Debora to be specific about the incidents. "Your first Yom Kippur, Debora, you disappeared on the congregation, not a word to anyone except Joni. Can you see how that was disturbing?"

"Yes," she said, "and I already apologized to you for being tired, not knowing the *minhaggim*, not being prepared to be made the target of Torah Truth."

"This is a longtime custom of ours," David Cahn, another board member, told her. David was a retired professor. He had an attractively weary look about him, and a kind heart. "I asked the lay leaders if it was on the schedule they created with you, and they said yes. So you knew about it. If you or anyone had actually been targeted with malicious intent, we would have stopped it. But the idea is to speak from the heart, and that's what Chana did."

"So this is my major crime, having a problem with Torah Truth?"

Debora made air quotes as she said the name, just as she had in her meeting with me.

"Can you explain why you thought it was okay to disrupt Sarah's class unannounced, insult her father, and scold her?" David asked.

"I thought I should visit Sunday School classes to get acquainted, and hers was the first. Why didn't she welcome me? Another teacher might have thought it was an honor to have the rabbi take an interest. And in case you don't know, Jonathan Fox is a hard act to follow."

This seemed a little surreal. Everyone was quiet for a minute. Then Alon spoke. "I'm having trouble reconciling your view with everyone else's, Debora. You gave us no reason to expect incidents like these. We ask about your prior work experience because it's hard to believe these came out of nowhere."

"Everybody has growing pains and adjustments," Debora said. "Haven't you?"

 Arlene Goldbard

"Yes," said Alon. "A disagreement with a team member or supervisor that had to be worked through, sure. But not like these, where a room is cleared by my remarks, where people go away offended, where I disappeared without a word when I was supposed to be working."

"Lucky you," said Debora, her mouth clamping shut. I could see Avi squeeze her hand. She pulled it away.

"I'm sorry you won't talk to us," said Eve in a calming social worker voice. "We have two choices now. "We can contact your references and dig deeper to find out if essential information was withheld as part of the search process. Or we can start to negotiate your resignation right now and skip that step."

That took me aback. Eve hadn't been prompted to go that far. No one had.

"So you want to fire me?" said Debora, suddenly furious.

Alon said "No. We want you to acknowledge where you've missed the mark, for one thing. So far, you don't seem to think your behavior has been a problem. And if that's where things stay, we want to give you a way out, a negotiated resignation that allows you to move on and get the help you need."

"There is something very wrong with you people," said Debora. She stood up, glancing at Avi. He rose, and the two of them walked out of the room. Mickey Katz blasted through the cat door into the room and looked around. No one said a word for several minutes, but I guess he felt the energy.

As the rabbi, Debora could post at will to the Or Chadash e-list. Up till now, her posts had wished people happy holidays, described classes, or offered resources that might interest the community, things like that. But this one was headed "Message to the Or Chadash community from Rabbi Debora." Here's what it said.

Dear Chevra,

In the short time it has been my honor to serve the Or Chadash community, I have enjoyed getting to know many of you and done my best to offer the care and knowledge a rabbi owes her congregation. Yet it has come to my attention that the board has found fault with my work and wishes to terminate our contract. I am surprised, hurt, and sad at being treated this way after trying my best to serve a community that lost a beloved leader and must also be trying to learn and adjust to new spiritual leadership.

I am unwilling to stand back while the board conspires to end my relationship with the congregation based on false charges and innuendo. I have been led to believe that the Or Chadash community prizes participation and democracy. I would like all of you to have a chance to decide for yourselves whether this attempted coup should stand.

I have reserved the community room for Wednesday evening at 7 pm. All members are invited to attend. I will be telling this story in more detail and answering questions. It is my hope that you will be satisfied with the information I provide, and will join in a vote to override the board's action. I look forward to years of partnership with you as Or Chadash's rabbi.

L'shalom/to peace,

Rabbi Debora

Our next emergency board meeting took place on Zoom, as there was no time to waste. We quickly agreed that all board members would show up on Wednesday. We couldn't and wouldn't stop the membership from convening and taking a vote. That would backfire bigtime. But we could tell our story and answer questions too. Our message to the community read like this:

Dear Or Chadash community,

As your elected board, we have been in dialogue with Rabbi Debora about a number of disturbing incidents brought to our attention by community members. It has been our hope to find a way to resolve the situation without creating a public disturbance, but sadly, Rabbi Debora has chosen to do just that. Please know that we will all be present at Wednesday night's meeting to ensure that the full story is made available to you and to answer any questions you may have.

We are sorry it has come to this. We had hoped to spare Rabbi Debora and the community embarassment. Our prayer is that this meeting is conducted respectfully by and for all, and that the best possible outcomes for all emerge from it.

With love and blessings,

Your board

All of us also signed our names.

We decided to speak individually with each of the people who had brought me complaints: Joni Bindler, who'd come to me first on behalf of the lay leaders;

     Arlene Goldbard

Sarah Fox, whose class had been disrupted; Ken Simon, whose reading had been hijacked; and Rachel Gold, our administrator, who could report on Debora's disappearance on Yom Kippur and its aftermath. No one was eager to speak publicly, but all agreed they would if it felt necessary. I told them I had a strong hunch it would be.

The board strategized how to handle things. We hadn't called the meeting, and beyond her offer to tell her story and answer questions, Debora hadn't described whatever process she may have had in mind. We decided to come to the meeting with a simple plan for how it could be conducted. Debora would be able to tell her story first. Then I would introduce the four people who could speak about their own experiences. Then all of us would be available for questions.

It was possible that Debora would try to reject this format: her meeting, her rules. I was counting on the basic fairness of community members to oppose that. I couldn't imagine a situation in which people would deny Joni, Eve, Ken, and Rachel—all respected members of the *shul*—the same chance to speak their own truth that Debora had requested. We'd see.

We also asked Saul Citrin to join the Zoom. He's a congregation member who does some legal work for us from time to time. He advised us to be prepared to offer an exit agreement as soon as possible after the meeting. I liked his optimism. He quickly drew up a severance offer and a non-disclosure agreement. Resignation was the best option, as it would still save Debora's face in the larger Renewal world. But just thinking that made me imagine someone calling me for a reference for her next job application. Debora wouldn't list Or Chadash, I was sure, but it would be easy enough to find out that she'd worked here and contact us. We'd called the rabbinic program head where she'd received ordination, and she hadn't listed him. I made a mental note to start rehearsing how to tell truth without doing *lashon hara*. I didn't want to be guilty of the same reticence that had gripped her references, which I was pretty sure we were paying for now.

I felt antsy and uncomfortable prepping for the meeting. Debora had slandered us—"a coup!" Did she see herself as queen of the community? Despite everything, I felt strongly that we had to be scrupulous and fair in our response. It would be terrible for the congregation if the encounter degraded into a shouting match. It would be terrible if we started talking about mental illness or anything like that. We needed to hold to decorum regardless of how rude or irrational Debora might be.

I decided to send her a note describing a simple format for the meeting. I told her that all the board members would see her Wednesday evening, that we too would be ready to tell our stories and answer questions. If she wished to go first with her story, we would follow up with ours. Then the meeting could be opened to questions for all. There was no reply, but that didn't worry me. I also wrote a short note to the whole list, describing that plan so whomever showed up would have an idea of what to expect. No one pushed back, which reinforced my hope that I could count on people's sense of fairness.

Board members and our allies—Rachel, Joni, Eve, Ken, and Sarah, who'd come in with her "aunties," Nomi and Sharon, who sat in the front row smiling encouragingly—met a little beforehand to encourage each other and go over our plan again. At 10 minutes to seven, we went to the community room. Debora and Avi were already there, setting up folding chairs in rows facing a single chair at the head of the room. Their dress was oddly similar: Avi's usual white shirt and black vest, Debora in a sort of black jumper with a white shirt underneath. Her hair was pulled back with a large tortoiseshell clip. She wore no jewelry. They made a solemn pair. I looked down at my black leggings and turquoise shirt and thought "Oh well."

Batya Stein was helping them. That figured. Batya and her many judgments had always tried Reb Jonathan's patience—and mine. She'd always taken the side of the aggrieved, whatever the issue, whatever the facts of the situation. What interested me was that so far, only Batya had shown up in the Debora bloc of this controversy. I was pretty sure that Debora would have gathered more allies, although Avi was the only person I'd seen her actually hang out with. She had charm when she wanted to, and Renewal always attracted at least a few people who transferred their resentments of the conventional Jewish world to the alternative one they'd joined. If so, they'd show themselves before long.

Rachel and I quietly added six more chairs at the front of the room, one for me and the rest for those giving accounts of their experience. Debora and Avi glared at us, but I guess the battle of the folding chairs wasn't the hill they were ready to die on. Rachel and I took seats, and the other three joined us as they arrived.

As people walked in, Avi led a *niggun*, a wordless melody to smooth people's way to their seats. He picked "The Rav's Niggun," composed by Rabbi Schneur Zalman of Liadi, the first Lubavitcher Rebbe. If this was an attempt to elevate

     Arlene Goldbard

Debora by association, it probably went over most people's heads. But a room like this would usually be buzzing before a meeting, and the solemn music overrode any tendency to chatter. At a few minutes after seven, Debora and I rose at the same time. She started to speak first.

"Chevra," she said, "this meeting is turning out differently than I expected. I thought that as rabbi, I'd be granted the decency of speaking directly to our community, but you can see that the board fears that, so they've horned in here. I have no power to stop them, but I can ask you to listen to me with open hearts and minds. If you do, you will know who to trust. Now…"

I cut her off before she launched into her story. "We, too ask you to listen with open hearts and minds. As I wrote to you, each of us will have the opportunity to tell our stories, and then there will be time for any questions you want to pose to anyone. Rabbi Debora, please go first."

"I want to tell you a story," Debora said, "about leadership gone wrong, about people who have let their power blind them to what is right, about a new leader who was chosen to help heal the grief that had gripped the community on the loss of their beloved Reb Jonathan, and about the way she has been mistreated."

The story she told was detailed and complicated. She started out narrating events such as her own version of Torah Truth and its aftermath. "I had never heard of a congregation allowing members to hold the *sefer* Torah as if they loved it, all the while spewing vicious attacks on the rabbi. I put my heart and soul into planning High Holy Days services, as Avi will tell you," she turned toward him with a tight little smile. "I was told that as rabbi, I would have full creative input in service planning. I was excited for my first High Holy Days and wanted to bring something different. And I was expected to sit there and take it when someone I've never met attacks me for not making her cry enough? How is this holy? How is this kosher?" Debora's voice rose with each question. "Our tradition says that the Temple was destroyed on account of *sinat chinam*, baseless hatred. That is what is being heaped on me."

As she paused for a breath, Chana Fuentes, who had offered the first Torah Truth on Yom Kippur, said in a clear, even voice, "I would like to take my turn later too."

"See?" said Debora. "It's never enough." She spread her arms wide, looking disturbingly Jesus-like. "Take another whack at me."

From where I sat, I could see Avi lay a soothing hand on the small of Debora's back, but she appeared not to notice. Debora looked at Sarah Fox, then turned to the audience. "Sarah Fox is a sweet girl, and I know you all hold a special place for her as Reb Jonathan's daughter. But what is the correct response when the rabbi visits your Sunday School classroom? Surely to be honored and welcome her! Instead, she shut me up and ejected me!" Debora's cheeks reddened as she spoke.

Then she looked at Ken. "It's not part of my job description to host book events, but I wanted to host Ken's as a way get to know the community better. What was my crime? I asked a question to open up the Q&A. It seems I should have praised the book instead. Are you starting to get the picture now? There are so many unwritten rules in this community, and it seems the penalty for violating them is expulsion." She glared at me.

"You can see for yourself that these are tiny disagreements. A rabbi can be fired for real misconduct—I don't know, embezzlement, sexual harrassment, things like that. But for doing services a little differently? For visiting a classroom? For asking a question? If I had understood that I was hired under false pretenses, just so these power-mad board members could have a scapegoat, I never would have come. But now that I'm here, I feel a responsibility to stay and protect all of you from their abuses." She swept her arm from side to side, indicating the assembled. Then she paused. "I'm sure you have questions," Debora said. "We'll come back to them." She sat down.

I went next. It felt very hard to stand up. "I really don't want to be doing this," I said. "I did not want to embarass Debora by publicly detailing her misconduct. I hoped we could come to an agreement for her to resign and get help. Instead, she called this meeting." I pointed to my five companions. "I've asked each person to say exactly what they experienced, no embellishment, no commentary. Since Rabbi Debora has characterized Chana's behavior, Chana would also like a chance to tell her story."

"That's not fair," Batya shouted from her seat in the fourth row. "Does everyone get to come up and tell whatever story they want? Rabbi Debora is so outnumbered here. Give her some *rachmones*!" *Rachmones* was mercy.

"Let's give us all *rachmones*," I said. "Debora wanted this. No one else did."

"I did!" Batya shouted. She moved to the back of the room, where two other members were standing. If I had to predict who would be in the aggrieved camp, Phil and Rhonda would have been my next two guesses. But their enduring grievances had nothing to do with this situation. Phil was mad because he hadn't won election to the board, despite putting himself forward many times.

     Arlene Goldbard

Perhaps he saw this as an opportunity to stick it to the board. Rhonda and Batya tended to show up together at workshops and events around town, always lingering for the post-event evaluation where their many criticisms would be sure of an audience.

Except for whispers emanating from Batya's corner, the room went silent. I asked Sarah Fox to tell her story. She kept glancing at Sharon and Nomi, who nodded encouragingly. When she described what happened in her classroom and repeated Debora's remark about Reb Jonathan—"Just because everybody around here thinks your father was a saint doesn't give you the right to tell me what to do!"—there were shocked gasps.

Then it was Ken's turn. As he spoke, he fixed his gaze on people in the room who had been present at his reading. Lucy was in the front row, right next to Nomi. "You saw for yourselves, right?" he asked. "I don't need everyone to praise my book, and I have a lot of experience with hard questions. But when Rabbi Debora called us a cult, that pretty much cleared the room. Jacob, you saw that, right?" Jacob nodded. "I asked a few people why they left, and they all said the same thing. They were embarrassed at Debora's outburst. They wanted to spare her shame. She was obviously distressed. They thought it was better to break up the event than prolong her misery." Ken looked around the room. "You who were there," he asked, "isn't that what happened?" No one contradicted him.

Chana stood in place for a minute or two to explain that she hadn't known who had cut out parts of the Yom Kippur service that she needed for her *t'shuvah*. She certainly hadn't intended to attack Rabbi Debora. "Torah Truth is to speak your heart," she said, tearing up. "That's all I did."

Before Rachel could go next with her account of Yom Kippur, Debora stood up again. She looked shaken. "This was a mistake," she said, her voice clogged with incipient tears. "Batya is right. This was a set-up and I was outnumbered. There's no point in answering questions."

That's when Alon and Ya'el, who were sitting together towards the back of the room, stood up at the same time. Alon went first. "Rabbi Debora," they said in gentle voice, "I need to remind you that *you* set this up. None of the board members wanted this public spectacle."

Ya'el started to make her way to the front of the room. "Let's bring this to an end now," she said as she walked. She looked directly at Debora. "Let the board offer you an honorable exit here."

"We were promised a vote," Rhonda said. "Let's have one. Many people may be afraid to talk because they don't want to invite the board's retribution."

Rachel, sitting at my side, laughed out loud. "Sorry for laughing, but let me ask you all a question? Who has experienced the board's retribution? This is a bunch of volunteers pouring their energy into holy community and having to face a very challenging situation. You want a vote? Okay, here's a proposition. All in favor of returning this matter to the board and Rabbi Debora to work out her exit in as fair and ethical a manner as possible, please raise your hands."

The vast majority of people present did just that.

"And all opposed," said Rachel.

Batya, Phil, and Rhonda raised their hands.

The next morning we sent Debora the proposed settlement agreement, saying that we'd included three months' severance to give her resources to seek help. We also sent her the non-disclosure agreement, saying we had no wish for any of this to go more public than it already had.

When a small group of us met with Debora in Saul Citrin's office that afternoon, she was alone, subdued, and ready to sign both documents, to have it all be over. I thought I knew how she felt.

I felt relieved for about an hour. Then I realized that while the lay leaders would be there as always through the spring and summer—and we could always have occasional visiting leaders, as we'd done since Jonathan passed—we'd need to do another search to hire someone in time for High Holy Days prep. Again. A letter to the community announcing Debora's resignation was set to go out first thing tomorrow. I wanted anyone who hadn't been at the meeting to see it before the rumor mill started grinding. I'd think about the future after that.

It was dark outside, but full moon dark. I could make out the shape of every leaf. The stars seemed closer than usual. I said a little prayer of gratitude and closed the curtains. I sat down in front of the TV. Mickey Katz jumped up next to me. I needed something truly distracting, a good detective show without too much blood. I went to the kitchen and surprised myself by making a giant martini—drinking wasn't usually the fun it used to be, but it sometimes did the trick. I also collected an ashtray and a joint to smoke later. Halfway through the program with no clue as to who did it, I decided I was in the right state to actually fall asleep. I made my way carefully into the bathroom, but instead of the overhead light I just switched on the makeup mirror, enough illumination to find my toothbrush and everything else I needed to get ready. I left my clothes on the towel rack and grabbed my nightgown off the hook. In bed, I found my Nina Simone playlist and set the speaker to click off in 20 minutes.

The next thing I remember is waking up feeling a little unsteady, but surprisingly, nothing coffee wouldn't cure. As I took my first sip, the most amazing thing happened. The phone rang. It was Ken Simon and Lucy Perelman, two voices on a speakerphone.

"We got the letter," Lucy said.

"Good outcome," said Ken.

"Thanks, you two. I don't think Debora cultivated a lot of loyalists in the congregation. You saw that only three were at yesterday's meeting, but I was half expecting an argument when the phone rang just now."

"Have you thought about next steps?" asked Ken.

"Another search?" asked Lucy.

"Thinking about it gave me a headache last night and I decided to wait till this morning. Just between us, I dread doing the whole search process again."

"Maybe you won't have to," said Ken.

"What do you mean?" I asked.

"You know Iz Goodman, right?" asked Lucy.

"Of course I know Iz. Jonathan loved him and vice versa. Jonathan always joked that if Iz kept up his Talmud studies, he'd succeed him."

"And now he's in rabbinical school," said Lucy. "Kind of synchronous, no?"

"But doesn't he have years to go?" I asked.

"Yes, yes," said Ken. "You know, he and I are close, he helped me tremendously with my book. Rivvy recommended him, which was really lucky for me. He's still helping me with promotional stuff, the website, like that. He's in that low-residency program, so he only has to be on campus a few days a year. He needs income while he's doing it. The curriculum is mostly distance learning, research and papers, taking classes at other institutions that count towards credit. Next he gets placed with a community, a kind of rabbi-intern. He gets the experience and the community gets a bargain leader. The placement starts in August."

"We can't know the future," said Lucy. "But it sounds kind of *bashert* to me, especially what you said about Reb Jonathan. I've heard Iz say that he could never aspire to Or Chadash because he isn't Jonathan, but the way he says it, you can tell it's his dream."

"It isn't like you'd be signing a five-year contract," said Ken. "You would enter into an agreement for the internship year, and that could be renewed. And once he's ordained, who knows?"

"Have you talked to Iz about this?" I asked. Whatever grogginess I'd been feeling had been replaced with a rush of blood through my veins.

"No, no," said Lucy. "It just popped into our minds when we got the letter about Rabbi Debora and wondered what next. But I have a strong feeling that he would love the idea. And I know he hasn't lined up his internship yet, it's months away."

"I'm getting goosebumps," I said. "I'm going to talk with the board. Don't say anything to anyone, okay? I don't want to get hopes up, but mine are already rising!"

The first person I called wasn't a board member. It was Nomi Riordan of the Khegev Project. She knew Iz very well. As a half-Okinawan half-Ashkenazi kid, he'd loved Khegev. He made it his bar mitzvah project, then interned there as an undergrad. I swore her to secrecy, then asked what she thought of the idea.

"Holy shit, sugar! I think it's fantastic! If Jonathan can hear us upstairs, he must be dancing with joy! Can I tell Sharon?"

"I haven't talked to the board yet, let alone Iz. If you absolutely have to tell her, please let it be between we three until it gets real. And if you can resist and hold onto the secret for a few days, so much the better."

All it took was a few days. Other board members were just as thrilled as I was. At 24, Iz was young, but we'd known him forever. People remembered how Jonathan had doted on him. He was knowledgeable and kind and just his presence and his connection with the Khegev Project would make Or Chadash an even more inviting space for Jews of color. For everyone. The lay leaders loved the idea of working with him. Once the board expressed consensus, a few of us were deputized to talk to Iz. He was excited, to say the least. We put it to the membership in democratic fashion:

"This opportunity has come to us. Many of you know Iz from Sunday School through bar mitzvah and beyond. If we apply by the deadline—more than a

     Arlene Goldbard

month away—Iz can start to work with us in August. Board members feel this is a good direction for Or Chadash. As a bonus, it avoids another long rabbinic search process right now. Is it right for the community? That's up to you."

We scheduled a community meeting the following Sunday afternoon. I was hoping it would be the last one for awhile. I was tired. But after the Rabbi Debora *balagan*, this gathering felt like a celebration. People brought food—there was a tableful of rugelach, cheesecake, and other treats—and this time, everyone ate. There were a few practical questions, but no objections, which felt like some kind of major milestone in the history of Jewish Renewal.

Back at home, I sat back on the couch and took a deep breath. I looked at the photo of Reb Jonathan with his wife Judy and little Sarah on the opposite wall. It was taken at a community Hanukkah party where everyone brought a *hanukiah* and the crowd was captured looking thrilled by the great light they'd made, dozens of candles blazing.

A thought came into my head. "Perhaps my work here is done." On the other hand, I *am* only 77. We'll see.

EPILOGUE: S'LICHOT

"I know," says Anya. "A dream come true." She gazes heavenward, one hand pressed to her heart. Jacob nods. He hasn't been able to stop smiling. Alon and Eve, not exactly the best of friends, keep hugging each other. What has got these Or Chadash board members so worked up?

Jonathan Fox here—or from your perspective, out there, in _olam haba_, the world to come. Since I'm not limited by the same things that affect Earth-dwellers, I have a bird's-eye view of events unfolding down there. So I'll be your narrator.

Right now, the great room at the Rachamim Center is packed. Members have come out to see Isamu Joseph Kaneshiro-Goodman—Iz, that is—leading the first service of his internship as the community's spiritual leader. There are also dozens of young people who are evidently new to the community, people who must have known Iz from graduate school or from other Jewish community gatherings, or just heard some buzz.

To the old guard, this is clearly thrilling: young people, all colors, all genders! A low hum of worry plagues many Renewal shuls, that the movement having come into being through the energetic urging of a cohort of sixties people might die out with them. This gathering suggests that the community's future might not be so precarious after all. That thrills me too.

People are gathering tonight for S'lichot. That means forgiveness in Hebrew. It refers to prayers we offer during the month of Elul, leading up to the _Yamim Noraim_, the High Holy Days each fall. But most of all it names the practice of coming together on the last Saturday night before Rosh Hashanah (the timing is an Ashkenazi custom, the Sephardim do it earlier in Elul). In community, we sing, chant, pray, and move in ways intended to open the gates of compassion. Having done our _cheshbon hanefesh_, the soul accounting that allows us to see where we have missed the mark and where we have hit it in the year just ending, S'lichot is an opportunity to offer and receive forgiveness as the holidays approach.

I always loved it. Still do.

The Or Chadash S'lichot plan braids old and new practices, a little differently each year. I've just been chanting along with some beautiful psalms, for instance. Iz is starting with Psalm 27, which is customary to recite every day during this time. I love the middle stanzas:

     Arlene Goldbard

Hear, YHVH, when I cry aloud;
have mercy on me, answer me.

In Your behalf my heart says:
"Seek My face!"
O YHVH, I seek Your face.

Do not hide Your face from me;
do not thrust aside Your servant in anger;
You have ever been my help.
Do not forsake me, do not abandon me,
O God, my deliverer.

Though my father and mother abandon me,
YHVH will take me in.

It's such a pleasure to *daven* with Iz. I've been kvelling and *davenen* so intensely I sometimes get the two confused. I hope he knows how proud I am of him.

During Elul, we recite the thirteen attributes of HaShem many times. At Or Chadash, we use the language of my old pal Dovid, Rabbi David Wolfe-Blank z"l, whom I see up here from time to time. We trade stories and argue texts, a little holy *chavrusa* he calls it.

Yud Hey, Vav Hey,
Compassion and tenderness
Patience, forbearance, kindness, awareness
Bearing love from age to age
Lifting guilt and mistakes and making us free

A ritual is always the central experience of our S'lichot service. I heard Anya saying the plan had been to seat everyone in a circle, but so many people have shown up, they need two concentric circles. Baskets of small smooth stones are being passed from hand to hand around the room. Everyone takes two while Avi leads the *Hashkiveinu* chant, asking HaShem to spread over us the shelter of peace. Avi seems over his broken heart, by the way. He came in tonight holding hands with someone new.

At the front of the room stand two large vessels containing water. People hold one stone in the left hand and concentrate on a place they missed the mark in the year gone by, something they want to heal and release. Then, holding the other stone in the right hand, they bring to mind something good—something beautiful, hopeful, inspiriting—they want to carry into the year to come.

After giving people a few minutes to pick up and focus on their stones, the tune changes to *Adon Haslichot*, a beautiful Sephardic melody asking the Master of Forgiveness for mercy. It's an acrostic poem. The first lines of three long verses begin in turn with each letter of the Hebrew alphabet, with a repeated chorus in between. That provides plenty of time for people to walk slowly to the *bimah*, depositing their stones in the proper receptacle, left and right.

There's more to follow, including people breaking into dyads to share *t'shuvah* and blessings. At the end everyone leaves quietly—no snacks, no schmoozing—solemnly happy, befitting the occasion.

It's Sunday now, and dinner at Rivvy's is shaping up to be convivial and noisy. It's a big group: Sharon, Nomi, my sweet Sarah, and Sarah's darling Yasmin; Ken and Lucy; Iz and his parents Shim and Eileen and his friend David; Rivvy and Sam, of course, bustling around; and Anya and Rachel in aprons, helping to get everyone settled with drinks and noshes. Fourteen in all. Tables are set end-to-end as we used to do for a big family Seder.

Rivvy stands at one end of the longest table waving her napkin like a semaphore, calling everyone to attention. She's wearing a brilliant blue dress, many scarves and necklaces. The kitchen light is on behind her, turning her hair into a halo. Or maybe hair on fire. She used to say that all the time, whenever she was in the grip of some enthusiasm. "Let's make *kiddush* and *motzi*," Rivvy says now. "Iz, will you lead the *kiddush*?"

"With pleasure." Iz stands and blesses the wine. Most people sing along, then click glasses, saying *l'chaim*.

"Anya," asks Rivvy, "will you make *motzi*?

Anya licks her fingers and wipes them on her napkin. "Chopped herring," she mumbles. She stands, holds two long loaves of bread aloft. She's wearing a bright red sweater and long dangly gold earrings, very festive. As is the custom, those nearby extend a finger to touch the challah. Everyone else touches one of them on the shoulder, making a chain of guests with the challah at the center.

"And *Shehechyanu*," Nomi calls out. "Let's do *Shehechyanu*. It's been a long time..."

"A long strange trip," Ken interjects.

"A long time," Nomi continues, ignoring the interruption, "since this group of people has broken bread together."

     Arlene Goldbard

They sing the blessing of gratitude to the Source of Life for allowing everyone to reach this moment. I sing too, but of course, no one can hear me.

Rivvy always likes to do some type of ritual when people gather. Nomi teases her about it, saying "Rivvy loves to go around the circle." Rivvy does love it, and she doesn't see anything wrong with that, so she doesn't take the bait.

On this occasion, Rivvy picks up on the gratitude that started with *Shehechyanu.* "While we eat, let's take turns and each share what we're grateful for, then share the blessings we hope will come to us in 5785, for ourselves, our communities, our world.

"I want to start by saying some things that are very close to all of us. One reason is that I hope we won't need to repeat the same ones 14 times." She clears her throat, a little *farklempt.*

Rivvy pauses for a moment as Anya and Rachel come out of the kitchen, each carrying a steaming tureen. "Stuffed cabbage," Anya says. "I've got the one with meat and Rachel has the fake meat."

"Thank you," says Rivvy. "I'm getting hungry." She takes a sip of wine. "My heart was full to bursting to see Iz lead last night. I remember your bar mitzvah, Iz. I remember how proud Reb Jonathan was of the way you made it your own. I remember he told me he could see great things ahead for you. I don't think he foresaw anything as *bashert* as this. I am sure he'd be as grateful as I am for your presence."

Rivvy was right. I hadn't. I'd imagined Iz either as a rock musician or some kind of professor in a Jewish school, a scholar. In truth, he is the latter. And now he is *this*!

Iz dips his head shyly. Eileen, sitting beside him, rubs her hand over his thick, short hair. Her baby. She kisses his head.

Rivvy continues. "I think we all need a boatload of blessings, *chevra.* Less than six weeks to the election. May Harris win, and may we all find a way to live together in peace. My stomach hurts when I imagine what could happen if Trump comes back."

"*Ameyn!*" rings out.

"Now dig down a little, friends, and think back on the time since last Rosh Hashanah. Each of us has been sustained and enabled to reach this season, *Baruch HaShem.* What stands out? What are you grateful for? What blessings do you desire? Eileen, would you like to start?"

Rivvy takes her seat and adds a big spoonful of chopped liver to her empty plate. I don't know if it's the real kind or the one Judy liked to make out of green beans and walnuts.

Eileen smiles, then looks suddenly serious. "I'm grateful for the way I have been welcomed into this community," she says, "many years ago and many times since." She looks slowly around the table, stopping at Nomi. "And especially by you, Nomi, for the way you helped my son and so many others to feel a true belonging that is so often denied. Every year, I take my middle school class on a field trip to the Kegev Center. My blessing is that the same spirit that inspires you will grow and spread everywhere, unstoppable."

There's a chorus of "Ameyn!"

Shim is next. He's just dipped a wedge of pita into some hummus. He lowers it to his plate, uneaten. Rivvy and Sam's little dog Hintele watches him like a hawk, hoping for an accident. Shim is the only man at the table wearing a suit and tie. Still dapper, brother.

"I'll try to obey Rivvy and not repeat," Shim says. "But she got me remembering that bar mitzvah too. Iz came to Eileen and me with a fully laid out argument for the kind of bar mitzvah he wanted. *Machloket l'shem shamayim*, he told me. Argument for the sake of heaven. I knew he found his calling that day, only I thought he'd wind up being a lawyer."

Lots of laughs at that.

"He told me that Jonathan had shared something Rivvy said, that one thing she loved about Judaism was disputation as a form of worship. So right now, I want to say that I'm very grateful our wonderful son didn't listen when we tried to discourage him, back then and not so long ago. And the blessing we need, I think, connects with that. May all of us be blessed with true freedom of choice."

"L'chaim!" *"Ameyn!"*

I visualize a glass of wine in my hand so I can join in the *l'chaim* chorus that follows every blessing.

David reaches down to spread the front of his white button-up shirt, revealing a Jewish Space Lasers T-shirt. He turns to the left and right, like a fashion model. "I borrowed this from Iz," he says, "without exactly asking. I'm very glad he got this gig, too, but the thing I want to thank him for is being my *chavruta*, my study partner. Coming here to Berkeley, meeting you, man, that made it possible to discover my true nature and identity, and to live into that.

"And my blessing? Well, I apologize, but it has to start with a worry. Back in New Mexico where I grew up, the drought years are piling up. Where my family used to live, there's an acequia, a shared irrigation system that allows people to water their crops on the regular by portioning out the water fair and square. Only a lot of the time now, there's not enough water because there's not enough rain. That makes the environment ideal for fires too; not so terrible this season, but last year...." David shakes his head, remembering. "I'm worried things will get worse if the wrong people get into power. So my blessing is that the people who have the power to really address the climate crisis wake up and make it happen like their lives depended on it. 'Cause they do."

All is quiet. Then a soft "*Ameyn*" from Sarah, and a second later, "*Ameen*" from Yasmin.

Sam picks up his glass and extends it to each person around the table, pausing a few seconds as his eyes rest on Sarah, Yasmin, David, and Iz. "I'm a professor, so I spend time with many young people. It's often hard to know them, though, because of the constraints of the situation. The grades I give have some power to affect their futures. And they have some power to affect mine with evaluations and so on. I've been fortunate not to have to deal with serious complaints about my teaching, but I've seen colleagues accused of things that jeopardize their jobs, whether that's inappropriate relationships with students or increasingly often, unpopular political opinions. So mostly we're careful, the students and I.

"But when I come to the Rachamim Center with my wonderful wife," here he gazes at Rivvy and smiles, "or we go to services at Or Chadash, I'm struck by the sense of equality I feel. All kinds of people, all ages, everyone contributes, everyone is treated with respect. So my gratitude is for these communities that have shown me what's possible if you start with loving intentions and an embrace of human dignity. Thanks to the young people. May they be blessed with true community and right relationship for all of their long lives."

Classes clink. "*Keyn yehi ratzon*," says Rivvy. May it be your will.

"*Davka!*" Iz calls out. "Truth! Malachi tells it: 'turn the hearts of parents to their children and the hearts of children to their parents.' And here we all are."

This earns him another kiss from Eileen.

Anya, up next, raises one finger to signal just a minute. She extracts an olive pit from her mouth, then clears her throat. "So touching," she says, looking at

Rivvy. "Honestly, I feel like *bensching Gomel*," she says, referring to the blessing we make after coming through danger—a perilous journey, a serious illness.

"I am so grateful that this past year, the community faced a test that could have destroyed us, when faith is placed in a leader who cannot sustain it. Just about all of you were there this past spring for the challenges we experienced with Rabbi Debora. My gratitude extends to so many, but the central thing is that we have built a community that can come together in the face of danger, maintain presence, distinguish the calling of the *yetzer hatov* from the *yetzer hara*, act with decisiveness and compassion." She drops the olive pit on her plate, wipes her hand, and runs a finger under each eye. "I still tear up thinking about it."

"So my blessing is this: that no matter what happens in the year ahead, individually and collectively we maintain our ability to learn from experience and our commitment to find a way forward in fairness and lovingkindness."

"*Ameyn, ameyn!*"

Rachel takes a sip of water, adjusts her ponytail. Rachel helped me so much back when I served Or Chadash. She's hardly changed. Judy used to say she looked like Donna Reed. She had to show me one of those old TV programs on YouTube, since I'd never seen that show. I agreed.

"I'm not the biggest talker, you know," Rachel says. "But I want to try to say something that feels important. Reb Jonathan of blessed memory..."

My heart squeezes whenever I hear that, even if I'm not wearing a body at the moment.

"...if anyone complained about conflict in the community, he always used to say that you can't make community—he said the same thing about peace—only with people who think like yourself. You have to be willing to accept differences and disagreements, and find a way to work them out that respects everyone."

"*Machloket l'shem shamayim,*" Shim calls out. "Twice in one hour!"

Twice in every hour, I find myself thinking. It's a hard lesson to learn when everyone wants to win.

"Rachel?" Rivvy gestures her to continue, then looks pointedly at Shim, who raises his eyebrows and makes a zipping his lips gesture.

"Shim is right," says Rachel. "I know people come to Or Chadash for many reasons: devotion, habit, learning, company, healing. But I don't think we give enough weight to what seems to me to be the biggest and best reason of all: to rehearse for life, which is full of differences.

"We take a pause from busyness, we take a break from thinking about all we have to do. Even if we can't leave our worries at home, we can at least put our attention on lifting them up, on blessing and helping, on our place in the long history of our people. We try to bring our whole selves, we do our best to act in harmony, we ask the most important questions about how to live in this moment, we reflect, we listen deeply and think before we speak—and all of this is the template for making community, which our society seems to find very challenging these days. I am grateful for this space in time, for Or Chadash. And not just because I have a job there!"

Everyone laughs, especially knowing Rachel could get a much better-paying job anytime she wanted.

Rachel picks up her glass and drinks the rest of her water. "So my blessing," she continues, "is that our awareness of this intention and its power grows every day, that our conscious intentions add to our ability." She exhales with a sigh.

Sam extends his glass with a "*l'chaim*." His cheeks are pink. Sam knows how to savor the moment.

"Whew!" Sharon fans herself with one hand. "I did not know the deep Torah I would hear when I accepted Rivvy's invitation to dinner tonight! Nor this incredible chopped liver. I'm hoping Rivvy will give me the recipe this time, but whether or not she does, I want to express my gratitude for her place in this community." Sharon throws Rivvy a kiss.

"Some of you weren't around or aware when—almost a decade ago now— Rivvy was targeted by a broken person trying to hold onto his position as a spiritual celebrity, and the Rachamim Center almost succumbed to his *lashon hara* campaign. I'm not going to drag out the details now." Sharon glances reassuringly at Rivvy, who nods and smiles back. "They don't matter.

"What matters bears a striking resemblance to the gratitude Anya expressed for the way the community came through its crisis this year. I'm not naïve enough to think that truth will always out, that the upright will always prevail. But that time, just like this past spring, they did, and I have to think that was the outcome at least in part because we have built up a reservoir of blessing in all these years of practicing, just as Rachel described.

"So I want to bless Rivvy and the Rachamim Center and all the people who have learned and grown there—including most of us around these tables—with open minds and hearts, with the strength of body and spirit to remain present even under extremely difficult circumstances, with a strong desire to live into the questions, even questioning our own assumptions, and with a thirst for truth and justice that can never be fully quenched."

"Whoo!" says Lucy. She puts two fingers in her mouth and blows a whistle so loud it rattles her hair. "*Ameyn!*" rings out.

Nomi, knowing she is next, pulls her braid over her shoulder, tugging at the end. She extends her empty glass in David's direction. "Just a little, please, sugar." He pours an inch of red wine into her glass. "I think most of you came up in a place where there were Jews, and maybe a place where you felt it wasn't dangerous to be one, and that is great. I wish every place were like that, not just for Jews but for all the colors and heritages and languages and ways of being." She laughs softly. "Don't worry, this isn't a commercial for the Keghev Center." People smile at that.

"I didn't know I was Jewish until I came to Berkeley, but I knew I was different, and I knew I had to get out of Dodge as soon as I could, that leaving home was the only way I would ever have a chance to belong somewhere. Kind of a paradox. So I want to say how grateful I always am to have been received. To Sharon, who helped me discover myself. To Reb Jonathan, who helped me become myself. To all of you, who've accepted me as myself and inspired me to help others who need that acceptance!

"My blessing is that we'll all be able to see the Divine spark in every person we encounter, even if it's sometimes dim or deeply hidden, even under layers of strangeness like I was."

"*Ameyn* to that," says David.

Nomi reaches across the table and clicks his glass: "*L'chaim.*"

Yasmin isn't Jewish, but she reminds me of some of the young *frum* wives I used to see while I was studying in Philadelphia a very long time ago: modest, a little shy, her head always covered. She and Sarah are holding hands under the table.

"Thank you," says Yasmin, "thank all of you for making me feel so welcome whenever we meet."

There are smiles and nods all around. Lucy makes a praying hands gesture in front of her mouth and lowers her head just a little bit.

"I am Palestinian, as you know. Things have sometimes been hard for Sarah and me since October 7th. For months, I was told that everyone had to pick a side and hate the other side. And that Sarah and I would always be on opposite sides even though we were both for peace and justice. It took us a long time to break through to what we wanted. One thing that really helped is when Sarah took me to a meeting of Or Chadash members who believe that Jewish and Palestinian lives have equal value, and who do their best to show up for both. I was welcomed there too, with all my tears and fears and grief and hope and confusion.

"Thank you for holding that space. My blessing for everyone is *Allahumma la tajeal fi qalbi karahiatan li ahad.* Oh Allah, don't let the hate of anyone reside in my heart."

I'm so happy that my girl found her true love.

Sarah stares adoringly at Yasmin. "It's hard to add anything to all the wonderful words that have been said. I want to talk a little about Yasmin and myself too. Yasmin's heart is big; she always focuses on the good. But over this past year, we've heard so much scary stuff, not only about Israel-Gaza, but right here in this country, the MAGA people who say they will end same-sex marriage like they're doing with abortion. We've been thinking we'd get married next year, when we both turn 21. But just today, we decided to do it before the election, in case we lose our chance."

Everyone gasps. My Sarah's grin lights up the room. "Nothing huge. We'll just go to City Hall, maybe have a little party at the house."

"A big party!" Nomi and Sharon, her honorary aunties, say it simultaneously.

I feel a flood of tears. I wish I could be there, not just watching from afar. I can't wait to tell Judy. She'll say they're young to make such a big decision. But she'll understand their reason for feeling rushed.

A little flurry of conversation wells up. From up here, it's startling, like when a school of fish suddenly takes off. Sarah waves her left hand for silence. "S-s-shh!" Her other hand is under the table, still holding Yasmin's. "I'm not done yet, you guys! Here's my blessing: that everyone should have love that brings them happiness and delight!"

This triggers a big *l'chaim*, lots of glasses clinking.

"I love your blessing," Ken says to Sarah when the sounds die down. I see he's still wearing his black uniform, but somehow the edge is softer. He looks at Lucy. "No matter how long it takes," he says.

"I guess that applies to a lot of things about my life," he continues, starting his turn. "It's not much more than a year ago when I consulted Sharon about feeling blocked in my writing." He looks at Sharon. "That was my second time asking you for help, and I still needed you to know I didn't really believe in that sort of thing. Belief-shmelief! It started me on a journey of exploration and study that led me to write my new book and to let myself fall all the way in love with Lucy and to take her advice and seek Iz's help. And that led to calling Anya up after the Rabbi Debora mess to suggest Iz do his internship at Or Chadash," Ken pauses. "Not that I'm trying to take credit for anything, you understand."

Lucy makes a funny face, the confusing kind where you think something your beloved does is both cute and embarrassing.

Ken shrugs. "So my big gratitude is to Sharon who is some kind of catalyst and energy source for so many of us. Thank you, Sharon, with all my heart." He raises his glass and Sharon nods, smiling. "And my blessing is for me as much as anyone, that we remember that there are mysteries hidden in ordinary things, that we keep using our brains even as we remember to listen to our hearts and our hunches too."

Lucy kisses Ken's cheek, just a peck. "I would like to express my gratitude to whoever made this stuffed cabbage," she says. "I would swear it was my Bubbe but she's been gone a long time." People raise forkfuls in a kind of toast to Rivvy, who makes a slight bowing gesture, accepting the accolades. Hintele, in her lap, offers a tiny bark.

"Has it all been said?" Lucy asks, looking around. "Never all, I guess. I want to tell a little story. Earlier today, I was at this senior housing place where an older friend of mine lives. It has all the railings and safeguards and a resident nurse, that kind of place. Just about everyone there is an old lefty. I've been working on an oral history piece about the Free Speech Movement. That was sixty years ago. A bunch of these people were involved back then."

She looks at the youngers. "Do you know about that? Big student demonstrations that practically shut down the Berkeley campus in 1964 and 1965. They won the right to have political meetings and information tables on campus—it was literally about free speech. Mario Savio was a major leader, a stirring speaker. He is famous for this rally where he said—I think I have this

Arlene Goldbard

part memorized: 'There's a time when the operation of the machine becomes so odious—makes you so sick at heart—that you can't take part.' Then this long metaphor about putting our bodies on the gears and levers."

Ken gives her a gentle dig in the ribs. I don't think anyone else could see it.

"Anyway," Lucy says, glancing at Ken, "leaving the long metaphors behind, there's a rumor that RFK Jr. is coming to the East Bay, and the people I visited this morning were talking about showing up to protest. They think his votes could tank Harris. One of them said they had the idea to all go with their walkers. I told her they should call it a walk-in."

"I like that," says Eileen.

Lucy smiles and carries on. "So my gratitude is for being in this lineage of people who stand up for things like free speech, and being inspired by the way they keep on keeping on!"

There's a round of applause.

"And my blessing," Lucy adds, "is that all of us, old and young, have the will and energy to persevere, to walk in and to walk on."

"*Keyn yehi ratzon*," says Rivvy, and everyone joins in. May it be your will.

Iz, last to go, shakes his head gently. "I'm sitting here thinking how lucky I am," he says. "How many people came up in a community that supported them and gave them room to grow, with a teacher like Jonathan, *alav ha-shalom*, with friends like all of you, and then get the opportunity to serve that community, giving back any way they can?"

"*Kinehora!*" Anya calls out, and others echo. There are a few superstitions left over from the shtetls, and this is one of them, to offer a charm against an evil force that seeks to obliterate any good fortune that is spoken aloud.

"That's my gratitude, friends," Iz continues. "That I have been privileged and helped to walk this path. And my blessing is that we can do Reb Jonathan justice, strengthening the community he helped us build." Iz raises his glass, and *l'chaims* and *ameyns* resound.

Iz takes a big breath. "I want to say more, because we are talking about a future that is always uncertain. I want to share something I've been thinking, and I ask you to tell me what you think about it."

I can see this isn't easy for him. He's wearing a T-shirt I've never seen: the *sefirot* traced on a background that looks something like a flower. Or maybe a Venn diagram. Very cool. I try to send him confidence.

"I've been thinking about our ancestors," Iz continues. "Take my family as an example. Both sides had to run away from a familiar world where they stopped feeling safe, and from everything I've read, the need to leave often came suddenly—like the Israelites having to escape from Egypt overnight. Like FDR issuing Executive Order 9066 setting up the internment camps two months after Pearl Harbor.

"I've also been thinking about our spiritual ancestors. Some of us see ourselves as part of a neo-Hasidic movement, trying to repair the big rupture in that lineage that occurred when the Hasidic communities were wiped out by the Nazis and their allies and collaborators. We've been lucky to have some teachers who escaped to this country—Reb Zalman, Rabbi Zalman Schachter-Shalomi, there isn't anyone in Renewal who hasn't been affected by him, who hasn't joined him in redeeming teachings that our enemies wanted to wipe out.

"I doubt there's any place that Jews have felt as safe for as long as in this country. Not that it's been perfect. There were insults and exclusions and falsehoods and threats all along, just like on my Mom's side. When my Mom's relations who lived on the mainland were rounded up and put in camps—that was like 80 years ago! Bad shit happened, but everyone stayed. Recently Jewish businesses and shuls and schools have been attacked by vandals and assassins. But I can't wrap my brain around the idea that we'll be forced out like our ancestors. I'm not predicting the worst. I'm not trying to scare anyone." Iz took a swallow of his wine.

"But the truth is we don't know if Trump will be re-elected. Some polls say yes. And we don't know what he'll do if he is. Just last week he said Jews will have a lot to do with it if he loses. We've already seen how he takes a loss. How he takes a win could be worse. I hope and trust Harris will win, but I think we need to be prepared for either outcome. I mean spiritually prepared, prepared to provide aid and comfort to people who are suffering, prepared by understanding the paths our ancestors carved out of history, prepared by finding the sources of our resilience.

"I am saying all this because a community has been built here. Earlier Rachel said that people come to Or Chadash for all kinds of reasons. But I think there's a big reason that covers them all. You know that line from *Hashkivenu*? '*Ufros*

Arlene Goldbard

aleinu sukkat sh'lomekha, Spread over us the *sukkah* of Your peace.' I'm just starting, and I've got a lot to learn. But here in this room tonight, just before the High Holy Days, just before the election, just among us, I want to ask if you are seeing what I am seeing, and if you agree that without panicking, it's time to rededicate ourselves to the bedrock project, the heart of what Or Chadash is about: creating community, community that can withstand whatever's coming."

There is silence for a minute.

I admit it, I'm kvelling again. I may not be able to see into the future, but I can definitely learn from the past and Iz is right: conscious community, facing into every possibility, preparing as best people can, these are what's needed now. These are our deepest reasons for belonging. I'm so proud of him. And so happy to see him stepping up to leadership, the kind where everyone supports each other.

So what do you think happens next?

My darling Sarah starts the singing: *Ufros Aleinu*, the slow, melodic version that I used to sing to her when she went to sleep. Everyone who knows it— which is just about everyone—joins in. Anya and Rachel don their aprons, and singing all the way to the kitchen return with plates laden with honey cake, taiglach, rugelach, a beautiful plate of dates stuffed with cream and nuts that Yasmin brought, the sweets that rhyme with the sweetness of the High Holy Days. No one knows what will happen, but it's crystal-clear that whatever comes—a long, hard time or a season of mixed blessing—what the members of this community have built will offer them shelter while they figure it out.

GLOSSARY

Ahavat Olam: Hebrew. Eternal love; the name of a congregation founded by Jonathan Fox.

Alav ha-shalom: Hebrew. Peace be upon him/her; Hebrew equivalent of rest in peace.

Al Chet: Hebrew. A prayer of collective responsibility for sins recited on Yom Kippur.

Aliyah, plural *aliyot:* Hebrew. Literally "ascend." Being called to read from the Torah in synagogue. Also "making aliyah," emigrating to Israel.

Ameyn: Hebrew/Aramaic. A word that ends a prayer or blessing, signifying "so be it."

Amidah: Hebrew. Literally "standing." A long prayer recited or davened silently while standing, part of every service.

Ashkenazim: Hebrew. Jews descended from European ancestors.

Assiyah: Hebrew. The most material of the four concentric worlds of mystical Judaism. Next is *Yetzirah* (formation/emotion), *B'riah* (creation/intellect), and finally *Atzilut* (emanation/spirit).

Avinu Malkeinu: Hebrew. Our Father, Our King. A key prayer key in High Holy Days liturgy.

Avodah: Hebrew. Service. Also the name of a part of the *Musaf* service on Yom Kippur.

Ba'al t'shuvah: Hebrew. Literally "master of repentance," but used to describe a movement of secular Jews returning to Jewish observance.

Balagan: Yiddish. A chaotic mess. A circuslike brouhaha.

Balbusta: Yiddish. An accomplished homemaker.

Bar/Bat/B'nai Mitzvah: Hebrew. Son/daughter/children of commandment. Describes a rite of passage many Jews undergo at 13, taking part in ritual and reading from the Torah to signify entering adulthood.

Baruch HaShem: Hebrew. Blessed be God, usually an expression of gratitude.

Bashert: Yiddish. Literally, "destiny." Often used to refer to a soulmate: "he's my bashert." But can refer to anything that feels foreordained.

Bet Din: Hebrew. Literally "house of judgment," a rabbinical court, including the assembly of three Jews (who may or may not all be rabbis) who certify a conversion.

Beit midrash: Hebrew. Study house.

Bimah: Hebrew. Literally "stage" or "platform," the raised surface on which the Torah service takes place.

Bris, brit: Yiddish, Hebrew. Covenant. Often used the describe the rite of circumcision, embodying a covenant with the Divine.

Bubbe: Yiddish. Grandmother.

Chabad: Hebrew. An Orthodox Jewish Hasidic dynasty founded in the 18th century. Its name is an acronym of *Chokmah, Binah*, and *Da'at*, three of the upper *sefirot* on the kabbalistic tree of life, representing wisdom, understanding, and knowledge. It is a sophisticated global movement with centers worldwide. Chabad recruits secular Jews to Hasidic study and practice.

Chavruta: Hebrew. The practice of engaging with a study partner or small group regularly to study Torah.

Chaya: Hebrew. To live, living person or animal. Also the fourth highest spiritual level of soul.

Cheder: Hebrew. Jewish religious elementary school.

Cheshbon hanefesh: Hebrew. Soul inventory, the process of searching one's deeds and thoughts in preparation for the High Holy Days.

Chevra: Hebrew. Friends.

Daven, davenen, davening: Hebrew. Pray, praying.

Dreidl: Yiddish. A four-sided spinning top with a Hebrew letter on each side, used in a Hanukkah game.

D'var Torah: Hebrew. Literally "word of Torah." Talk, essay, sermon.

Eco-kashrut: English and Hebrew. Also eco-kosher. Moving beyond traditional laws of *kashrut* such as separating meat and milk and eschewing pork and shellfish to take the human and environmental cost of food production into account, choosing organic, humanely, and sustainably raised food sources.

Elul: Hebrew. Hebrew month preceding the High Holy Days.

Erev: Hebrew. The evening that precedes a holy day. Jewish days start at sunset, so Friday night is Erev Shabbat, for example.

Frum: Yiddish. Highly observant, pious.

Gematria: Hebrew. Jewish numerology. Every Hebrew letter is given a numeric value, and words and meanings are drawn and often connected based on that value. The numerical value of the word *chai* (life) is 18; Many Jews give gifts or make charitable contributions in multiples of 18, thereby wishing long life to the recipients.

Ger: Hebrew. Stranger, also convert.

Gevalt: Yiddish. An expression of dismay or shock, *Oy gevalt!*

Gilgul neshamot: Reincarnation of souls.

Haftarah: Hebrew. A reading from the prophets assigned to each Torah portion, generally including something that resonates with the *parshah.*

Haggadah: Hebrew. The book that guides the order of the Passover Seder.

HaGilgulim: Hebrew. The reincarnated.

Halacha: Hebrew. Jewish law.

HaLev: Hebrew. The heart.

Hanukkiah: Hebrew. The nine-branched menorah used to kindle Hanukkah lights.

Haredi, Haredim: Hebrew. Literally "to tremble, tremblers." Used to refer to the Ultra-Orthodox.

HaShem: Hebrew. Literally "the name." A word for God.

Hasid, Hasidism: Hebrew. Members and practices of an Orthodox Hasidic sect such as Breslov or Chabad, marked by study, specific costumes, usually dynastic leadership, and ecstatic communion with the Divine such as dancing.

Havdalah: Hebrew. Literally "separation." The ceremony that marks the passage out of sacred time, such as Shabbat or a holiday, into ordinary time.

     Arlene Goldbard

Hazzan: Hebrew. Cantor.

Hechsher: Hebrew. A label or stamp indicating rabbinic certification of a kosher product.

Jewish Renewal: English. A Jewish grouping originating in the 1960s, typified by feminist egalitarianism, ecstatic worship, creative liturgy, and liberal/progressive politics. It is not a denomination like Conservative or Orthodox, although some communities use it as their identifier. The movement typically welcomes many different levels of observance.

Kabbalah: Hebrew. Jewish mysticism incorporating esoteric writings and practices.

Kaddish: Hebrew. Usually refers to the mourner's *Kaddish,* an ancient Aramaic prayer that mourners say three times a day for eleven months following the death of a parent. It is also included in daily services.

Kiddush: Hebrew. Literally, "sanctification." The blessing that sanctifies wine on Shabbat or a holiday. Can also mean a small meal following a prayer service.

Kinehora: Yiddish. A contraction of the Hebrew keyn ayin hara, no evil eye. It's said as a charm against evil befalling someone who boasts of good fortune, expressing the hope that the evil inclination will pass by without responding to the provocation.

Kippah: Hebrew. A skullcap worn by observant Jews.

Kittel: Hebrew. Literally, "shroud." A white garment worn over clothing on certain occasions such as marriage or Yom Kippur, also ultimately used as a burial shroud.

Kol isha: Hebrew. A woman's voice. Sometimes used to mean the Orthodox prohibition against women praying or singing aloud at services.

Kol Nidre: Hebrew. Literally, "all vows." An ancient sung prayer opening services on Erev Yom Kippur, the first night, annulling all vows made with the Divine.

Kosher: Hebrew. Literally "proper." Foods that are permitted and prepared according to Jewish dietary law. "Glatt kosher" literally means "smooth," referring to specific aspects of meat, but has taken on the popular meaning of "super-kosher." When dishes, pots, or utensils are rendered fit according to Jewish law, the verb is "koshered" or "kashered."

Kvelling: Yiddish. Boasting, especially concerning family members; rejoicing and taking pride in accomplishments.

Lashon hara: Hebrew. Literally "evil tongue." Evil speech, gossip, slander.

Latkes: Yiddish. Potato pancakes traditionally eaten on Hanukkah by Ashkenazi Jews.

L'chaim: Hebrew. Literally, "to life." A common toast.

Leyn: Hebrew. To chant Torah, using a trope—tune, rhythm—appropriate to the occasion.

L'malah: Hebrew. Upstairs, also indicating a heavenly realm.

Machloket l'shem shamayim: Hebrew. Argument for the sake of heaven. A dispute animated not by the desire to win, but by the desire to find truth.

Magid: Hebrew. Retelling of the Exodus story as part of a Passover Seder. Also a storyteller or preacher.

Mazal: Hebrew. *Mazel:* Yiddish. Literally, "constellation." *Mazel tov* means good luck, and also suggests an astrological origin.

Mechitza: Hebrew. Partition. The divider of cloth or other material that separates men and women in Orthodox synagogues.

Melitz Yosher: Hebrew. Intercessor. Someone who pleads for help from a heavenly court for a person who is suffering an illness or a problem.

Mensch: Yiddish. Literally "person," but used almost exclusively to describe a good, honorable person.

Midrash: Hebrew. Stories, parables, commentaries that go beyond actual Torah text to add plot, color, interpretation. There are several volumes of compilations.

Mikveh: Hebrew. Ritual bath used to purify before holy days and for other purposes such as conversion to Judaism.

Mincha: Hebrew. Literally "offering." Afternoon prayer service.

 Arlene Goldbard

Minhag, plural *minhaggim:* Hebrew. Jewish religious customs such as how a community traditionally handles *aliyot.*

Minyan: Hebrew. A gathering of ten adult Jews deemed necessary for reciting many prayers, including the mourner's *Kaddish.* Many Orthodox communities will not count women in a minyan.

Mishegas: Yiddish. Craziness, outlandishness.

Mishpacha, mishpocha: Hebrew, Yiddish. Family.

Mitzrayim: Hebrew. Straits, narrow places, also Hebrew for Egypt.

Mitzvah, Mitzvot: Hebrew. Commandment, commandments. Sometimes used to denote a good deed: "he did us a mitzvah."

Mizrachim: Hebrew. Jews descended from North African or Asian ancestors.

Mohel: Hebrew. The person who performs ritual circumcisions.

Moshiach: Hebrew, Yiddish. Messiah.

Motzi: Hebrew. Literally "brings forth." The name of the blessing before eating bread, which ends with *"hamotzi lechem min ha'aretz,"* who brings forth bread from the earth."

Nefesh: Hebrew. Soul. The most basic of five levels of soul.

Ne'ilah: Hebrew. Literally "closing." The concluding part of Yom Kippur services in which the gates of prayer are said to be closing.

Nephilim: Hebrew. Precise meaning unknown. Sometimes giants, sometimes hybrid offspring of angels and humans.

Neshama: Hebrew. Soul or spirit. The third of five levels of soul.

Niggun, Niggunim: Hebrew. Wordless spiritual tunes or melodies.

Nu: Yiddish. Many meanings such as well, what's up, go on.

Oneg: Hebrew. Literally "delight." Oneg Shabbat describes a gathering with food and blessings following a Shabbat service.

Parshah, parshiot: Hebrew. A section of the Torah assigned to be read for a particular Shabbat or holiday.

Payess: Side locks, long dangling curls worn in front of Hasidic men's ears.

Pesach: Hebrew, Yiddish. Passover. Jewish spring holiday commemorating the exodus from slavery in Egypt.

Pirke Avot: Hebrew. Ethics or Chapters of the Fathers, a compilation of ethical teachings and maxims.

Purim: Hebrew, Yiddish. Jewish spring holiday observing the rescue of the Persian Jews by Queen Esther.

Rachamim: Hebrew. Compassion, mercy.

Rachmones: Yiddish. Mercy.

Rosh Hashanah: Hebrew. Literally "head of the year." New Year celebration, the first of the fall High Holy Days.

Ruach: Hebrew. Spirit, breath, wind. Also the second of five levels of soul.

Schmooze: Yiddish. Chat.

Sefirot: Hebrew. A configuration of ten Divine emanations or qualities used and studied in *kabbalah*. Each expresses a powerful quality emanating from the highest realms and suffusing existence, for instance lovingkindness/*chesed* and constraint/*gevurah*.

Sephardim: Hebrew. Jews descended from Spanish and Portuguese ancestors.

Shabbat, Shabbos: Hebrew, Yiddish. Sabbath.

Shabbaton: Hebrew. A multi-day event spanning Shabbat, featuring prayer, study, and celebration.

Shaliach Tzibbur: Hebrew. Literally "messenger of the community." Can refer to anyone who leads prayer, including a cantor or rabbi.

Shalom: Hebrew. Peace, wholeness.

Shavuot: Hebrew. Spring holiday commemorating the receiving of the Torah on Mt. Sinai.

Shelshelot/shersheret neshamot: Hebrew. The chain or necklace of souls; the generations stretching into the past and future.

Shema: Hebrew. Literally "listen." A foundational Jewish prayer asserting the oneness of the Divine.

Shiksa: Yiddish. A non-Jewish female.

Shmita: Hebrew. Literally "release." Every seventh year, the land is left fallow, debts are forgiven, the enslaved are freed, holdings are returned to their owners, moving toward equity by keeping people from perpetually buying up others' land.

Shoah: Hebrew. The Holocaust, mass murder of European Jews by Nazis and their allies.

Shul: Yiddish. Synagogue, school.

Shvat: Hebrew. A winter month on the Hebrew calendar.

Siddur: Hebrew. Prayerbook.

Simcha: Hebrew. Gladness, joy, celebration.

Simchat Torah: Hebrew. One of the last of the fall High Holidays on which the annual reading of the Torah scroll is completed and the new cycle begins.

Sinat Chinam: Hebrew. Baseless hatred.

Sitra Achra: Hebrew. The other side, the realm of evil.

S'micha: Hebrew. Ordination.

Ta'anit Esther: Hebrew. The fast of Esther, taking place the day before Purim.

Tallit: Hebrew, *Tallis:* Yiddish. Fringed prayer shawl.

Tanakh: Hebrew. A book containing the first five books of the Hebrew bible plus prophetic and other writings.

Tikkun: Hebrew. Repair.

Tikkun olam: Hebrew. Repairing the world. Current main usage describes social action. Can also refer to undertaking spiritual practices to repair the vessels of holiness shattered in the kabbalistic creation story.

Torah: Hebrew. Jewish sacred texts. Often comprising the first five books of the Hebrew bible. *Sefer Torah* is the Torah scroll, as opposed to a Chumash or Tanakh, a book holding the same content plus prophetic and other important writings.

Treyf: Hebrew. Non-kosher.

T'shuvah: Hebrew. Reorientation, repentance, the process of self-examination, apology, and forgiveness undertaken for the High Holy Days.

Tzimmes: Yiddish. Literally, a stew or braise with multiple ingredients. A brouhaha.

Tzitzit: Hebrew. Fringes, specifically the fringes on a prayer shawl or a *tallit katan*, an undergarment worn by many Orthodox Jews.

Tsofah: Hebrew. Watcher, sentinel.

Tzedakah: Hebrew. Righteousness, charity.

Unetanneh Tokef: Hebrew. An ancient and beautiful poem recited as a prayer on Rosh Hashanah and Yom Kippur.

Yahrtzeit: Hebrew. Anniversary, usually anniversary of a death.

Yasher koach: Hebrew. Traditional congratulations upon having an *aliyah* or completing other rituals. The equivalent of "more power to you."

Yechida: Hebrew. The spiritual essence of the human soul. The highest of five levels.

Yeshiva: Hebrew. A Jewish academy of higher education.

Yetzer hara: Hebrew. The evil inclination.

Yetzer hatov: Hebrew. The good inclination.

Yikhes: Yiddish. Lineage or pedigree. Usually in terms of family, but also giving credit to others' teachings. "That idea has *yikhes*."

Yizkor: Hebrew. Literally "remember." The memorial service for the dead recited on holy days.

Yovel: Hebrew. Jubilee. Every fiftieth year—after seven cycles of *Shmita* years—a year of complete rest for the land and remission of debts.

Yom Kippur: Hebrew. The day of atonement occurring ten days after Rosh Hashanah in the cycle of High Holy Days.

Zaftig: Yiddish. Plump, full-figured.

Zohar: Hebrew. Foundational books of *kabbalah*, Jewish mysticism.

     Arlene Goldbard

ABOUT THE AUTHOR

Arlene Goldbard is a writer, visual artist, speaker, social activist, and consultant. She and her husband, the artist Rick Yoshimoto, live just outside Santa Fe, New Mexico.

Arlene's essays have appeared in many journals and anthologies. Her books include *Crossroads: Reflections on the Politics of Culture*; *New Creative Community: The Art of Cultural Development*; *Community, Culture and Globalization*; *The Culture of Possibility: Art, Artists & the Future*; *In The Camp of Angels of Freedom: What Does It Mean to be Educated?*; and two prior novels, *Clarity* and *The Wave*.

Arlene has offered hundreds of talks and workshops and helped many organizations make plans and solve problems. They include nonprofits such as the Independent Television Service, the National Campaign for Freedom of Expression, and the New Museum of Contemporary Art; foundations such as the Rockefeller Foundation and the Paul Robeson Fund for Independent Media; a score of state arts agencies; and many others.

Until 2019, she served as Chief Policy Wonk of the U.S. Department of Arts and Culture and president of the Board of Directors of The Shalom Center.

Many of her talks, essays, and paintings can be found on her website, www. arlenegoldbard.com, where you can also subscribe to her blog.

ACKNOWLEDGEMENTS

I am more grateful than I can say to the kind readers who read this book in draft and offered me their excellent advice: Barry Barkan, Rabbi Phyllis Ocean Berman, Rabbi Diane Elliot, Betty Farrell, Amber Hansen, Judith Marcuse, François Matarasso, Minna Scherlinder Morse, Marc Weiss, and Rick Yoshimoto.

Any errors are of course entirely my own.

www.ingramcontent.com/pod-product-compliance
Lightning Source LLC
Chambersburg PA
CBHW031304120726

47906CB00003B/875